17948

D0038826

X

	DATE DUE	
JUN 16 1999		
AUG 21 1999		
SEP 11 1999		
SEP 29 1999		
MAY 03 2000		
JUL 01 2000		
NOV. 29 2005		
JUL 02 2011		
SEP 21 2016		

GILBERT MORRIS

Chariots in the Smoke

Tyndale House Publishers, Inc.
Wheaton, Illinois

Library of Congress Cataloging-in-Publication Data

Morris, Gilbert.
  Chariots in the smoke / Gilbert Morris.
    p. cm. — (Appomattox saga ; 9)
  ISBN 0-8423-5553-7 (sc)
    1. United States—History—Civil War, 1861-1865—Fiction. I. Title.
II. Series: Morris, Gilbert. Appomattox saga ; 9.
PS3563.08742C48   1997
813'.54—dc20   96-43215

Printed in the United States of America

02 01 00 99 98 97
9   8   7   6   5   4   3   2   1

17948

*"The Lord give mercy
unto the house of Onesiphorus;
for he oft refreshed me. . . ."*

*This book is dedicated to a man who,
as much as any other Christian I've ever known,
encouraged me during a time
when I needed it greatly.
Every young pastor desperately needs
a man to refresh his spirit—
and I've always believed God
sent such a man into my life.
To my dear friend and fellow pilgrim*

JIMMY LLOYD

CONTENTS

Part Four: Chattanooga

GENEALOGY OF

THE APPOMATTOX SAGA

THE ROCKLINS

Noah Rocklin
(1767–1842)
m.1797
Charlotte Minton
(1780–1847)

Stephen
(1798–)
m.1816
Ruth Poynter
(1797–)

Gideon
(1819–)
m.1840
Melanie Benton
(1821–)

- Tyler (1841–)
- Robert (1842–)
- Frank (1843–)

Laura
(1818–)
m.1839
Amos Steele
(1816–)

- Patrick (1840–)
- Colin (1841–)
- Deborah (1842–)
- Clinton (1843–)

Thomas
(1800–1863)
m.1819
Susanna Lee
(1801–)

Melora Yancy
(1834–)
m.1863
Clay
(1820–)
m.1840
Ellen Benton
(1820–1862)

- Denton (1842–)
  m.1861—Thomas (1863–)
  Raimey Reed
  (1843–)
- David (1842–)
- Lowell (1843–)
  m.1863
  Rooney Smith
- Rena (1846–)

Amy
(1822–)
m.1839
Brad Franklin
(1810–)
m.1835
Lila Crawford
(1818–1842)

- Grant (1840–)
- Rachel (1842–)
  m.1862
  Jake Hardin (1836–)
- Les (1844–)
- Vincent (1837–)

Burke
(1830–)
m. 1863
Grace Swenson
(1836–)

Mason
(1805–)
m.1825
Jane Dent
(1807–1833)

Marianne
(1810–)
m.1830
Claude Bristol
(1805–)

Paul
(1831–)
m.1862
Frankie Aimes
(1844–)

Austin
(1832–)

Marie
(1837–)

Mark
(1811–1863)

Allyn Griffeth
(1845–)
m.1863
Jason Larrimore
(1835–)

THE YANCYS

Buford Yancy
(1807–)
m.1829 ───────
Mattie Satterfield
(1813–1851)

─ Royal
  (1832–)
  m.1854
  Margaret O'Hara
  (1835–)
─ Melora
  (1834–)
  m.1863
  Clay Rocklin
  (1820–)
─ Zack
  (1836–)
  m.1859
  Elizabeth Stuart
  (1841–)
─ Cora
  (1837–)
  m.1855
  Billy Day
  (1835–)
─ Lonnie
  (1843–1863)
─ Bobby
  (1844–)
─ Rose
  (1845–)
─ Josh
  (1847–)
─ Martha
  (1849–)
─ Toby
  (1851–)

PART ONE
Vicksburg

CHAPTER ONE
Barrel Staves and Salt

As the tall, rangy, iron-gray gelding plodded wearily down the road, plumes of dust lifted as he planted each foot. The rider, almost as rangy as his mount, glanced up at the sky, which looked hard enough to strike a match on, blinking his eyes against the sun that stared unwinkingly down from above.

"I believe Mississippi's hotter than Virginia!" he murmured through parched lips. Glancing up ahead, he saw a line of trees gathered to the left of the road. Spring had come, filling the trees' bare black branches with green buds, and the rider was drawn to the sight. His face was covered with a film of fine, white dust that formed again as soon as he wiped it with the soiled handkerchief he drew from his inner pocket.

Tall, lean, and wide at the shoulders, David Rocklin had a broad forehead and deep-set eyes. His mouth was wider than most, and his square jaw made him look rather determined. When he removed his gray, low-crowned hat to wipe the dust away again, his hair, as startlingly black as his eyebrows, had a crispness to it that didn't seem to go with the fatigue hooding his dark eyes. Replacing the hat, he slapped his shirt, raising a small cloud, and shook his head. "I don't reckon I'll ever get clean again," he said, eyeing again the line of trees that paralleled the road. "Ought to be a creek over there." Turning the gelding's head, he rode slowly toward the line of trees.

When he reached the line of willows, he was pleased to see a stream almost twenty-five feet wide, and at once he moved upstream to find a place to water his weary horse. The trees were thick and the bank so high that it was ten minutes before he finally pulled in at a bank that sloped gradually to the water. Stepping out of the saddle, he loosed the saddle girth to give the horse a breather, then led him down to where the water gurgled over smooth, rounded stones. The horse lowered his head at once, sucking the water in eagerly.

Rocklin leaned against the horse, watching him drink, then finally pulled him away. "Not too much, Ace," he said softly. "Wait awhile and you can have some more." He pulled the reluctant horse around, tied him to a scrub sapling, then walked slightly upstream, where he tossed his hat on the dry grass and lay flat on his stomach. The water was cool and delicious, and Rocklin had to fight off the temptation to gulp it down, realizing that doing so would bring on stomach cramps. He sipped carefully, the water relieving the dry tissues of his mouth, then sighed and sat back to wait.

Rocklin was so tired that fatigue cramped his bones. He'd left his home in Richmond five days earlier, and now both he and his mount were worn thin. He'd left on a search for salt and barrels, a strange combination. But the Confederacy had been stripped clean, at least in the Richmond area, of these two items. David reached down, picked up a handful of pebbles, and began tossing them out, his mind blank for the moment. He was a man who didn't speak a great deal. In this way he was quite unlike his twin, Denton. As he sat, soaking up the quiet atmosphere of the glen and enjoying the shade that shielded him from the burning sun, he became aware of the whistling cry of a small flock of birds. "Guess you fellows are Mississippi birds," he said, not recognizing them. They flew downstream, their cries echoing back like tiny trumpets. Glancing down at the water, he saw silvery minnows, rank on rank of them, packed closely together. They all moved together as a body—darting more quickly than a man could ever hope to move, stirring the yellow-brown sands of the stream. When they moved away, he took another drink, then watered the horse again. It was almost three o'clock, he judged by the sun, and he had no idea how far he had to go to get to the Cathcart plantation. The small town of Jackson lay twenty miles east, but that was no help for his present problem. He was a stranger to Mississippi, having never been in this part of the world, and had been misled by bad directions.

As he thought again of the long hot ride, he suddenly realized, *By George, a bath wouldn't go down too bad!* He let the horse drink more, then pulled him back and tied him again. He went to the edge of the trees and glanced at the road. It was more a trail than a road, rutted with old wagon tracks made in the mud during the winter. There was no-body in either direction and not a farm, not a house, not even smoke in sight. Eagerly he moved back to the stream, lifted his saddlebag cover, pulled his bedroll from behind Ace, and took out a towel and a bar of pale gray soap. He had no clean underwear, but at least he'd be clean. Quickly he moved to the edge of the stream, stripped down, shook his clothes out as best he could, then waded out. The cool water struck him with a force, swirling around his knees, and the soft, sandy bottom yielded under his bare feet. Sinking down to his chin, he lay there floating, letting the water run over his body. For a long time he soaked up the coolness, so welcome after the hot, dry day. After a while, he soaped up and washed his hair. Then, tossing the soap back on the bank, he sat down so that only his head was above water. Downstream a small, furry, brown animal emerged, holding itself upright with only its head out of the water. Rocklin watched curiously as the lithe body of the otter moved from spot to spot along the creek.

It seemed warmer now, and he grew more and more drowsy as he sat there. *No hurry,* he thought lazily. *I'll get there when I get there* . . . and continued to watch the otter's comic antics.

★   ★   ★

As Leah Cleburne guided her mare through the huge pecan trees, some at least eight feet in diameter, she slapped at the gnats that rose from the ground to swarm around her face, saying sharply, "Get away from me!" She slapped the flank of her horse with a braided crop, and the mare, a small roan, protested by humping her back, then breaking into a fast gallop. Her sudden movement didn't disturb Leah, however, for she was an expert rider. She clamped her right leg more forcefully against the horn of the ladies' riding saddle, thinking, somewhat irritatedly, *Men can ride astride, but women have to hang on with one leg hooked around a blasted horn!* She pulled the mare up sharply as she cleared the grove, then glanced ahead, seeing the dusty road that wound alongside the river and led to the Cathcart house. Her horse was thirsty, so she turned to cross the road and headed for what Ora Mae Cathcart, her best friend, had identified as the Eleven Point River. When Leah had asked her why it was called that, Ora Mae had shrugged, saying blandly, "That's what it's called. I don't know why."

Leah moved across the field toward the river, swaying with the animal's movements. Tall for a woman of that day, Leah somehow managed to appear less than her five-foot-seven-inch height. Her bright red hair was exposed under her black riding hat, and the dark green gown matched her greenish eyes. She had an oval face with a wide mouth and a smooth fullness of neck and figure pleasing to the eye.

Crossing the road, she glanced back to the south, seeing no one, and thought again what an isolated place this part of Mississippi was. She had left Vicksburg to get away from the city's frantic activity, but after a week in this isolated area, where the most exciting event was the Sunday morning service at church, she felt a surge of impatience. She'd spoken sharply to Ora Mae when she'd left for her ride and now was sorry for it. An impulsive young woman, Leah often found herself doing things like this. As she approached the river, she thought, *I'll have to apologize to Ora Mae when I get back. It's not her fault I'm so impatient!*

Noticing a clearing to her left, she led the mare forward. When she reached it, she pulled up short, shocked to see a horse tied to a sapling back away from the stream. Quickly she looked around, but the trees lined the river so thickly except for this one clearing that it would be impossible to see far. She'd been warned about the danger that existed from marauders, both from Confederate and Union troops, so she advanced cautiously. The mare threw up her head, whickering tentatively at the gelding, then stopped at the water's brink.

Looking both downstream and up, Leah wondered at first if someone had fallen in and drowned. But the stream was relatively shallow and not that swift. She then decided that someone had tied the horse and gone hunting along the edges of the river, where squirrels abounded. She tightened her hands on the lines, preparing to turn the mare aside and return to the road, when she remembered she hadn't allowed the animal to drink. Nudging the horse forward with her heel, she sat quietly on the sidesaddle, still alert. When the mare had drunk her fill, Leah realized she too was thirsty. Stepping out of the saddle, she held the lines firmly with one hand, stooped down, and cupped her hand into the water. It was awkward trying to drink like this, but she had nothing to drink with.

Suddenly, a movement caught her eye and she gasped involuntarily as fear jolted her. She saw a man in the water—at least a man's head. He was almost hidden behind some willow branches that leaned out over the stream.

"Woman, will you please get out of here!"

The voice was filled with exasperation, but there was no threat in it that Leah could discern. She blinked with surprise, then grew stubborn, as she sometimes did.

"I'll go as soon as I've finished getting a drink," she said

7

curtly. Deliberately she turned back and took another scoop of water in one cupped hand and then another.

"Will you kindly get yourself out of here!"

The voice was raspy with irritation, and this pleased Leah since she'd been upset for most of the day without any way to manifest it. She turned deliberately to stare at the man whose startling hair, longer than usual, glimmered wetly in the bright sunlight. "It's not my fault if you decide to do your bathing at a public place," she said coolly enough. Now that the fear had passed away, she examined the face of the man more carefully. He was extremely good looking, at least the part she could see. His hair was black as a crow's wing, as were the heavy eyebrows that shaded his dark brown eyes. His face, a slight wedge with a broad forehead, sloped down to a prominent chin that now jutted forward aggressively. Because the planes of his face were smooth, Leah judged him to be no more than twenty-one or twenty-two. She could tell from the muscles in the width of his neck that he was a strong man.

As he stared at her with a mixture of anger and embarrassment, she tormented him a little more. "This is a public place," she said again. "If you had any sense you'd know better than to take a bath here."

"It wasn't public when I got in here. There was nobody in sight. Now, get out of here!"

Leah found the situation amusing. "What will you do if I don't? You don't have a gun on, I see."

"I'll—I'll come out of here. That's what I'll do!"

Leah turned to face him, holding onto the lines of her mare tightly. "Why, come right ahead," she said sweetly. "What's keeping you?" And then she was frightened because the man did suddenly move in the water. He came up, the water just over his waist, and she could see the strength in his chest as the muscles in his arms tensed. However, she wouldn't be bluffed and held her ground, hoping to last him out. She was successful; he stopped abruptly, sank back down into the water, and glared at her.

"You won't come out?" she said, arching her eyebrows in mock surprise. "Well, then, I'll just have to be moving along." She mounted her horse gracefully and turned the mare's head around. As she left, she said, "Don't forget to wash behind your ears!"

"Hey! Wait a minute!"

Leah turned to see that the man had edged around so he could see her leave. His shoulders glistening with the water, he queried, "Which way is it to the Cathcart place?"

"Oh, you're lost as well as unwise about where to take public baths!" Leah hesitated, then pointed with her riding crop. "Go down that road four miles. Then you take a smaller road off to the side. It leads to the Cathcart house."

As she rode off she heard him calling out, "Wait a minute! What's your name?" But she didn't turn.

When she was out of range of the trees, she laughed aloud. The encounter had pleased her, driving away the bad humor. Then, as she slowed her mare down, thinking about the incident, she said aloud, "What would I have done if he *had* come out of that water?"

She shrugged, knowing she would have been in trouble, but then, after a time, she smiled and said reluctantly, "He *is* a handsome thing! Wonder why he's going to the Cathcarts?"

★ ★ ★

From the parlor window, Florence Cathcart had watched the man ride up to the front porch and swing out of the saddle. She studied the stranger carefully as he moved up to the house and past her sight. When she heard his knock on the door, she touched her hair, then walked out of the front parlor into the wide foyer and to the door. "Yes?—What can I do for you?" she asked.

"My name's David Rocklin. I'm looking for Leon Cathcart."

"I'm Mrs. Cathcart. Won't you come in?"

"Thank you." David stepped inside the house, noting

with approval the smoothly polished pine floors and rag rugs scattered about the entrance for muddy feet. The walls were papered, and he saw by glancing around at the portraits on the wall—all framed in gilt—that he'd come to a well-to-do family. "Is Mr. Cathcart at home?" he inquired.

"Why no, he's not, Mr. Rocklin." Florence hesitated, then asked, "Did you have business with him?"

"Yes, ma'am, I wrote him last month. I'm looking to buy a large number of barrels. He wrote back, saying he'd be able to supply me."

"I'm sure he would. . . . Won't you come into the parlor? I've just made some lemonade."

"That would be good. Mighty hot and thirsty out there," David said, smiling.

Florence Cathcart escorted him to the front parlor, which was well lit by tall windows, and nodded toward a horsehair sofa. "Have a seat, Mr. Rocklin. I'll be right back."

She moved to the kitchen, where she quickly procured a pitcher of lemonade and two glasses. Putting them on a tray, she went back to set them on a low table beside her desk and poured one glassful. "Not too cool, but wet."

David picked up the glass and tasted it, his eyebrows lifting with approval. "That's very good," he said. "I've had a dry, thirsty trip. Is it always this hot in Mississippi in April?"

"No, not at all." Mrs. Cathcart spoke about the weather, then said, "I'm sorry you missed my husband."

"Well, when are you expecting him back?"

"He'll be back tomorrow, I'm sure."

David thought of the long road he'd taken, then asked, "Is there a village or someplace ahead where I could get a room for the night?"

"Oh, no, we're very isolated here." Mrs. Cathcart looked at the young man, noting that his dusty clothes were finely made. There was an aristocratic air about him as well, and Florence Cathcart prided herself in knowing quality when she saw it. She made an instant decision. "I'm sure Mr. Cathcart would want you to stay here. We have plenty of rooms in this house—six bedrooms as a matter of fact." She let this fact drop to let her guest know he wasn't the only person of quality in the room. "If you'd like to stay, we'd be glad to have you."

"That would be kind, Mrs. Cathcart. I'd hate to be a bother. . . ."

"No bother at all. Come along and I'll show you to your room."

"Let me unsaddle my horse. If you have a place I could put him out to graze, I'd be grateful."

Fifteen minutes later, David was shown into a room on the second floor. He looked around with appreciation, noting the good furniture, mostly walnut. There was a fine rosewood table beside the bed, which had a massive headboard, and pictures of castles, knights, and ladies on the wall. "This is very nice, Mrs. Cathcart," he said, turning to her.

"I decorated it myself. I'm glad you like it. I'll have one of the servants bring you fresh water so you can clean up. We'll be glad to have you take dinner with us."

"I didn't bring any fancy clothes."

"We're informal here. Perhaps you'd like to lie down and rest awhile. Dinner will be at six."

"Thank you, Mrs. Cathcart."

Ten minutes later, a mulatto woman brought water up and David at once pulled off his shirt and moved to the washstand. He lathered his face, took a straight razor, and blinked as it rasped through the whiskers. He had a tough beard and it was torture for him to shave. His eyes watered, but he worked carefully to avoid slicing his face. Finally, he did a credible job, cleaned the razor, put it back in the leather case, then wrapped the soap up in oilcloth and dried his face carefully. He removed his one change of clothes from the bedroll. Although they were wrinkled, they'd be better than the ones he'd worn for the past three days. "Have to wash them tomorrow," he muttered.

Then he lay down on the bed and dozed off. David had the gift of going to sleep almost instantly under any circumstances, and yet he was a light sleeper. Sometime later a tap on the door sounded and a voice said, "Mr. Rocklin, Miz Cathcart say you come downstairs to eat now."

"Thank you."

David rose quickly and dressed, studying his reflection in the wall mirror as he brushed his hair into place. The shirt was new and bright, with a ruffled collar and a slight ruffle at the sleeves. It was a little fancy for his taste, but these days clothing was at a premium in Richmond. He slipped on close-fitting brown trousers and calf-length boots, and after adding a string tie, left the room.

When he got downstairs, Mrs. Cathcart was waiting for him. "This way to the dining room," she said.

As they entered the dining room, she continued, "My daughter will be down in a moment." Even as she spoke, he heard voices and turned toward the double-wide French doors that opened to the hallway. Two young women suddenly appeared, one in front of the other, and Mrs. Cathcart commented, "This is my daughter, Ora Mae. Ora Mae, this is Mr. David Rocklin."

Ora Mae, a rather plain girl, was wearing a light pink dress that showed off her good figure to the best advantage. Smiling, she said, "How do you do, sir?" Then she stepped aside and added, "I'd like you to meet my friend, Miss Leah Cleburne."

The smile on David Rocklin's face froze, and the greeting he was about to speak so lightly hung in his throat. The young woman who stepped forward was, without doubt, the woman who had caught him bathing in the stream!

"How do you do, Mr. Rocklin?"

Leah's face was smooth and there was no hint of agitation. However, her green eyes were gleaming with humor.

Why, she's laughing at me! David thought with astonishment. He wanted to be angry, but something about the audacity of the young woman caught his fancy. He smiled more broadly and bowed from the hips. "I'm delighted to know you, Miss Cathcart, and you, Miss Cleburne."

"Haven't we met before?" Leah asked, putting her finger on her chin and tilting her head to one side inquisitively.

"I'm sure I would have remembered *you*," David said, half bowing. He couldn't resist smiling even more broadly.

Mrs. Cathcart said, "Come now. Let's sit down and eat."

Soon the table was covered with platters of fried chicken, fried steak, bowls of butter beans, potato salad, mashed potatoes, and pickles of almost every kind imaginable. There was buttermilk, sweet milk, and lemonade to drink.

During the meal, David stole glances at Leah Cleburne. She was witty, he discovered, several times hinting at the encounter they'd had, daring him to speak of it.

After the meal was over, they retired to the sitting room, where they drank imitation coffee and spoke of the war.

After an hour, Mrs. Cathcart rose and said, "It's time for you girls to go to bed. You have to get up early for church in the morning. You can find your room, Mr. Rocklin?"

David took his dismissal and after saying good-night to the women, went upstairs to bed at once, for he was exhausted from his journey. But he lay awake for a while, thinking what a pleasant combination red hair and green eyes made in a young woman.

The next morning he rose and dressed, then went downstairs to find the three women waiting to have breakfast with him. It was a large breakfast and he complimented Mrs. Cathcart profusely.

On the way to church, he sat in the backseat of the carriage with Leah Cleburne while Mrs. Cathcart and her daughter occupied the front with the driver, a tall man with a face the color of ebony. "You're here on a visit, Miss Cleburne?"

"Yes, my home is in Vicksburg."

"How long will you be staying?"

"I'll be going home at the end of the week. What about you, Mr. Rocklin?"

"My family has a plantation outside of Richmond."

"Oh, you raise cotton, I suppose?"

"No, there's no point in raising cotton," David said, shrugging. "Not when Jefferson Davis has forbidden us to sell it." He referred to Davis's plan to create a market for cotton by refusing to let England have it until they recognized the Confederacy. The plan had backfired, however, because England was in the doldrums economically and had cotton to spare. Besides, they had found another source in Egypt where cotton could be obtained at a reasonable price.

"Is your land lying fallow then?"

"No, not exactly," David said, grinning. "We're raising hogs." When he saw her startled expression, he added, "We plant corn and feed hogs out. That's what I'm doing here. We have a contract to furnish salt pork to the Confederate army, but we're out of salt and barrels to pack the meat in."

They talked on the way to church, and when they got out he reached his hand out and took hers. It was warm and firm in his, and she smiled at him. He knew she was still thinking of how she'd caught him in the river, but he dared not say anything in front of the other women.

The service was long and loud. The preacher seemed to have bellows for lungs, and though the building was small, he preached as though there were five thousand people in an amphitheater. His sermon was on hell, and David felt the impact of it, for he was the target of the man's iron-gray eyes.

On the way back home, David commented on the service and Leah smiled, answering, "You might not agree with what the reverend said, but he certainly said it loudly and positively enough."

When they arrived at the house, Leon Cathcart had returned. A tall, heavy man with sharp brown eyes, he greeted David with reserve. But later on, when the two men had talked business, he became more open. "I can furnish the barrels," he said, "but it will take a few days. I just sold the last batch I had. We've got the staves already formed, though. They just have to be hooped."

"Well, I'm going to have to find someone to freight them back to Richmond. Perhaps I can get a room at a town close by."

"No need of that!" Cathcart insisted. "Plenty of room here. I'll be around and there's good hunting here. Perhaps you'd like to try a little of that."

David quickly agreed, and for the next few days he got to know Cathcart well. The two men went hunting several times, then sat in the parlor with the family in the evenings. Both girls were musical, Ora being a fine pianist and Leah possessing a rich singing voice. The third night was the first time he was ever alone with Leah. Ora Mae had been feeling ill and had gone to bed early, and the older people had left at nine, admonishing them to turn the lamps out when they went to bed.

David talked with Leah for some time and finally queried, "I've been wondering if you were ever going to say anything about our first meeting."

Leah smiled instantly. "I don't think I'd better, Mr. Rocklin. It wasn't exactly the proper thing a young woman should do."

"I don't think it's the first time you've ever stepped out of that role. You enjoyed it!"

"Why, Mr. Rocklin! Are you insinuating I'm not a proper young lady?"

"Do you claim you are?"

Leah shrugged. "I get tired of the way women are forced to be what men want them to be."

Interested, David leaned back in the Windsor chair and examined her carefully. She was wearing a plum-colored dress with a bodice cut lower than usual. *A daring dress,* he thought, *except at a fancy ball.* He was fascinated by the redness of her hair, which was touched by gold. "I think you enjoy breaking traditions, don't you, Miss Leah?"

"Yes! I wish I'd been born a man."

"I can't join you in that. Much better to sit here with an attractive woman than some dull man."

The more they talked, the more intrigued David was. Leah refused to take the usual mind track most women followed. There was a boldness about her that wasn't arrogance but a willingness to take the less popular side of issues. She could be blunt, as he found out almost immediately.

"Why aren't you in the army, Mr. Rocklin?"

David blinked with surprise at the audacity of her question. It was true that most men of his age were in the army, and he knew people often wondered, especially strangers, why he wasn't. But no one had ever braced him so straight with the question. "I—my family's pretty well represented," he said carefully. "My father and my twin brother are both officers in the Army of Northern Virginia. I have a younger brother who's also served, until he lost a leg. . . ." When he'd finished, saw she still wasn't satisfied. "As for me . . . well, I can't exactly say. My other brothers were never interested in farming and I was, so I was practically in charge of the plantation when the war came. Then, when my father and brothers went off to the army, there was nobody to take care of it. It seemed to me more important to get food to the men who are fighting." This explanation sounded lame, even to him, and his face grew tense as her steady gaze remained fixed on him. Somewhat angered by her obvious refusal to accept what he'd said, he offered no more reasons and instead said, "I suppose I'd better be getting to bed."

They rose to their feet and she said coolly, "Good night, Mr. Rocklin."

"Good night, Miss Leah."

The next morning, however, she seemed to have forgotten the coolness between them. She enjoyed his company, that was obvious, and he enjoyed hers—more than he had any woman's in a long time. He'd never been in love, and he found Leah's beauty and differentness enticing. As the days moved forward, he spent more and more time with her.

On the following Saturday, Ora Mae and her mother

spoke of this. "I think he's fallen in love with her, Mama," Ora Mae said firmly as the two were alone in the kitchen making a cake. "For a while he wouldn't do anything but go hunting with Pa. Now all he does is take Leah riding."

"You may be right," Mrs. Cathcart said, nodding. She was a great matchmaker, and if her own daughter hadn't been engaged to a young officer stationed with the Army of the Tennessee, she might have done more in that direction. However, she was interested in Leah. "I wonder what her mother would think of Mr. Rocklin for a match?"

"Oh, you know Claire. She's not going to be satisfied with anybody. I never saw such a picky woman!" Ora Mae said sharply. She looked out the window to where Leah and David were walking slowly along. "He is the handsomest thing! It's too bad he'll be going back to Richmond."

"Well, she'd never have him anyway," Mrs. Cathcart said. "You know what a fiery Confederate she is. Whoever Leah falls in love with and marries will be wearing Confederate gray, you can depend on that."

The next day Leah said good-bye to the family, thanking them for their hospitality. "Now," she said warmly to Ora Mae, "you've got to return my visit. When will you come to Vicksburg?"

"I don't think that would be a wise idea," Leon Cathcart said at once, shaking his head gravely. "Things are looking grim there with Grant trying to take that place."

"He'll never take Vicksburg," Leah said definitely. "Why, they call it the Gibraltar of the South. I wish the Yankees would try it!" Her eyes gleamed with anger for a moment, then she kissed the two women. Mr. Cathcart stepped outside to speak to the driver as David opened the door for Leah. Once outside, Leah turned to David and extended her hand. "I'm glad I got to see so much of you, Mr. Rocklin." Again there was an impish light in her eyes, though her words were demure enough.

David laughed aloud. "Maybe I can return the compliment some day, Leah." The two had gotten very close, on a

66

superficial plane at least, and as he held her hand, he said, "I hope to see you again."

"I doubt if you will. Mr. Cathcart's right. Vicksburg's not a safe place these days."

David couldn't help but wonder if she were referring to his own lack of courage. "If I didn't have to chase all over the country looking for salt, I'd pay you that visit," he said firmly.

Leah stared at him. "Salt! Is that what you're looking for? I thought it was barrels."

"That, too, but we're out of salt in Virginia. You can't have salt pork without salt. It's hard to get in the South, what with the blockade and all."

"Why, I have a neighbor in Vicksburg," Leah said slowly, trying to remember, "who said . . ." She thought for a moment, then continued, "He said he had a whole warehouse full of salt that came in on a ship. It was to be shipped, but then the Yankees blockaded the river."

"A lot of salt?" David asked eagerly.

"Oh, he said it was." Her eyes studied him and then, when Mr. Cathcart called, she said, "Well, good-bye. It's been most entertaining, Mr. Rocklin." She boarded the carriage and David watched as it drove off.

"Salt—a whole warehouse," he murmured. "And in Vicksburg! Now, that's downright interesting. . . ."

CHAPTER TWO
A Soldier of the Confederacy

"William Dabney came by to check on you while you were gone, Leah," Claire Cleburne mentioned, watching her daughter's face sharply. The two of them were sitting on the front porch watching a group of soldiers drilling down on the street. All of them were dressed in ordinary working clothes and seemed clumsy. One of them dropped the musket he was attempting to manipulate, and the sergeant, clad in a Confederate gray uniform, barked his displeasure profanely.

Leah shook her head at the ineptness of the soldiers, then turned to her mother. Well aware that she and her mother didn't hold similar views on the young man mentioned, she asked quietly, "Did he?"

"Yes, he seemed real interested." At forty, Claire Cleburne looked ten years younger. Her auburn hair and clear gray eyes were a complement to her fair skin. She was wearing a well-cut, modish gray dress and sat upright in an oak rocking chair.

Before Leah could comment, a petite woman with light brown hair sprinkled with silver joined them. She had brown eyes and was plain in appearance, but she walked with dignity. She was wearing a simple blue cotton dress, and her hair was done up in an old-fashioned way. This was Amelia Seaton, Claire's aunt. She seated herself in one of the cane-bottomed chairs and began at once to knit a sock out of green yarn.

"I was just telling Leah that William Dabney came by," Claire said. "Such a fine young man—and I think he's very interested in you."

"I suppose so." Leah didn't sound particularly interested, which she wasn't. She continued to watch the soldiers, who attempted to start and stop on time without conspicuous success. "If that's what we've got to stop the Yankees with," Leah remarked petulantly, "I think we have difficulties."

"Where is Grant now?" Amelia kept her eyes on the face of the young woman, listening closely as Leah began to speak of the approach of the Federal general who had been sent by Lincoln with a large army to capture Vicksburg. It was common enough knowledge that Grant, who had been the victor over Fort Donelson, was Lincoln's best chance of subduing Vicksburg.

Claire listened as Leah spoke, then changed the subject. "You haven't said much about your visit with the Cathcarts."

"It's a dull place with nothing at all to do. I was glad to get back home." Leah leaned back in her chair, rocked tentatively, and said, "I did meet one interesting man."

Claire looked up quickly. She was, as most women in her position, keenly interested in her daughter's prospects. After all, she thought, what was there for a young woman to do except marry? And of course, marrying involved a ritual as formal as the mating of cranes. Some things had to be said, other things had to be done, arrangements had to be made. And Leah was so exasperating about it all! So now Claire asked eagerly, "Who was it? One of the Cathcarts' friends?"

"No, his name is David Rocklin. He's the son of a wealthy planter close to Richmond," she said innocently enough, with a glitter of humor in her eyes. "I saw quite a bit of him."

"What was he doing in an isolated place like that?" Amelia inquired.

"He'd come to buy barrels from Mr. Cathcart." She hesitated, thinking about the young man, then added, "He

20

may be coming here to Vicksburg. He's looking for salt. I told him William Dabney had a whole warehouse full of it."

"Is he acceptable?" Claire asked. By *acceptable*—a code word all three women understood perfectly—she was asking, Is he single? Does he have money? Is his family respectable?

Leah smiled sourly. "I suppose so. He's not married and not too old. He's got all of his arms and legs and doesn't chew tobacco that I know of."

"What a thing to say!" Amelia exclaimed, amused by Leah's ribald remarks. "Was he handsome?"

"He looked very well. I don't suppose he'll come here, though. Not with Vicksburg about to be descended upon by the Yankees. . . ."

★ ★ ★

When Amelia answered the door, a tall man removed his hat and asked in a pleasant voice, "I wonder if I might see Miss Cleburne? This is her home, is it not?"

"Yes it is, sir."

"My name's David Rocklin. I met Miss Cleburne at the Cathcart home."

At once Amelia opened the door saying, "Come in! She did mention that." As he entered, Amelia's sharp eyes took in the strong figure, the well-cut clothes, and she said at once, "If you'll wait in the parlor, Mr. Rocklin, I'll send her down."

Amelia walked upstairs immediately and knocked on Leah's door.

"Yes? What is it?"

Opening the door, Amelia said, "It's David Rocklin. He's come calling on you."

Leah stared at her blankly, then got to her feet, a smile on her face. "What did you think of him, Aunt Amelia?"

"Very handsome!"

"Yes, he is. Has Mother seen him yet?"

"No, not yet."

"Well, try to keep her from proposing, will you? She's so anxious to get me married off, I don't think she'd mind doing that in the least."

Amelia smiled but said nothing as she followed Leah downstairs. She didn't go into the sitting room with the girl, however, but went outside to the backyard where Claire was talking with Deets. Although the black man had put in gardens more years than Claire had been alive, Claire still felt it important to give instructions. When she saw Amelia, she asked, "What is it?"

"That young man Leah talked about—David Rocklin— he's here! They're in the sitting room." A light appeared in Claire's eyes as Amelia continued, "He looks very well. You don't see many men as fine looking as this one."

Inside, Leah had gone at once to the sitting room and, upon seeing David Rocklin, had held out her hand saying, "You did come! I'm glad to see you, sir."

He took her hand, bent over, and kissed it suddenly. It was an unexpected thing—something he'd rarely done. The sight of Leah affected him strongly. He'd thought of her steadily for several days and now he said with more fervency than usual, "You look lovely, Leah."

Leah was taken aback and said lamely, "You've come a long way for salt!"

"I didn't come for salt. I came to see you. The salt's just an excuse."

Leah was pleased with his compliment. "I'm always glad to be esteemed more than a load of salt. Sit down . . . or do you have to go buy the salt right now?"

"Oh, no. There's no hurry at all. Matter of fact," David said as he took a seat on one of the satin-covered chairs that was backed against the wall, "I hope it takes quite awhile to get the dickering done. I'd like to see Vicksburg while I'm here."

The two sat there talking and finally Leah said, "I'd like for you to meet my family."

"I'd be very happy. I've already met one lady."

"That was my Aunt Amelia. I'll go get my mother."

Leah disappeared and soon returned with Claire in tow. "May I present Mr. David Rocklin—and this is my mother, Claire."

David wasn't surprised to see Leah's mother was attractive. He bowed, saying, "I'm happy to meet you. Your daughter has made me feel very welcome in Mississippi."

"Are you in Vicksburg on business?" Claire asked. As David explained his mission, she summed up the tall young man carefully. He was fine looking, as Leah had said, and had a pleasant air about him. As soon as he'd finished, she said, "We'd be happy to have you take dinner with us tonight, if it would be convenient."

"Oh, quite convenient. I don't know a soul here," David responded instantly. "What time shall I return?"

"Come back about six. We'll look forward to seeing you then."

As soon as David left, Leah turned to her mother. "What did you think of him?"

"A well-set-up young man. Tell me more about his family." She sat listening while Leah, amused, told what she knew about David's family, then spoke aloud what was troubling her. "He's not in uniform. That's rather unusual."

"His father and brother are in the army," Leah said. "He says his family urged him to stay home and keep the plantation running. They've started raising pigs now, packing salt pork for the troops."

"Very necessary, and I'm sure he does an excellent job. Well, I'd better go talk to Sissy about supper, if we're to have guests."

★ ★ ★

That evening after supper, they all sat on the porch. It was a beautiful night, with a clear display of the stars. A slight haze settled over the Mississippi, which lay east of them. As they spoke, their voices soft on the night air, lights twinkled from the Vicksburg hillsides. The conversation was pleasant, and

23

David talked more than was customary for him. Claire, who was intense and wore an expression David couldn't quite understand, was nonetheless skillful. David realized she'd learned a great deal about him during the evening.

Finally, at nine o'clock, David was about ready to take his leave when a sudden burst of noise shattered the peace of the evening. "It's the guns!" Leah cried. "The gunboats guarding the Mississippi!"

David stood up, confused. "Who are they shooting at?"

"Grant! It must be Grant and his gunboats. They're trying to run the Mississippi—come on!" Without even pausing for a coat, Leah ran down the steps.

Her mother called out, but she ignored her. At once David said, "I'll watch out for her, Mrs. Cleburne." He leaped off the porch, ignoring the steps, and caught up with her. She flashed a look at him, her face intent. *She loves this,* David thought. *Any kind of excitement or challenge stirs her up.*

They joined a yelling crowd of people as Vicksburg suddenly swarmed out into the streets. They were all running, and most of them were shouting. Among them were ladies in their most fashionable evening attire, for a grand spring ball had been interrupted. The hoop skirts made it difficult for them, but they ignored this and plunged toward the river. Shrieks rang out when sections of masonry crumbled under the impact of Federal shells.

"They're shooting back!" David said in surprise.

"Of course they are! What did you expect!"

David, feeling foolish, made his way with Leah to the river as shot and shell continued to scream overhead, exploding among the buildings of Vicksburg.

★ ★ ★

The architect of the advance of the gunboat armada down the Mississippi, Ulysses S. Grant, was standing on the deck of a river transport, his wife, Julia, and children with him. One of the children sat on his knees with her arms around Grant's neck, and as each crash came, she clasped her father closer. Finally she became so frightened that Grant murmured, "Time for bed!" and a servant took the child away.

Frederick Dent Grant, then twelve years old, later recalled, "On board our boat, my father and I stood side by side on the Hurricane Deck. He was quietly smoking, but an intense light shone in his eyes."

Grant had first attempted to take Vicksburg by land, but the bayous of the swampy country had bogged his army down. Now, in cooperation with Adm. Porter, he'd devised a plan to break the long, frustrating deadlock. Grant's army was to pick its way through the swamps on the western side of the Mississippi to a point well below the city. Porter was to take the fleet directly past Vicksburg's batteries in the night. Then, once it met Grant's army, he was to ferry it across to the western banks where an attack could be made on Vicksburg directly. As Grant sat quietly watching the shells explode among the fleet that churned in the muddy waters of the Mississippi, some of them struck by shot that set them on fire, he must have known his reputation rested on this one venture. But he was a bulldog of a man, his chief virtue being the ability to concentrate totally on whatever lay before him. As one man described him, "Grant habitually wears an expression as if he had determined to drive his head through a brick wall and was about to do it!"

★ ★ ★

A strange sense of depression settled over the entire city of Vicksburg on April 16, 1863, after Porter's fleet successfully ran the batteries of Vicksburg. All understood that the ships would ferry the Union army across the Mississippi—and that that same force would soon be knocking at the gates of the city. It was as if a fatigue drained the energies of the townspeople. During these two days, David got a good sense of the city of Vicksburg itself. On his first day, he went out and made his way through the city. It was a neat town, a river port, laid out in precise geometric patterns. Most of the streets were straight, made right angles, and the buildings and plots were neatly measured into squares. He quickly found, however, that it was different from most cities, being sprawled across an undulating landscape of hills. It was sometimes called "A City of a Hundred Hills." David made his way down roads where houses were found on many different levels, like flotsam scattered over crests and hollows of waves. And, dominating all, on the highest hill, stood the new courthouse, its cupola lifted to the sky. It was an impressive structure, standing in eminent solitude. He walked around its freshly stuccoed pillars, ignoring the cannonade that still vibrated through the air from time to time from the wandering gunboats. But the city was silent. Even the bright flag, with its two broad red stripes hedging the single white one, hung limply on the pole, high on the courthouse cupola.

To David, Vicksburg was completely different from Richmond. Along the waterfront, black stevedores worked at the slowest possible rate while white overseers, drained of energy, chewed their cheroots. All along the streets idlers moved silently, if at all, and on the roads, drivers and riders moved in slow motion. All of them, from time to time, stared at the river in dismay.

David found a room, putting off the meeting with William Dabney, for he wasn't anxious to leave Vicksburg. Sunday morning he went to church with the three women. All the denominations were represented, and he supposed each would be praying for deliverance from the villainous Yankees. The various churches were crowded with civilians and off-duty soldiers. Saint Paul's, the Catholic cathedral they passed, was no exception. Those who attended mass left as part of the throng that flowed sluggishly down the church steps and onto the streets.

The Methodist church, where the Cleburnes escorted him, was filled to overflowing.

With a salty tang in her voice as she entered the church beside David, Amelia said quietly, "Our church was never this crowded in peacetime. I guess people get more religious when their skins are in danger."

David grinned down at her. She was a cheerful woman but he'd learned her life hadn't been easy. She'd been married to a man whom she never mentioned except indirectly, calling him "he" without using his name. "He" had been a cotton broker who had died and, after his death, Amelia had discovered he'd wasted his small fortune on women and gambling. Now she lived on a small fund that came from the wreckage of the estate, making her home with her niece and Leah since there was nowhere else for her to go.

During the service, Claire was very much aware of the attention David Rocklin drew. She saw William Dabney straighten up in his chair and frown as they passed, but she only smiled at him courteously.

The service was conducted by a tall, thin minister with a shock of white hair and light blue eyes. He had a soft accent and, unlike most preachers of that denomination, was not a shouter or a ranter. Most of his sermon was given over to exhortation to accept the will of God and to endure hardship with grace and humility.

After the service, David shook hands with the pastor and complimented him on his sermon.

"I don't believe we've met?" Rev. Simms inquired.

"No sir, I'm a visitor. First time I've been in Vicksburg."

He turned at a touch on his arm and Mrs. Cleburne said, "I'd like for you to meet Mr. William Dabney."

At once David recognized the name Leah had given him. "Why, I'm happy to meet you, Mr. Dabney. I believe you're the man I came to Vicksburg to see."

Dabney was a middle-sized man, tending to overweight. He blinked and said, "Sir, I don't believe I understand?"

"This is no time to conduct business," David said, "but if I may, I'll call upon you in the morning."

"Certainly, sir. Certainly." Dabney quickly moved to take Leah's arm and escort her down the steps. "Who is this man, Leah?"

"Oh, I met him last week. He was at the Cathcarts."

"What's this business he has with me?"

Leah smiled and teased him by assuming a pious expression. "It's not right to talk business on the Sabbath, William. Come along, I know Mother's expecting you for dinner."

The dinner was excellent, and Dabney tried every way he could to find out as much as he could about David Rocklin. David was just as determined to keep him from it. Leah understood the duel at once and enjoyed it.

After the meal was over and the two men had left, Amelia observed candidly, "You've got a mean streak in you, Leah Cleburne."

"Mean?" Leah looked innocently at Amelia, raising her eyebrows. "I don't know what you mean, Aunt Amelia."

"Yes, you do. You tormented those two men! You know how jealous Dabney is. I thought he was going to turn absolutely green."

Leah laughed. "It'll do him no good—or harm either."

Claire had come in to hear this last remark. "William Dabney's a good man—I want you to be nicer to him."

"All right, Mother." Leah had long since stopped arguing with her mother. Although she wasn't interested in Dabney as a suitor, he was persistent. For a year now he had come calling regularly as if it were a duty, although he enjoyed her company well enough. He was not at all romantic, which pleased her greatly since she wanted none of that from Dabney.

"We'll have to show Mr. Rocklin our favorite places in town," Leah said, smiling. "All he's seen so far is the Yankees blasting us off the hillside. But we'll do better, I trust."

★ ★ ★

The next few days were pleasant for David. He'd never met a young woman as charming as Leah Cleburne, and he was in no hurry to get back home. Things were not pressing there and, to be truthful, he was tired of raising hogs. At one time it had been a joy for him to farm, but somehow raising hogs didn't have the romance others apparently saw in it.

His quest for supplies was nearly done, but he felt no inclination to return home. He wasn't needed—Josh was an able manager for the time being. *I might as well stay and enjoy myself,* he thought to himself one afternoon as he dressed, preparing to take Leah to a party. *Better than looking at those pigs back home.*

He left his hotel room and made his way to Leah's house. When he entered, she met him at once. "You're right on time!" he said with a smile. "I didn't know women could do that."

"Women can do all sorts of things you don't know about, David," Leah retorted. She was wearing a pale green silk dress, complete with hoop skirt and snowy white lace along the neckline and at the cuffs. She wore small jade earrings, and her red hair hung down her back in heavy waves. As they got into the carriage he had brought, she said, "I think you'll enjoy this party tonight. You'll get to meet most of the officers in charge of the defense of Vicksburg."

This proved to be true for, when they went inside the white three-story house where the party was being held in a massive room, the room was bright with the colors of women's dresses, set off by the ash-gray uniforms of Confederate officers. Gold buttons and braid sparkled under the lights of the chandeliers, and the air was filled with laughter and talk.

"You'd never know this place was in such danger," he said quietly to Leah.

"I suppose people would have a party in the evening if the world were coming to an end the next morning. Come along and let me introduce you to my friends."

In the next hour, David met the most illustrious guest, Gen. John C. Pemberton, the Confederate commander. Pemberton was a tall man and rather nervous—as he had every right to be, David thought.

The names, of course, went by David as quickly as they came, but he did remember a young captain of artillery named Raymond Finch. At twenty-five, Finch was husky and had brown eyes and brown hair. His uniform was exquisitely cut, obviously made by a private tailor, and upon finding out that David came from Richmond, he began firing questions about the situation there. A crowd soon gathered about them, and David became the center of attention. He felt out of place without a uniform but was accustomed to that.

"What's Lee going to do?" Finch demanded.

David said, shrugging, "Well, Gen. Lee hasn't let me in on his plans, but I suppose everyone is convinced he's going to invade the North." A murmur of approval went around the room and Finch nodded emphatically. "It'll be a difficult thing," David continued, "but everyone in Richmond thinks it'll happen."

For some time he fielded questions, and finally Finch asked the one he'd been anticipating. "You are a believer in the cause, Mr. Rocklin?"

"Yes," David said. "Of course, I'm not in uniform, which is unusual for a man of my age—"

He saw agreement in the eyes of Finch, who waited for his explanation. When he gave it, it wasn't satisfactory. Finch studied him carefully and commented, "Well, I suppose someone needs to raise pigs while the fighting men go out and do the work."

David's cheeks reddened at the blatant insult. Quietness fell around the little circle as Finch waited for David to take it up. David Rocklin, however, was a mild young man and he'd always been so. When the war had come he'd had none of the fiery zeal to join as had most young men his age. As the war had dragged on, more and more he was aware there would be no happy ending in this struggle for the South. He was convinced that sooner or later the ponderous weight of the Federal war machine would lead to a dire and tragic disaster. Now, however, he knew he had to answer, and he said quietly, "I respect all those who wear the uniform, Captain. Several members of my family serve in the military." It was all the explanation he made or intended to make. As he waited patiently, he was glad to see Finch relax.

Later, on their way home, Leah complimented him on his

tact. "It must be very hard for you," she said. "I suppose you get that kind of challenge all the time." They were riding along the deserted streets; the skies were velvet with fiery points of light that burned and vibrated. From time to time they would pass a soldier on guard, but other than that, all was still.

"I don't take offense easily," he responded. "I never did. If you want that, go to my brother Dent. He'd fight a buzz saw or a bear—and give the bear the first bite."

"He sounds like an exciting fellow. Tell me more about him." She listened as David related how his twin had been terribly scarred at the battle of Manassas—and how he'd married a blind girl named Raimey. "They're very happy," he said, nodding as he ended the story.

"He must love her a lot . . . to marry a blind girl," Leah murmured.

"I don't think he even notices that—not anymore." He thought for a time, then added, "She lives in fear Dent will get killed, but she never lets him know it."

"Tell me about the rest of your family."

By the time they arrived at the house, Leah knew a great deal about the Rocklins of Virginia. Finally they reached the house, where he stepped down, went around, and handed her to the ground. When they were back at the steps, she turned to say good-night and he surprised her—and himself.

"Leah," he said, "I'm not a ladies' man."

Startled, Leah looked up at him. The silvery moonlight bathed her face in its warm beams. The air was filled with the smell of honeysuckle from the vines that draped a wall to the right side of the house. She was taken off guard and said so. "Most men don't want to admit that!"

"Well, it's true enough."

He was so tall that he seemed to tower over her. Although she herself was more than average height, she looked dainty and fragile in the frilly dress she wore, almost like a mist in the moonlight. "Why are you telling me this, David?"

He made no attempt to touch her. All of his life he'd been compared to his twin, Dent, usually unfavorably. Dent was dashing, romantic, adventurous—and David was the quiet one. . . "the dull one," he usually translated that to mean. Although he had the same good looks as Dent, he'd never been attracted to women, nor had they been attracted to him, strangely enough. Oh, there had been some, but none he really cared for. Now as he stared at Leah, he said haltingly, "I don't know why I wanted to tell you that. It's obvious enough, I guess. Anyway, I did want to say that it's been wonderful, this time with you. You're a fine young woman."

He spoke so simply and without affectation that Leah was speechless for a moment. She was accustomed to more aggressiveness from young men. She had fully expected that by this time, certainly tonight, he would attempt to kiss her, but he made no attempt to do so. He stood there, the masculine planes of his face outlined by the starlight, and a strength and solid quality about him that she didn't often see. "Why . . . thank you, David. It's been fun for me, too. And, it's not over," she said. "You're not going home right away, are you?"

"No, I'm arguing about the price of salt with Bill Dabney. He's so jealous of you, I think he'd *give* it to me to get me out of town. But he's too tight for that!"

"He's close with a dollar, all right. You just keep bargaining. There's lots more I want to do with you." Leah looked up, smiled, and whispered, "Good night, David," then turned and went into the house.

David stepped to the carriage, then drove it back to the livery stable. He walked back to the hotel, undressed, and got into bed, where he lay quietly for a while, thinking of how her face had looked in the moonlight. He smiled and said aloud, "No question what Dent would have done. Maybe I should have had him give me lessons on how to be romantic."

★ ★ ★

Another day passed, then two. By this time most of Vicksburg, at least those in the inner circle, knew David Rocklin was not staying to buy salt. He'd already done that, paying a fair price and arranging for the freighting all the way back to Richmond. Dabney had been grudging enough about it and, when he had wished David good-bye, after the deal had been closed, had been disgruntled when David had said cheerfully, "Oh, there's no hurry. I'll stay around for a week or two to see what happens."

During that time, David Rocklin had experienced the most enjoyable time of his life. Away from the pressures of the plantation at Richmond, not having to face the crises that constantly seemed to envelop that city, he felt differently about Vicksburg. After all, it was not *his* city!

He and Leah had a grand time together. They went on picnics, and she even took him fishing once on a cutback from the Mississippi where they caught catfish. She shuddered properly over baiting a hook with a worm. They went down to the river to watch the gunboats every day and then had supper at her home. This was usually followed by a time of sitting in the parlor.

David Rocklin was engaged in something new to his experience—falling completely in love with a young woman. He'd always assumed this would come to him sometime, but not so soon. But it was happening now, although he dared not mention it to Leah. The young people in Vicksburg watched all this carefully because who married whom was the big game in Southern society. Here in Vicksburg, even with the war machine about to grind them to pieces, it was no different.

It was on April twenty-fifth that David stepped out of character. He had gone with Leah to visit one of the two farms Dabney owned outside Vicksburg. Dabney himself had escorted them around. The purpose of the visit was, according to Dabney, for Leah to see to the decorating of the large room for a party, then to be the hostess.

While the two were inside, David wandered around. It was not a well-kept farm, he saw. The slaves looked sullen, and it was with one of these that he was shaken out of his composure.

David was watching when Dabney came out of the house with a white man, evidently the overseer. They went to a barn where Dabney spoke loudly to a tall slave who stood silently. When David moved closer, he heard Dabney cursing the man. The slave merely shook his head. Dabney yelled, "Tie him up! I'll teach him who owns him!"

David watched as they tied the slave to a fence. The overseer came forward, grinning, a black snake whip in his hand. "Let him feel a taste of that!" Dabney commanded.

"Yes sah!" the overseer said and at once brought the lash down on the slave's bare back. It left a pale streak that immediately rose up the size of a man's finger, and the lash struck again, crisscrossing the first mark.

David was sickened by the sight. He'd heard of such things and when he was very young had even seen one slave whipped. But this never took place at Gracefield, his own plantation.

The whip rose and fell, and David saw pleasure on Dabney's face as he stood back and watched.

Finally, David moved forward and Dabney caught his eye. "That's enough," he said, turning to David. "You know what this nigger says? He says he won't work! I suppose you got this kind on your place, too?"

David's face was set but he said evenly, "We usually don't have to whip our people."

"Then you must have a different kind of niggers. I paid four thousand dollars for this 'un and he's not worth spit! But he will be by the time I get through whipping him."

"He won't be much good to you if you beat him half to death," David said. "Maybe you might try another way."

Dabney stared at him, his face full of contempt. "You come all the way from Richmond to tell us how to treat our slaves? You think you could do better? Then you can buy him—just what I paid for him."

David instantly said, "Why, of course, Mr. Dabney. He looks like a good hand. If you'll make out the papers, I'll write you out a check."

Dabney was aware that Leah was now standing to one side. He took one look at her face and said quickly, "You don't want this nigger!"

When David didn't answer but simply stood there, Dabney knew he had to go through with it. "All right," he said, grumbling. "I'll go make out the papers."

As he left, his back stiff with anger, David looked at the overseer, who was staring at him with wide eyes. "That's all," he said, dismissing him brusquely. Then he stepped over and pulled his knife from his pocket. After slitting the rawhide that held the slave's hands together, he closed the knife and stepped back. The slave turned slowly to look at him. He had not flinched during the terrible beating, and now he stood looking at his new owner, hatred gleaming out of his eyes. He was six feet tall, powerfully built, and a rich brown color. But it was his eyes that attracted David the most. They were intelligent—and bitter.

"What's your name?" David asked quietly.

"Corey . . . Corey Jones."

"Well, Corey, I think we'd better see about that back of yours."

"I'm all right . . . sah." The last word was slow in coming and there was resentment in the slave's attitude.

"Don't be foolish. I'm sure there's something to put on it. My name's David Rocklin. You'll be going back to Virginia with me." He hesitated, then said, "I'll see you don't have to go through this anymore."

Unbelief blazed out of the slave's eyes, but he was silent.

On their way home, Corey sat in the back of the carriage, glowering, a sack of meager possessions in his hands. The two in front were intensely aware of him but said nothing. Finally, when they got to the house, Leah said, "Why don't you leave Corey here with us until you're ready to go?"

David said at once, "That would be a help. I don't really have a place." His eyes warm, he turned to the slave. "Corey, I'll be here a few more days. You help Miss Leah all you can, and I'm sure she'll see you're well bestowed."

The slave stared at him, then at Leah. Without a word he got out of the carriage and stood waiting. Leah turned to David, saying, "Well, I doubt if William will want me to grace his party now. He was embarrassed about all this."

"So was I . . . and humiliated. I never could stand to see anybody mistreated."

"Even a slave?"

He stared at her. "Yes, even a slave!"

She studied him carefully as if seeing something she hadn't seen. Then her eyes grew gentle. "You're very nice," she said. "There's a goodness in you that I love to see, but don't often find." Then she got out of the carriage, saying, "Come along, Corey. I'll show you where you can stay."

★ ★ ★

On April 30, Grant and his army were ferried across the Mississippi by the navy of Adm. Porter. As soon as word got to Vicksburg, every person there knew what it meant. David was eating supper with the Cleburnes, and it was Claire who said nervously, "I feel we'll be all right. Gen. Pemberton will certainly be able to keep those Yankees from taking the city."

Amelia, who kept up with military news better than Claire, shook her head. "He's got a big army, and Sherman will be joining him. It's going to be close."

David watched and listened, saying little. Later that night, as they sat on the front porch after supper, all felt the pressure that seemed to be closing around the town like a fist. The women talked of old times.

"I wish you could have known my father, Thaddeus Rayborn," Claire said. "Have you heard of him?"

"I've heard of a Congressman Rayborn."

"That was him; that was my father." Her face glowed as she continued, "He was the best lawyer in the state of Mississippi, maybe in the whole country. He was so wonderful! I used to go watch him in the courtroom. He hardly ever lost a case."

David listened for some time as Claire talked about her

father. He found it strange she never mentioned her husband. David had made the mistake once of saying something to Amelia about Claire's "late" husband, and Amelia had answered instantly, "Her husband isn't dead. His name is Matthew Cleburne and he lives in New York. They're separated."

Now as Claire talked eloquently about her father, with great spirit and longing, David realized Leah was listening intently, her eyes fixed on her mother. *I wonder what she feels?* David wondered. *I can't ask her about it, though. Maybe I can ask Amelia later on.*

Later he did ask Amelia about Claire's marriage, and she replied, "It was tragic. The marriage didn't last long. After Leah was born, Claire grew more and more unhappy and finally separated from her husband. He moved to New York and went into business there."

"What was it, Amelia?" David asked, feeling he could ask her honestly.

Amelia looked down at her hands, reluctant to answer. "He drank some . . . and there was talk about a woman."

There was something in her voice that drew David's attention. "But that wasn't all of it?"

Again a silence, then Amelia looked up at him, misery in her eyes. "She worshiped her father—my brother. She saw everything in him that she admired in a man—and afterwards, when she grew up, she demanded those same things from other men." Silence fell again, cutting across the room like a knife. From somewhere a bird called out in a lonesome fashion, and Amelia waited until the mournful tone had died away. "I don't think," she said in a whisper, "Claire would ever have found what she saw in her father in any other man. I—I liked Matthew very much—but now Claire won't let his name be mentioned."

"Hard on Leah."

"Yes—very hard!"

As the week progressed, David picked up other hints of this situation. When he asked Leah she said restlessly, "I haven't seen him since I was fifteen years old. Before that, I don't remember when he lived with us. I saw him a few times when I was a child and he came and visited. He took me to a fair once and bought me everything I wanted. But he left after that. Now he writes and sends money."

"I'm sorry," he said. "I know that's hard for you."

She turned to him and David saw tears in her eyes. They'd been walking along the street after supper, and now that they'd reached the porch, she seemed depressed. He said quietly, as if he were saying nothing of particular importance, "Leah, I have something to say to you."

Surprised, she looked up. Thinking about her father always saddened her, although she usually covered it better. But there was something about David Rocklin, something she hadn't felt with any other man, perhaps because she saw no threat in him, that brought out this willingness to share things. Now, as she looked at him, she saw his face was utterly serious.

"I love you, Leah, and I mean to make you love me."

"Why, David—!"

"I know," he interrupted, shaking his head, "I'm not very romantic, am I? I wish I were."

"But you can't . . . you can't mean it! We've only known each other a few days!"

"I don't think that matters. I've known other women for years but I've never felt like this. I'm not asking you for anything, but I think it's only fair to tell you how I feel."

Suddenly, Leah was confused. *Here's a man Mother would at least accept. He's rich, he has a good family, and he's young, nice-looking, and has good manners.*

But that wasn't enough for Leah Cleburne. She looked at him and said gently, "I hate to say this to you, David, but I could never let myself love you."

Her words cut him and he stared at her. "Never?" he asked. "Are you sure?"

"Oh, David," she said compassionately, "It's not *you.*

You're one of the most gentle men I've ever known, perhaps the most gentle. You have so many good qualities, but—"

Suddenly he realized what she was saying. "It's because I'm not in the army, isn't it?"

Leah's lips pressed tightly together. "I believe in the Confederacy," she said. "Those of us who do have risked everything we have—and you've risked nothing, David. Two people couldn't live together unless they agreed on the important things, and this is one of the *most* important things."

David stood looking down at her. Her skin was like alabaster in the moonlight, and he could smell the slight jasmine fragrance she wore in her hair sometimes. Finally, he said slowly, "I can see that."

"You can? Then you understand?" she said eagerly.

"Yes, of course I can." He stood there quietly and then said, "Good night, Leah."

He turned and walked away, leaving her alone. As she watched him go, a sense of loss flooded her. "Have I made a mistake?" she whispered aloud. He disappeared into the darkness, and still she stood there, feeling a strangeness she couldn't explain. If he'd been more aggressive, it might have been easier. But now she felt somehow that she'd failed, and she didn't know why. Slowly, she turned and went into the house, not even hearing when Amelia spoke to her.

★　★　★

David stayed away from Leah the next day, May 8, and walked the streets of Vicksburg in silence. He thought of Corey, the slave he'd purchased, and wondered what would become of him. He thought about taking him back to Richmond. He slept poorly. Finally, on the ninth, he appeared at the Cleburne house late in the afternoon. When Leah opened the door, her hand flew up to her lips.

"Here I am, Leah."

"David," Leah whispered, "I can't believe it."

David Rocklin was wearing the uniform of a private in the

Confederate army. It was an ill-fitting uniform made for a smaller man and seemed to pinch. He stood there looking awkward and ill at ease, but he smiled at her saying, "I've come courting, Miss Leah. May I come in?"

Leah shook her head in disbelief. She put out a trembling hand and he took it. Leaning over, he kissed it and said, "I had to do it, Leah, but I must tell you, I just enlisted for ninety days. At least I'll be able to do something in this battle that's shaping up."

"Why did you do it, David?" Leah said, although she knew.

Then, for the first time, he reached out and pulled her close so she was leaning against him, with her face turned up. He kissed her slowly, savoring the softness of her lips. Her hands gripped his arms, and she was aware of the strength of the man who held her and the way it made her feel safe and secure. But she was also filled with shock at what he'd done and thought, *A man who would do this for a woman must really love her.*

As if in answer to her thoughts, he lifted his head and said, "I love you, Leah. I won't ask you for an answer now, but you mean more to me than anything in this world."

Leah's eyes grew misty. She said softly, "Come in, David, and let's tell Mother and Amelia."

CHAPTER THREE
A Taste of Fear

On May 11, David Rocklin was introduced to his share of the Confederate army. He'd been connected, in a way, with soldiers and camps before, having spent much time with his father and brothers with the troops in Richmond. This, however, he quickly learned, was far different. Early Monday morning, he found himself in front of Capt. Noland Devers, who was in charge of Company C, and the heavy, profane, balding man who looked him over seemed displeased. As a political officer, Devers had never actually seen a battle. He was the sort of officer who was the curse of both the Confederates and the Federals, since neither Lincoln nor Davis learned to avoid such men.

Devers looked across at Capt. Raymond Finch, who'd brought David into headquarters, introducing him as a new recruit. Finch smiled superciliously, saying, "Pvt. Rocklin is somewhat late coming to the service of his country, I fear, Captain."

Devers stared at the tall soldier before him dressed in the ill-fitting uniform and grunted, "What brought you to your senses, Rocklin? Finally see the light?"

With Finch's eyes fixed on him, David felt he couldn't speak the truth—that he'd joined to please his sweetheart. Then he suddenly realized he had no choice. "I'm in love with a young woman," he said evenly, meeting Devers' eyes. "I'm joining the service to prove I can be a loyal soldier."

Devers burst out in uproarious laughter. He cursed color-fully, then slapped the table before him with his meaty hand. "At least we got the truth out of you." Then, his eyes crafty and sly, he said, "See to it that he has plenty of opportunity to prove his courage, Capt. Finch."

"Yes, sir, I'll certainly do that," Finch replied readily, a grin forming on his lips.

After the two left the tent, he said, "All right, Rocklin, I'm putting you in with a good company."

He took him to a street where some men were drilling and they met Lt. Jacob Turnbridge. "Lieutenant," Finch said, "this is David Rocklin. See to it that you make a soldier out of him."

Turnbridge, a slim man with blond hair, was no more than twenty-three. His blue eyes examined David critically. "After the jailbait we've been having to use, I believe you got a good one. He's big enough. Can you shoot, Rocklin?"

"Yes sir."

A smile played over Turnbridge's thin lips. "Well, you're not overburdened with modesty. We'll see about that. Ser-geant?"

Ballard, a skinny man with blue eyes and red hair, disen-gaged himself from a group of privates and came to stand before the lieutenant. "Here's your new replacement," Turnbridge said. "Says he can shoot. I guess he'll get some opportunity to prove that, but you better check him out."

"Yes sir."

"This is Sgt. Ike Ballard," Turnbridge said. "Take him, Sergeant, and make a soldier out of him."

When Sgt. Ballard led David away, Turnbridge turned to Finch and said, "Better quality than we're used to."

"I doubt it," Finch said coolly. "He'll malinger if he can and run away if he gets a chance."

Turnbridge stared at him. "How do you figure that, Captain?"

"He joined up to please a young woman. First smell of powder and he'll be gone. If he'd been any kind of a man, he'd already have been in the army. Keep your eye on him. Let me know if he makes a break. We'll have him shot as an example for the rest."

"Why, yes sir."

Meanwhile, Sgt. Ballard said to his squad, "You fellows come on. We'll get a little exhibition of shooting from our newest recruit. This here's David Rocklin."

David didn't miss the smirks on the faces of a few of the men, but he followed along to a makeshift rifle range. A target was set up 150 yards away. Ballard picked up a musket and said, "See if you know how to load this thing."

David had loaded guns all his life. All the Rocklin boys were good hunters. Quickly, he bit the end off the cartridge, dumped the black powder down the barrel of the musket, then quickly added the lead bullet, tamping it all down and then priming the weapon. "Yes sir," he said.

It had been expertly done, and Lon Gere, a small man with intense black eyes, said, "Well, he knows how to load up. Let's see if he can shoot."

"Give you two-to-one odds he misses dead center," someone else called.

"No takers," Ballard said. "All right, see what you can do."

Without comment, David swept the rifle up, held it steady for a fraction of a second, and pulled the trigger. There was the hiss as the cap exploded, setting off the charge, then the musket cracked, kicking back against his shoulder slightly. He lowered the rifle and stood there calmly.

"Dead center!" Lon Gere said with surprise. "Where'd you learn to shoot like that?"

David shrugged; it had been an easy shot. "My father taught me and my brothers."

"See if you can do it again. This time we'll back away to two hundred yards."

They repeated the process, and David put his next bullet within two inches of the last.

Ballard nodded with satisfaction. "That's enough. We

43

don't have powder to waste. You're a sharpshooter, and we've got use for a lot of them." He looked over at a skinny man in his late twenties and said, "Bones, maybe you need to take some lessons from this fellow."

Bones Detwiler grinned languidly. "I don't figure to be that far away when I shoot," he said.

After David had been tested, he was put to work drilling with the rest, but the drill didn't last over thirty minutes.

Harold Ficker, a seventeen-year-old farm boy with big hands and feet, complained, "Sarge, I don't see what good it does, all this here drilling. Them Yankees ain't gonna come to watch us parade."

Ike Ballard opened his mouth to reprove the young man, then smiled. A tough, mountain man from Tennessee, he felt the same way. "You might be right about that, Harold." He looked downriver and said, "Grant has crossed this river. I'm thinking he's headed our way."

The next two days, David was kept under close surveillance, not only by Sgt. Ballard but also by Lt. Turnbridge. Turnbridge reported to Finch, "He's a good soldier; he can shoot better than any man in the squad, maybe in the whole company."

Finch, displeased, said, "Keep your eye on him, Lieutenant. Mind what I tell you. He'll run away if he gets a chance, no matter how good he shoots. It's one thing to shoot at a target—another thing to be shot at."

Three days after he'd joined, David got time off. Late that afternoon, he walked down to the Cleburne house and was welcomed gladly not only by Leah but by Claire and Amelia. They went to great extent to put a fine supper on the table, and he ate heartily, for the army food had been bland and there hadn't been much of it.

They were halfway through the meal when Amelia said, "I guess the whole Confederacy's grieving today."

David looked up. "Grieving? About what, Aunt Amelia?" With her encouragement, he'd taken to calling her by this name.

All three stared at him. "You haven't heard?"

"Heard about what?"

Leah's eyes filled with grief. "It's Gen. Jackson. He's dead."

Grief, pain, and shock stabbed David Rocklin. "Stonewall Jackson?" It was as if she'd said, "The sun fell this afternoon." Stonewall Jackson, of all the generals in the Confederate army, had been the best. His men in the Stonewall Brigade and other larger units had won against impossible odds.

"My father and brothers are in the Stonewall Brigade," he said quietly.

"I know," Leah said. "I hated to tell you." She seemed to lose her appetite. "We couldn't afford to lose him. But we did."

The announcement put a damper on the dinner, and only by great effort did Aunt Amelia bring the conversation around to a more cheerful subject.

At last David asked, "What about Corey?"

The three women exchanged careful glances and it was Leah who answered, "He's very sullen."

"Hasn't offered you any insolence, I trust?"

"No, except he just won't say anything. Does what he's told," Claire said, shrugging, "but you'll never break him. We've seen that kind before. They'll die before they'll give in."

"I'll have a talk with him after we're done eating."

After supper, David found the tall slave sitting outside on a box, watching the sun go down. "Hello, Corey," David said.

The man's head turned slowly, his eyes hooded. "Hello, Mr. Rocklin."

David saw the anger had somewhat faded. "How are you?" he said. "Getting plenty to eat?"

"Yes sah." Bare monosyllables were all Corey offered.

"Well, I hope you're able to give the ladies help. It's hard on women having to take care of a house all by themselves."

"I do the best I can."

David sat down, and for a long time there was silence. Finally, David said heavily, "When we get back to Virginia, there won't be anything like what happened to you with Mr. Dabney."

Again, disbelief showed in Corey's eyes.

"Where are you from, Corey? Tell me about yourself."

"What difference does it make, Mr. Rocklin?"

"Why, I just like to know something about a man."

"I ain't no man—I'm a slave."

David clenched his teeth together. It was a matter he'd often thought about, but he had no answer and finally said so. "I tell you this, Corey. I look on you as a man and not a possession. I can't reconcile that with slavery. I don't understand it. I'm in the army now; you know that from the uniform. But I'm not in it because I believe slavery's right."

"What are you in it for then, Mr. Rocklin?"

"Because I'm a fool, I suppose." He found himself talking to the slave as he wouldn't have thought possible. He spoke of how he'd always been fearful of the war, that it was for the wrong cause. "People talk about it being for the states' rights." Then he said, almost in a murmur, "But if a state wants to do something wrong . . ."

He left the sentence hanging, not seeing the intelligent eyes of the slave fixed on him intently. For a while, Corey didn't speak, filing David's words away in his mind. But after some hesitation, he began speaking of his own life. It wasn't an unusual story. He'd been overworked, mistreated, had run away, and gotten the name of a rebellious slave. When he'd finished the short recitation, he was quiet for a moment, then turned to the man across from him. "I thank you for what you done, Mr. Rocklin."

Shocked at the slave's words after seeing such bitterness in his eyes, David nodded. "Well, don't repeat this to anybody else, Corey, but you'll be a free man one day. I'd like to see you free right now, along with all the other slaves. It's what God wants for people. . . . If you tell anybody this, they'll probably have me shot as a traitor. So, there's your chance to get even."

Corey Jones looked at David in a way he'd never looked at a white person. There was something in this tall, dark-haired man he'd often sought in the faces of the white race. He'd found it from time to time, but usually in the faces of women. He couldn't put a name to it, but he knew one thing: Here was one man who wouldn't beat him! Here was one who looked at him as a *man,* not as a piece of property or just another body to be used up to make money. When David rose to leave, he hesitated slightly and then said to Corey, "I want to give you a letter and some papers. If anything happens to me . . . I want you to go to Virginia. Go to my grandmother if my father's not there. Give them to her."

"What do them papers say?"

"One of them will say I've purchased you. It's a bill of sale. That will show whose . . . property you are."

Corey stared at him intently. "And the other one, Mr. Rocklin?"

"I'll write a letter to my grandmother, instructing her to give you your freedom at the end of one year's service."

Corey froze, as if turned to stone. When Rocklin saw that Corey wasn't going to speak, he turned and left. Slowly Corey rose and, for the first time since he'd been a small child, his eyes misted over. He couldn't believe what he'd heard, and yet there was truth in young David Rocklin's face. Corey turned blindly and walked away, his eyes fixed on the horizon as he thought about Virginia—and freedom.

★ ★ ★

Gen. Ulysses S. Grant's army didn't move all that quickly. Nevertheless, for its time, there had been fewer more rapid advances and sudden victories as that of the Union army in its swift approach to the citadel city of Vicksburg. Grant had sent Col. Benjamin H. Grierson sweeping through Missis-sippi, down into Louisiana, to throw the Confederates off stride. There was no Confederate cavalry on hand to oppose this move, and the raid caused great alarm, diverting attention away from Grant's operations.

Grant's army, including Sherman's corps, still at Vicksburg, numbered about fifty thousand men. The Confederate strength in that area was approximately thirty thousand, most of it concentrated in or near Vicksburg. Only two brigades opposed the crossing, and these were decisively and thoroughly defeated at the battle of Port Gibson on the following day. The Union forces pushed forward, seized the ground, and awaited Sherman's corps, which arrived a week later.

Gen. Pemberton left two divisions idle at Vicksburg instead of concentrating his forces. Furthermore, when some reinforcements reached Jackson, he left them to guard that area. In effect, he strung his forces out on a line all the way from Vicksburg east to Jackson—an impossible area to defend with his smaller numbers.

Gen. Grant proved too swift a thinker for Pemberton. He made for Jackson, where he cut the Confederate supply lines into Vicksburg.

On May 12, Union forces defeated a Confederate brigade at Raymond. On the sixteenth, the Union army won a hard-fought battle at Champion's Hill, the decisive engagement of the campaign.

On the following day, the Union forces lined themselves up at a crossing on Big Black River Bridge, ready to launch the final assault that would lead to the very doors of Vicksburg.

The assault commander was Gen. Michael Lawler, a mountainous man weighing over two hundred and fifty pounds. Lawler was so huge that a sword belt couldn't fit comfortably around his waist. Instead, he wore his sword suspended by a strap from one shoulder. But Grant once said of this man, "When it comes to just plain hard fighting, I would rather trust old Mike Lawler than any one of them."

On the morning of the seventeenth, Lawler moved his brigade through the woods to within four hundred yards of the enemy line. He found a natural gully deep enough to hide his men. "From right here, men," he said, "we'll smack the Rebs so hard they'll never know what got 'em! To get to it, though, we got to cross that open field." He motioned to a field exposed to fire from the Confederate forces. He didn't hesitate, however, and leaving one regiment behind to protect his artillery, he dashed across at the head of the other three regiments, losing only two men. Then he gave a startling order. "Don't bother firing, men. Fix bayonets!" Pouring sweat, he heaved his great bulk up on his horse. Spurring the animal forward, he yelled, "Forward, men!" and the regiments roared out of their shelters toward the Confederate line and took them completely off guard. The shocked Confederates had time to get off one volley before Lawler's column hit them. The charge was one of the shortest in the Civil War, lasting just three minutes. Completely outmanned, and with bayonets and the stocks of muskets raining on their heads, the Confederates turned and fled, throwing down their guns as they ran.

★ ★ ★

David Rocklin was one of the men who had approached Big Black River. It was his baptism under fire, and as the men were placed in a thin line by Lt. Turnbridge, his heart began to beat faster and his hands grew sweaty. Looking around, he didn't see that the other men were going through this sort of struggle. Harold Ficker was arguing with Lon Gere about a horse race that they'd planned as soon as the Yankees were whipped. Ficker wore a wild daisy on his tattered hat, and his brown eyes were wide and fearless as he argued.

Bones Detwiler put himself in the line and grinned as he looked at Rocklin. "Gonna see the elephant, I reckon, ain't you, Dave?"

This was a common expression for a man's seeing battle for the first time. David started to speak and found that his throat was dry. He cleared it, then managed to smile back. "I guess so, Bones. You reckon they'll be coming soon?"

"I say yes," Detwiler said, nodding almost carelessly.

Sgt. Ike Ballard came by, checking their muskets. "This ain't gonna be no revival meeting," he said crossly. "There's more Yanks out there than weevils in a cotton patch."

Nervously, David checked his musket. He lay there, his muscles tense. He heard a small, shrill sound and turned quickly to see a huge cricket not far from his head. Almost invisible, this creature was issuing a tiny chorus, almost like a song. Somehow it stirred David's imagination, and he wondered if the cricket would survive the battle that was surely coming.

Suddenly a loud voice roared across the line and through the air, "All right, boys, forward!" And then Lt. Turnbridge came striding along, his eyes gleaming with excitement and his saber drawn. "Get ready, men! They're coming! Don't shoot until—!"

There was a slight thudding sound as the lieutenant's words were cut off. David looked around curiously and saw that a black spot had appeared on the right side of Turnbridge's forehead. The officer stood there one moment, as if thinking deeply, but his eyes had dimmed and he fell face forward, not catching his fall.

"H'yar they come!" Ballard screamed, and then David saw them. He hadn't imagined there would be so many. The Union army swept ahead, a solid blue mass, and broke into small groups, all of them bearing a bayonet on the end of their rifle.

Somehow the sight of those bayonets frightened David worse than if they had come shooting. He'd always disliked knives and had never seen how any man could stand up and face cold steel in a knife fight. As Sgt. Ballard moved back and forth yelling, "Shoot! Shoot, men!" he threw his rifle forward, but his hands were trembling so much that he couldn't draw a bead on any of the approaching enemy. He pulled the trigger and knew he had fired wildly over the heads of the charging Yankees.

Then, suddenly, the blue wall was upon them. A tall man

with the eyes of a maniac appeared before him, the bayonet held straight at David's stomach. David Rocklin couldn't move. The sight of that bayonet was too much. He could feel it sliding into his stomach, and fear rose like nausea in him. The soldier drew back the bayonet, screaming and lunging at him, but he was driven sideways as a bullet caught him in the jaw. He fell to the ground, clawing at his jaw, scattering great drops of blood on the leaves.

Ballard stepped forward and struck him once in the head with the butt of his musket and he lay still.

"Load! Load!" Ballard cried, but it was too late. All along the line, the Confederates who had fired the only shot they would get off were facing the steel. Suddenly one man threw his gun down and turned, running as fast as he could. It was a signal for the others, and David, without thought, whirled and ran blindly. He didn't do so consciously, nor perhaps did the others, but they ran. They left the field to the Yankees. It was a blind insanity, and David never remembered running. He heard the screams behind him, and as he fell and scrambled along with the others, he felt no shame, only a determination to get away from what was happening in the battle.

CHAPTER FOUR
The Net Closes

The shattered Confederate army tumbled back into the trenches, breastworks, and redans of the city as though an invincible blue tidal wave had washed them back. Emma Balfour, wife of a prominent physician, poured out the spirit of most of the city in a letter to a friend:

> My pen almost refuses to tell of our terrible disaster. From six o'clock in the morning until five in the evening the battle raged. We are defeated! Our army is in confusion and the carnage—awful! Awful! Our poor fellows passed through the streets and every house poured forth all it had to refresh them. We carried buckets of water for them and everything edible was put out. I fed as many as I could. Poor fellows, it made my heart ache to see them. What is to become of all of the living things in this place when the boats begin shelling—God only knows. Shut up as in a trap, thousands of men and women have fled here for shelter.

David and the remains of his company were part of that broken army that stumbled back into Vicksburg. They were as beaten as men could be, and Capt. Raymond Finch pulled them up in front of their barracks, his face red with rage, and berated them for being cowards and traitors. "You're not soldiers!" he spat out, venom practically dripping from his lips. "You're cowards and a disgrace to the uniforms you wear! If we didn't need men so badly, I'd have you all shot for cowardice in the face of the enemy."

David stood with the rest of his squad, noting that the loss of Lt. Turnbridge, along with several enlisted men, had hit them all hard. Finch's ravings had little effect on David. He was so shaken by his part in the battle that he could hardly separate the officer's words.

I ran away! The shame of what had happened burned in him, and he thought of his father and his brothers who had gone through much worse and hadn't fled at the first threat to their lives. He'd always supposed that if he had been in the army he could at least have managed to do as well as Dent or Lowell.

But now that illusion had been torn from him. As Finch walked back and forth, stamping his feet so that small clouds of dust rose, David went over the scene again and again, wishing it had been different. But even the thought of those bright flashing bayonets chilled him. *If it had only been bullets,* he thought desperately, *I could have stood it. But I can't stand the sight of that steel!* Later, he talked with Lon Gere about it, not revealing his own fears, but asking the small gambler what he felt about their behavior.

"Well, we cut and run," Gere said and shrugged, his features showing nothing. His profession had schooled him to keep emotions hidden, so if he was ashamed of what he'd done it wasn't apparent in his dark features. "It's happened before to better men than us," he continued. "Just ask some of the fellows that's been in the bad battles—the big ones. The fellow that's a hero today, well, something comes over him and he ups and runs—especially when everybody else is running!"

"That's no excuse," David muttered.

Gere looked at the tall, strong young man whose shoulders now were slumped. He had known Rocklin only a few days but had seen quality in him. Now he added as helpfully as he could, "We'll get 'em the next time, Dave. Don't worry about it. You'll see the bluebellies turn and run when *we* get the upper hand."

They had the chance to prove their courage, for Ulysses S. Grant, flushed with success, made a tactical error. Convinced he could take the city, he launched an attack on May 19 and was repulsed. Three days later, still hoping he could finish the campaign without a drawn-out siege, he ordered another assault. His troops, as anxious to end the fighting as Grant, rushed forward to the attack. Vicksburg, however, was a naturally strong position, surrounded by steep ravines that were difficult to climb. The defenders had further strengthened the natural defenses, and on May 22, the blue waves of Yankee uniforms were met by a solid sheet of terrible fire that drove them back down again.

Grant, realizing that Vicksburg could not be taken by direct assault, settled down to siege warfare.

★ ★ ★

David made his way down through the streets of Vicksburg, noting the damage that had been done by the heavy guns of the warships in the river. They had sent shell after shell screaming up in the air to fall on the defenseless. Now details were at work everywhere, rebuilding and repairing the work plowed up and torn down by the firing of the enemy's batteries. It was no light task, and he himself had struggled for a week with the other men. After Grant's second assault had been repulsed, David had become a day laborer, and after fighting all day beneath the rays of the summer sun, spent the rest of his strength using pickax, spade, and shovel. He carried heavy sandbags and strengthened the torn-down breastworks with timbers and cotton bales—protection for the next day's combat.

Now as he reached the Cleburne house he was relieved to see it was undamaged. Just down the street he saw one house—a three-storied mansion—gutted, apparently by explosive shells, and the sight depressed him. He moved up onto the porch and was met before he knocked by Aunt

Amelia, who greeted him warmly. "Come in, David." She was wearing a plain brown dress, and her thinning body showed signs of the siege, although it was only the sixth day. "You're late! We waited supper for you, though," she said, a fond light in her eyes. She touched his arm as he stepped into the house. "You look tired. You need more rest."

"Not much of that for any of us," David commented as lightly as he could.

He followed Aunt Amelia into the dining room, where she pushed him into a seat, saying, "Now, you just sit there and we'll all be ready to eat in a minute. I'll get Claire and Leah."

She disappeared and almost instantly Leah came in with a bowl of mashed potatoes and a tray of fresh baked bread. Noting the fatigue that lined his face, she only said, "I'm going to fatten you up, soldier. We've got plenty tonight."

"Better save it," David warned. "There won't be anything coming in from the outside now that the line to Jackson's been cut."

Leah smiled and shrugged. "We'll worry about that tomorrow. Tonight, we feast."

Claire and Aunt Amelia came in and set the table with beef, corn, peas, pickles, and slaw. "Would you ask the blessing, David?" Leah asked.

David hesitated, then bowed his head and mumbled a few words. Then he looked up and smiled. "I cleaned up as best I could, but it doesn't do much good."

"What's happening, David?" Claire asked as she took some of the beef, then passed the plate along to him. "Are we going to be able to hold out?"

"The officers tell us we will," David said noncommittally. He was determined not to reveal his depression to the three women, so he forced a smile. "We'll last the Yankees out. They can't stay here forever. We've heard that Gen. Lee might send part of the Army of Northern Virginia to take Grant on. That would make a difference."

As the others talked, Amelia watched Leah's and David's

faces closely. She took little part in the conversation although she missed nothing of what was said.

"What will happen if the Yankees do win?" she asked finally. It was a question they had all thought about although none had voiced it. It was as if they were afraid to mention such a possibility. But now Amelia's brown eyes were filled with a doubt that hadn't been there before the siege began.

"I suppose all the soldiers would end up in a prison camp or else would go on parole," David said, shrugging. He took a bite of a dark green pickle, flinched, and said, "That's strong. Did you make this, Aunt Amelia?"

"Yes. I always say pickles need to be strong or there's no sense fooling with them," she replied firmly. Then she pursued her question. "Well, what would happen to the town? To us?"

"Why, it'd be like New Orleans or Baton Rouge—any other town the Yankees have taken. It'd be under military jurisdiction. Things would be pretty different."

"I couldn't bear to live in a town where a man like Beast Butler ruled over us," Claire said sharply. "Such a man's a disgrace to any uniform, even a Yankee uniform!" She referred to Benjamin Franklin Butler, who had given a special order that any woman in New Orleans who insulted a Federal soldier would be treated as a woman of the streets. It was doubtful you could find a man in the South more hated than Butler. Claire toyed with the slaw with her fork, took a tiny bite, and chewed slowly. She was a woman who liked things to remain the same.

And yet, David sensed an unhappiness in her that was rooted deeper than the siege itself. He had noticed it in her before and assumed her life had been unhappy. Aside from the fact of her separation from her husband, he knew little about what went on behind her smooth, attractive face.

Leah said quickly, "We're not going to talk about losing. Let's talk about when we run the Yankees all the way back to Washington." Her red hair caught the reflection of a lamp behind her, giving off golden glints. Dressed in pale green, with short sleeves and white ribbons at her neck, Leah was vivacious—even under the terrible circumstances. "Tell us what you've been doing," she added. "They won't let us go out to see the fighting."

David didn't want to talk about the war. It was a boring, dangerous, dirty sort of fighting. The Yankees circling the city were throwing up their own breastworks, and now all a man had to do was lift his head—or even part of it—and one of the sharpshooters would end his part in the war immediately. Both sides had sharpshooters posted to inhibit the digging of breastworks. Since David was known as a fine shot, he'd done his part of that duty. But it didn't require courage, and he felt ashamed of shooting the men on the other side as they showed themselves. So far as he knew, he hadn't killed any, but he had winged three and had tried to take satisfaction in putting three Yankees, at least, beyond doing more to root the citizens and soldiers of Vicksburg out of their fortress.

After supper, Leah said, "Come on, David. I want to show you what we're doing now. We're keeping chickens. I bought six of them, and three of them are already laying. Corey built a pen for them. He's as proud of them as I am."

David rose at once and the two left. Claire stared after them and shook her head slightly. "I hope she doesn't get too caught up with him," she said quietly.

Amelia looked up quickly. A spasm of emotion crossed her face, very slight but obvious enough that Claire saw it. "What's wrong?" she said instantly. "Certainly you don't see him as a suitor for Leah?"

"He's a fine young man. I like him a lot."

"Why, I like him, too, Amelia, but we're not talking about a casual acquaintance. We're talking about a possible husband for Leah."

"I think he'd make a fine husband."

"But he's not even an officer . . . and we don't know anything about him, really. We don't know anything about his family—and you know how important the bloodline is."

Amelia had picked up the platter containing the meat. Very seldom did she say anything that would cross her niece's opinions, but now she said evenly, "Bloodline's not everything."

Claire stared in astonishment at Amelia. So rarely had the woman taken a position opposite to her own that she couldn't remember the last time. "Why, Amelia, what do you mean by that? Of course it's important! Look at my father! We've got his bloodline and that's important. We know what he was. We don't know anything about the Rocklins, except that they apparently have money." She had risen and picked up the vegetable remains on two separate plates. Sadly she said, "If only Father were alive, we wouldn't be here in all this. I miss him so much!"

Amelia's eyes narrowed; her lips grew tight. She started to say something and then shook her head, almost imperceptibly. She was accustomed to Claire's almost idolatrous feelings toward her father, Amelia's brother. More than once, long ago, Amelia had tried to tell Claire that she needed to put these feelings for her father in the proper perspective but had been so sharply rebuked that she'd ceased mentioning it. Now she saw there was no hope of changing her niece's mind, so she cleared the table and then went to her room to read.

Claire sat on the porch outside, and from time to time, there would be an explosion. The boats on the river had the range and dropped shells on the helpless city in a regular cadence. *I suppose,* she thought, *they've been commanded to do that so we won't be able to sleep.* She leaned her head back, closed her eyes, and thought of earlier days when things had been better. It was a habit she'd fallen into lately. Mostly, she thought of her girlhood. She rocked slowly, the chair creaking on the boards of the porch, and smiled as she thought of the times she and her father had made trips together. He had treated her like an equal even when she was a child, and those days had been the best of her life.

Then she thought of her marriage, and her smile vanished abruptly. Her brow wrinkled as she thought of the early days

59

when she'd been so in love with Matthew. But those days hadn't lasted long, and slowly she had drifted apart from her husband. She wondered suddenly what he was doing, what his life was like. He lived in New York now and was apparently successful. He'd been generous with her financially, but the shadow of those days of her marriage when he had proven himself to be unfit as a father—and even more unfit as a husband—had disturbed her. Quickly she turned her thoughts to other things.

Later, when David and Leah came back, she said goodnight to the young man, who then trudged away. "Sit down, Leah," she said. "Tell me, what did David say?"

"Why, nothing, really," Leah answered. She took a seat, and for a while the two women talked, their words punctuated by explosions. "Isn't it strange," Leah continued, "that once an explosion would have had the whole town up, running outdoors to see what it was? Now it's no more than as if a limb fell off a tree. Just part of our way of life." Her voice grew still and a quietness fell over the two. They had been close when Leah was younger, but for the past year or two she had noticed how unhappy her mother was. After a while she said, "I don't suppose we'll be hearing from Father since no mail can get in?"

"No, I suppose not."

The coolness of her mother's tone troubled Leah. She was disturbed by her mother's life and somehow, although she'd never voiced it, had a faint resentment for the way she'd been brought up. Her mother had never given her a full explanation for the breakup of her marriage, although Leah had asked many times. Now as they sat together on the porch, she tried again. "What does he say, Mother? He's never married again. That's strange for a man his age as fine looking as he is and with money."

"He wants his freedom. He doesn't need to be married anyway. He's . . . he's not made to be a good husband."

"Why do you say that? What really happened, Mother? You've never told me."

Claire turned to her daughter. The silver light of the half moon washed across her daughter's face, and Claire was quiet for a moment, as if seeking for words. Finally she said, "He wasn't the man I thought he was before I married him, Leah."

"Were you in love with him? Before you married him, I mean."

"Of course I was." The answer was quick and almost sharp. Then Claire sighed and leaned back in her chair. She rested her head and closed her eyes for so long that Leah thought she wouldn't speak again. When Claire did speak, pain threaded her voice, something that hadn't happened in Leah's remembrance. Her mother, whatever else, was a strong woman who didn't complain often. But now she seemed to be off guard and spoke softly of her engagement. "He was romantic and fine looking, as you know. He was full of fun—I've never forgotten that." Then her voice grew bitter. "He thought too much of fun—that was his problem. There comes a time when you have to be more serious. But I didn't find that out for a long time." She hesitated, then said, "My father tried to warn me against marrying Matthew, but I was a fool and didn't listen to him."

"Grandfather didn't like him?"

"No. He said he had some bad seed in him."

"Bad seed? What does that mean?"

"He was a man who wasn't strong as your grandfather was strong. He was weak."

"Weak in what way, Mother?" Leah leaned forward, her eyes fixed intently on her mother's face. She'd never heard her speak like this, and now a lifetime of questions about her father surfaced. "What kind of weakness was it? You can tell me now. Surely I'm old enough."

Claire opened her eyes and sat up straighter. "Perhaps you are, Leah," she said. "You're a woman now and before long you will be having to make a decision about a husband. . . . Marry a strong man." She put her hands together and gripped them firmly as if gathering strength. There was a

61

rigid quality in her back as she continued, "I have to tell you, it was drink and women. Matthew couldn't handle either one."

Leah considered this and asked finally, "Wasn't he in love with you?"

"Yes, he was, in his way. I tried to curb his drinking. . . . He drank too much. Oh, he wasn't a drunk or anything like that! But that wasn't the worst. He was unfaithful to me, Leah." She turned in the gathering darkness. "I know it's painful for you to hear you have a father like that, but it's true enough."

Leah felt a sharp pain of disappointment, yet she couldn't let it go. "Did he have . . . many women?"

"No, not that I know of. Only one, but that's enough."

"Was he in love with her?"

"No, he said not and I believed him. He was just weak." She suddenly rose and turned her back, going to the edge of the porch and staring up to the skies. "Look up there, Leah."

Overhead the black velvet sky was spangled with stars that glittered like fiery points of white light. Claire stood studying them for a moment, then pointed upward. "See those stars right there? That's the Pleiades. Come and look at them."

Leah moved to stand beside her mother. "Where?" she asked.

Claire lifted her arm and pointed. "You can't see them if you look directly at them. They're almost invisible. But turn your eyes just to one side and you'll see them."

She described the constellation and finally Leah saw them. "How did you know that, Mother, about the Pleiades?"

"Matthew told me. He knew all about the stars, was fascinated by them. He kept a telescope, and in the summer at night we'd go out and look at them and he'd tell me their names." There was a softness in her tone, and she looked up at the skies again, unaware of her daughter's presence. The warm breeze ruffled her auburn hair, and she said in a voice filled with something Leah couldn't identify, "It's strange about the Pleiades. When you try to look right at them, you can't see them. You have to look to one side. Matthew always said that fun and happiness is like that. If you try to have it, keep your eyes on it, you can't see it or have it. But if you look at something else, it'll come to you."

"I think that's wonderful," Leah whispered. She thought of her father and the few brief days she'd had with him. During their last visit she'd been grown and no longer a little girl. Although both had tried hard, the meeting had been stiff. Now she asked, "Did he often talk about things like that?"

"He was always talking about something. I have to say, he was one of the most interesting men I've ever known, one of the wittiest—and he had great good in him." Claire hesitated and then, as though a bell had sounded, she stiffened her shoulders. "But he couldn't be what a man ought to be. I wish I didn't have to tell you these things." She turned abruptly and walked into the house, leaving Leah standing on the front porch.

For a while Leah stood there, looking at the stars and thinking about her mother's obvious unhappiness. After a few minutes, she entered the house and walked to the parlor, where Amelia was reading. She went in for a moment and sat down. After talking about household details, finally Leah said, "Tell me about my father, Aunt Amelia."

"Your father?" Amelia looked up, startled, to see a wistful longing in the eyes of her niece. "What shall I tell you?"

"Tell me how he was. Did you like him?"

Amelia hesitated, then nodded. "Yes, I liked him. Everyone did."

"Tell me some things about him."

Amelia put down her book and talked for some time. Her features grew soft talking of days long gone, and she lost herself in nostalgia. Finally she blinked and gave a high laugh. "I don't know when I've gone on like this. Why do you ask about your father, Leah?" But she thought she knew.

"Mother says he was . . . weak."

Amelia felt a chill as she looked into Leah's troubled eyes. She was a dependent. If it hadn't been for Claire's generosity, she would have had no place to go. For that reason, she had said little to Leah about those days when Claire was married. Now she said simply, "An outsider never knows about what goes on inside a home. Your father and mother did not get on."

"But he took mistresses?"

"I don't . . . like to say. He was disappointed in his marriage." She hesitated for even longer and then said something she'd never admitted, "Claire loved her father very much. My brother was a great man, but he had weaknesses, too."

Instantly Leah looked up. "What kind of weaknesses?"

But Amelia grew reticent. "We all have weaknesses, Leah. I more than most. Your mother will have to tell you what she wants you to know." She added one more thing: "Don't expect the man you fall in love with and marry to be like anybody else. He'll be who he is. You can change your dress and the way you wear your hair, Leah, but you can't change who people are. The man you marry will have flaws. So do you. The thing to remember is that we love people in spite of their flaws."

She got up as if embarrassed by what she'd said and left hurriedly, leaving Leah wondering what her words meant.

When Amelia Seaton got to her room, she did something she hadn't done for many years. She gave in to the tears. As she sat down on her bed, thoughts running through her head, the tears began to flow. She struggled for some time with them, then lay down on the bed, face down, and her shoulders shook as she thought of the wasted years of the past.

★ ★ ★

Rumors continued to fly about relief coming to aid the beleaguered city. Pemberton received word that Johnston and Loring were coming with thirty-one thousand men.

That was greatly needed good news, for on the thirteenth

day of the siege the world looked very dark in Vicksburg. It was on that day, June 3, 1863, that David was sitting outside the small chicken house with Corey, talking leisurely. "How are the chickens doing?"

"Fine, Mr. David," Corey said. He had put on weight and looked strong and hearty in the clothes Leah had found for him—a light green shirt, dark brown trousers, and a pair of brown boots. Corey's face was smooth as he asked suddenly, "What's gonna happen, Mr. David?"

"I reckon we're gonna get whipped!"

The simplicity of Rocklin's reply surprised Corey. "Well," he said slowly, "if it happens I guess it happens."

David, who'd been watching children playing down the street, now turned to Corey and said, "You remember, if anything happens to me, go back to Gracefield."

"Yes sah, I remember. I don't 'spec nothin's gonna happen to you, though."

"It can happen anytime. Yesterday the fellow not twenty feet down the line from me was just sitting there. A shell went off, and one little fragment hit him right in the throat. He bled to death; there was nothing we could do. And it could happen to any of us."

"I guess that's right," Corey said in a deep resonant voice. He was sitting down on a box and now took a knife out of his pocket and began to whittle slowly on a piece of cedar. He handled the knife easily and carefully, sending long shavings that curled up uniformly. "I always like to smell cedar," he said softly. "Best smelling wood they is."

"You ever married, Corey?"

"No sah, never was. And you never was either, Mr. David?"

"No. Not yet." David studied the smooth features of the black man and asked, "What will you do when you're free?"

"I don't think about it, sah."

"Well, it will happen, one way or the other. Either the Yankees will win and all the slaves will be free; but even if that doesn't happen, I've told you, after a year you'll be free."

"I guess I'm just 'fraid to hope," Corey said evenly. When he looked up, his eyes had a curious glint. "Why you doing this for me? I'm worth a lot of money. You don't have to set me free. You didn't have to buy me from that man."

"I guess I need something on my account. I got some things I'm not exactly proud of, so I try to even it up from time to time." Without changing expression or tone, he asked curiously, "Corey, what's it like to be a slave?"

Corey watched the cedar shavings that were curling up beneath the keen blade of his knife. "You remember yesterday, Mr. David, when you touched that hammer that'd been laying out in the sun and it burned your hand?"

"I remember."

"Well, I touched it before that." Corey glanced up and said briefly, "Burned my hand, too."

David instantly smiled. "So, we're both alike, you and I?"

"Well, at least we hurt the same when we touch something hot."

"No, there's more to it than that," David said slowly. "The whole system is wrong. You know what I've thought. A slave can't help it if somebody owns him, but when I own a human being that means I don't see any difference in that human and something else I own. So I'm the one who's made some kind of decision about what men are like."

Corey's interest was held. "I never thought about it like that." He sat there watching the young man who'd come into his life so abruptly and finally said huskily, "Thank you, Mr. David. I ain't much for saying thanks," he said, grinning ruefully. "Ain't had a whole lot to say thanks about, I guess. But now, I want you to know that no matter what happens from here on, I ain't never gonna forget what you done for me."

Embarrassed by the slave's words, David stood up. "Let's see if those chickens have done their duty. I could use a good fried egg."

★ ★ ★

"Wake up! They're coming!"

David had been leaning against the wall of the trench, dozing off. The hours had gone slowly and he'd missed a great deal of sleep. Now, however, as yells ran up and down the trench, he grabbed his musket with both hands and called out, "What is it? What's wrong?"

Sgt. Ike Ballard said, "Look out! They're coming! They're gonna take this trench!"

David looked out, checked his musket, and heard the screams of the enemy as they were running. Ballard was screaming and Finch was calling out from somewhere down the line. *It may be a full-scale attack,* David realized, knowing that the Federals' plan was to slowly squeeze in on the city. His palms grew wet and his hands began to shake. "Stop it!" he said viciously under his breath and slowly raised his head. He received a shock, for it *was* a full-scale attack. Instantly he threw his rifle over, drew a bead, and fired. His man went down and he straightened up and began reloading. He'd heard the Yankees had a breech-loading rifle, that they could just shove a cartridge in and fire, but that wasn't what he had. His hands trembled as he reached into his pocket and pulled a cartridge out. He bit it off and poured the powder down the muzzle, then went through the procedure of ramming home the wads and the musket ball. All the time the screams of the charging Yankees rent the air. Up and down the line, muskets exploded and Ballard screamed out, "They're coming with the bayonets! Fire! Shoot 'em down!"

David straightened up and began to chill as the sun gleamed on the naked steel that flowed toward him in great waves. He straightened his arm out but trembled so violently that he couldn't hold the rifle still. He pulled the trigger and knew he'd fired high—and then there was no time. A Federal soldier suddenly appeared to his left. Harold Ficker was reloading his musket and didn't see him. David

67

seemed to be frozen as the Yankee, a tall brown-faced man whose teeth gleamed in a wild grin, shoved the steel forward, catching Ficker in the side. The young man screamed, dropped his musket, and reached around. The Yankee pulled out the bayonet, which was bloodied almost to the muzzle, and drew it back again. Ficker held his hands up as though he could stop the flashing steel. On the other side of Ficker, Lon Gere appeared. His musket wasn't loaded either, but he swung the weapon viciously through the air, striking the Yankee in the face. The force of the blow drove the soldier backward, and Gere reversed the weapon, smashing the man's face over and over with the butt.

All up and down the line individual battles took place. But David could do nothing because his hands wouldn't hold the musket steady enough. Only the fact that on his particular section of the line no Federal came at him with a bayonet saved him. He heard echoing screams of rage and pain, the clash of steel, the explosion of the muskets, and then someone said, "They're giving up! Let 'em have it!"

As David watched the Yankees retreat down the hill, he stood still, unable to move. Soon Bones Detwiler came to stand beside him, his face pale. "They nearly got us that time, didn't they, Dave? I wasn't ready for it." Detwiler looked up and saw that David's face was dripping with sweat. "Are you hit?" he demanded. "Did they get you, Dave?"

David Rocklin shook his head. "No, they didn't get me." His voice was thin and reedy, and he couldn't control the shaking of his hands so he moved away from Detwiler and fell on his knees beside Ficker. Lon Gere, who was trying to stop the flow from his side, looked up. "We got to get him to the hospital, Dave. Can we get a stretcher?"

"No, I'll take him." David reached down, picked up Ficker, and said, "Come on, Harold."

He bore the weight of the heavy young man easily, and when he got back to where the doctors were already working on the wounded, he laid him down carefully, saying, "You'll be all right, Harold."

"I don't want to go to the hospital," Ficker cried out, his big brown eyes wide with fear and pain. "Don't leave me, Dave!"

"I won't leave you, Harold." David sat there, regaining control over his body. His hands ceased to tremble and his face slowly relaxed. Inside, however, his nerves were still screaming. He knew he'd never forget the sight of those bayonets coming up the hill!

CHAPTER FIVE
The Last Straw

Food had become the big question in the besieged city. Cowpeas, small beans, were usually cultivated as feed for animals. However, as regular food supplies dwindled, great ingenuity was expended to use the large supply of cowpeas for table use.

Making peas into bread followed the same process that one uses for corn. The peas were ground into a large amount of meal and sent to the cooks, who mixed it with cold water and baked it. But the nature of cowpeas was such that the longer they were cooked, the harder they became on the outside and the softer on the inside.

When the Federals found out the populace was eating peabread, David had to listen as the bluebellies hollered for several nights, making fun of them. "Come on over and have a cup of coffee and a biscuit with us," one of them with a shrill tenor voice called loudly.

David hadn't lost his appetite, but he was troubled with nightmares about bayonets. In one of them he was walking on a carpet of green grass with a breeze blowing gently when suddenly, out of the sky, thousands of bayonets appeared, all glistening in the sun—and all headed straight for him! The dream occurred many times and always woke him up as the bayonets were just about to pierce his body. Ike Ballard, tired of David's awakening and thrashing around and mumbling, said in disgust, "If a little thing like being besieged bothers you, Rocklin, you need to become a preacher or something else where there ain't no problems!"

On June 24 David marked the calendar he'd saved from a magazine and noted it was the thirty-fourth day of the siege. He had put in a hard day's work on the reinforcements of the redans and decided to go to the Cleburne house. He was worried about them, for the shells were falling faster and thicker than ever. There seemed to be no limit to the ammunition the gunboats spat out, and the town itself was battered almost beyond repair. As he made his way through the shattered streets, he noticed the magnificence of the courthouse, which caught the sun and glistened pristinely out of the rubble. *I wonder if the Yankees are deliberately leaving it standing so they can use it as a headquarters when they capture the city?* he thought, then realized he'd already given up on Vicksburg enduring the siege successfully. Somehow he knew—and suspected others did—that it was only a matter of time before the city fell.

He made his way first to the hospital, where Harold Ficker was glad to see him. "Hello, David," he said in a faint voice.

Since his wounding, Ficker's face had grown slender and he had none of the health and strength he'd had when David first met him. The brigade hospital was filled, and even now aides carried out the still form of a man who'd died in the night. Turning his eyes away from the sight, David sat down and spoke cheerfully. "You're looking well, Harold," he said. "I brought you a little something special from the mess." He had salvaged a piece of so-called cake and un-wrapped the paper from it, holding it up. "Not like your mother used to make," he said, grinning, "but better than cowpea bread."

Ficker tried to smile and reached out a thin hand. As he held the bread, not trying to eat it, he whispered, "They say I've got an infection, David."

"Well, they'll soon take care of that."

Ficker's eyes were fixed on him piteously, almost as if he were begging David for something. "That fellow they just took out. His name was Colin Symington. He's from Alabama. He had an infection, too—and he died last night."

David bit his lip. He knew the dangers of infection were terrible, especially in the hospital. The surgeons moved from man to man, never washing their hands, and it seemed that once infection did set in, it swept through the whole ward. He saw the fear rising in the boy's face and said, "You'll ride it out, Harold."

"I ain't—I ain't really ready to die." Ficker's face was pale, and his mouth moved spasmodically as he spoke. "Most of my friends got saved in a revival we had back home just before I joined up. But I didn't." He held the cake and looked at it, but his eyes weren't really focused on it. He seemed to be looking back in his past, and finally he whispered, "I guess I'll go to hell if I die."

"Why, you can't do that, Harold! I tell you what, I'll have the chaplain come and talk to you."

"Couldn't you do it, Dave?"

David Rocklin swallowed hard. "I don't claim to be much of a Christian. But my people are and I've heard good preaching all my life. I've thought a lot about it myself. The preachers all say you have to repent and turn to Jesus."

"How do you do that?"

Fervently, David wished he'd paid more attention. He was a Christian himself but had been timid about speaking to others. Now, however, he breathed a quick prayer and began to explain how to become a Christian. He was surprised to find the sermons he'd heard and the talk around his table at home before the war suddenly bear fruit. The wounded boy looked at him with hungry eyes, and finally David said, "What I think we ought to do is just pray right now that you'll be right with God. I'll pray for you and you call on the Lord to save you."

It was an awkward thing for David Rocklin, but after he'd said a prayer, he looked up and saw tears running down Ficker's face. "Thank you, Dave," he said. "I did it. I called on the Lord. I feel like something happened to me."

David sat for nearly half an hour beside the wounded young man, encouraging him, and finally Ficker dropped off to sleep. He left, making his way out of the hospital.

The scene had disturbed him, and he rebuked himself sternly for not being of more help. He consoled himself by saying, "I'll go back later and sit with him. I'll take the chaplain with me, just to make sure."

When he turned off on Cherry Street, where the Cleburne house was, he was strangely drawn to the place. His feelings for Leah hadn't changed, but the cowardice that had sprung up in him had blotted out all thoughts, except what he might be able to do about it. When he reached the house, he found Corey out back chopping firewood and spoke with him for a few minutes. "Everything all right, Corey?"

"Yes sah. You all right, Mr. David? You ain't been shot or nothing?"

"Not yet!" He grinned faintly and said, "I'll be glad when this is over."

"So will I, Mr. David. A man don't know when he'll live or die and I sure hate to see this house get hit like that 'un down the street there. Be bad to see one of them ladies get hurt."

This had bothered David, too, and he nodded. He left saying, "I'll talk to you before I leave, Corey." When he knocked on the door, Amelia was in the kitchen shelling cowpeas. He sat down beside her and joined in, teasing her about what a bad cook she was.

Amelia replied, "I never noticed you turning down any of my cooking!" She sniffed and gave him a straight look. "I suppose all of you fellows are hungry out there."

"Food's pretty scarce. We're down to mule-meat steaks now."

"I swan! I never thought I'd see the day! Soldiers of the Confederacy, eating mule meat."

"It's better than some I've seen. Some of the fellows had what they called a squirrel stew the other night. I tasted it and found out it was made of rats!"

"Oh, my stars!" Amelia said, shocked. "I can't think what would make me eat a rat!"

"Where's Leah and Mrs. Cleburne?"

"They're upstairs, trying to go through all the old clothes. Some of the neighbors lost everything they had. A shell tore up their house completely."

Suddenly David had a strange feeling. Everything happened instantaneously: His ears rang and he wondered if he was getting malaria. The world seemed to rock and the roof to his left caved in. Then he heard a tremendous explosion.

David leaped forward and grabbed Amelia, yelling, "Get out of the house! It's going to fall in!" He quickly shoved her toward the door, then turned and ran down the hall calling, "Leah! Mrs. Cleburne!"

Another shell struck in the house somewhere. This one was even more disastrous than the first. He ran to the stairs and saw Leah and her mother almost falling down. "Come on! We've got to get out of here!" The two women reached the landing and all three of them ran out the front door. Evidently a barrage from the gunboats had been aimed at this spot, for even as they dashed away from the house, two more shells struck it and blew the walls out. The roof fell in with a tremendous crash.

"Where's Amelia?" Leah cried.

"She went out the back door. I'll go see about her. Go take cover in that ditch!" David ran around the house and found Corey pulling Amelia along in his strong hands.

"Get her out of here! They're dropping a barrage on us!" he yelled.

Corey picked up the woman and ran. David ran alongside and, as the three dropped in the ditch, the barrage increased in intensity. It went on for five minutes, their ears ringing with the force of the explosions.

Then a quiet fell and Leah said, "Look! That house! It's gone, too! We've got to see if they're all right!"

For two hours after the barrage, pandemonium reigned. A little girl had been killed, three houses down. Her body was brought out by the weeping mother and Claire went over at once to comfort her.

David stood looking at the devastation of the house and said to Leah, "You'll have to go to one of the caves, Leah. Let's go through the wreckage and see what we can salvage. I'll go round up a wagon." He looked down and saw she was crying silently. Without thinking, he put his arm around her and squeezed her. "It's all right. Everybody's alive and that's what matters."

"All my things—gone," Leah whispered. Then she looked up at him and nodded. "You're right, though. *Things* can be replaced. I'll start looking while you get the wagon."

★ ★ ★

David and Corey stopped working and stood to examine the cave they'd carved out with some help from a few others. It had to be quick, but fortunately Leah and Claire had found enough money in the wreckage to hire other laborers. Now David looked at it with some pride. He winked at Corey and said, "I guess as cave diggers go, we're just about at the top of the list."

Spared from frontline duty, David had thrown himself into the job with all of his strength. They had made the cave in the shape of a T, with a straight entrance being the bottom part and the top part spreading into two compartments. The bottom leg was already being used for cooking and also served to store the furniture they'd been able to salvage. They'd even brought carpet for the two bedrooms and found enough tables and lamps to furnish them. The roof was arched and braced, the supports taking up some of the room.

David now walked in with Leah, and Aunt Amelia came out from one of the side units that served as a bedroom for her and Leah. "Welcome to our new home," Amelia said, trying to smile. A shell went off somewhere down the line and she looked up at the roof. "If they don't score a direct hit," she said, "I think it ought to be all right."

Claire had come out from the other room and added, "One of the caves took a hit." A worried look came into her eyes. "It collapsed and one man died before they could get him out."

Leah walked over and hugged her mother. "We'll be all right, Mother," she said. Then she turned to David. "You and Corey have done miracles. Now, then, let's see if we can have our first supper in our new home!"

An hour later they were sitting down to a table just off the opening to the cave. Aside from the cowpeas, Corey had managed to salvage the chickens. One of them had been butchered, and Amelia had fried the chicken over an open fire. There were also some dandelion greens—another of Corey's contributions. When they sat down to eat, Corey waited on them, saying, "I guess I'm a house slave now. Don't know how good I'll be at that."

David took a plate, put three pieces of chicken on it, along with some of the dandelion greens, and offered it to Corey. "Here—you sure earned your keep this time!"

Corey's smile was filled with admiration for David. "You and me could become gold miners," he said. "You sure do know how to dig."

David looked down at the blisters on his hands. "I'd hate to do it for a living."

The meal was pleasant enough. Outside, the air was hot, but inside the cave it was much cooler. This was June 27, the thirty-seventh day of the siege, and David mentally rebelled against going back to the trenches. However, after he finished, he said, "Well, this is all the time the sergeant would give me. I'll have to go back now."

"I'll walk part of the way with you, David," Leah said. She got up and the two left the cave. All along the hills caves had been cut out by homeless citizens, and they had become a community. Leah commented, "You know, we're closer to the people here than we ever were in a house with walls and a roof. We have to trust each other to get along, and we have to help each other."

77

He looked down at her slightly sunburned face and her red hair tied back in a single braid and smiled. "I guess that's not a bad way to live. Most people never do get to know each other."

They walked along, speaking from time to time. "This is far enough," he said finally, then added abruptly, "I hate to go back. Leah, I hesitate to tell you this, but I'm not much of a soldier."

Leah stared at him. "I expect you're as good as the others," she said quietly.

"No, I'm not." Then he told her what he'd never told anyone. "I think I can stand musket fire and even cannon fire—"

"What is it, David?"

"It's those bayonets. . . ." An involuntary shudder made his body twitch and his lips thinned. "I can't stand the thought of them!"

Leah watched him closely. "Maybe it'll be over soon," she said. "They can't stay here forever."

"I think you know better than that, Leah." David tried to pull himself together. "It's just a matter of time. We can't hold out here. Surely even Pemberton knows that by now."

Still Leah tried to be positive, as were many others. "It'll be all right," she said. "We'll make it."

David reached out, took her hand, and studied it. "You're getting blisters," he said, looking into her eyes. "I said once that I love you and that I'd make you learn to love me, too. But I haven't had much time for that."

She smiled. "No, you haven't. How do you go about making women love you? I've been waiting for you to turn on the charm."

He answered lightly enough, "I'm afraid to let all my charm out at once. Why, it's been known to stun a young woman at fifty feet."

"Really? I wasn't aware I was with such a man. Why don't you try just a little—not full force, of course," she teased him. Although her dress was faded and needed washing, her body was strong and youthful as she looked up at him. She was intensely attractive and, to some extent, unaware of the impact she had on him.

David held her hand, then grew more serious. "I've got to go. Somehow we'll talk about this later. May I kiss you good-bye?"

"Why, you're only going a mile away."

"I know, but it would be nice."

She lifted her head and, taking it for permission, he leaned down and kissed her lightly on the lips. Her lips were warm, full, and firm, yet still soft and yielding, speaking of her femininity. He turned without another word and walked away, afraid to trust his voice.

★ ★ ★

Three days of incessant barrages had frayed the nerves of all the men. Explosive shells went off continually, and now David jumped each time one did. He checked his calendar and saw it was June 30. "Forty days trapped in this place," he muttered, stretched almost full-length against the walls of the trench. It had been quiet for a while now, but he heard the popping of a musket every now and then, reminding him to keep his head down. The Yankees evidently had brought in more sharpshooters, for now all a man had to do was stick his hat up on a stick above the level of the trench and instantly it was shot off. David had tried this himself and pulled off his campaign hat to see a hole right through the brim. He put the hat back on his head and looked up at the sun, which was almost overhead. He lay there for a long time thinking mostly of Leah, who'd come to occupy a large part of his thoughts. He'd managed to block out the thoughts of the bayonets and had had a good night, without nightmares.

But late that afternoon he was jerked out of his ease when another attack was made. Again, the sergeant was yelling, the officers were crawling around, keeping down below the parapet, and once again, it happened. David was caught in the full fury of a barrage with mortar shells exploding around him. Then he heard the dreaded cry, "They're coming! Get ready!"

As he'd done before so many times, he got off one shot and was loading frantically when Sgt. Ballard hollered, "They're coming with bayonets! Attach bayonets, men!"

David had hated the bayonet he'd been issued. He couldn't imagine himself using it, plunging it into the body of another human being. Now as he fumbled for it, he was aware again that the lines were being broken. It became a melee as men fell and shouted and cursed.

David couldn't attach the bayonet on his rifle because his hands were trembling. Then he heard the screams of men who were dying from bayonets just like his, and something seemed to fall before his eyes.

He had no memory of it later, but somehow he found himself behind the trench, running. He heard a curse and a shout, "Rocklin, come back . . ."

But he didn't cease running. He ran until his lungs were scorched and burning. He ran until he got away from the sound of those cries. He couldn't face the thought of cold steel. And, even as he ran, blindly, mindlessly, something deep down inside told him he had turned a corner from which he would never quite recover.

★ ★ ★

July 1 and 2 were days of helplessness for the Confederate officers. Pemberton spent sleepless nights trying to think of a way to achieve some sort of good terms from Grant. He knew that Grant, however, would take the city, no matter what he said. He met his staff, and there was a tremor in his voice as he said, "We're beaten, gentlemen. I'd rather die a thousand deaths, but we must ask Gen. Grant for his terms." Several officers disagreed violently, but Pemberton knew the end had come. "I will write the message to Gen. Grant," he said.

★ ★ ★

David was in no condition to think about surrender terms. Something terrible had happened to him. When he'd finally stopped running, finding himself on the far side of Vicksburg from the trenches where his flight had begun, he'd stayed out all night staring emptily at the skies.

He'd gone back the next day and had been cursed soundly by Finch, who called him worse names than ever before. Lon Gere had met him with a blank stare, and David saw the contempt in the gambler's eyes. Bones Detwiler had been killed in the attack, so he was not there to know. David had been unable to cope with his world and now, as Gen. Pemberton wrote his letter to his opponent, all he could do was endure. Inside there was an emptiness, a hollowness, and he knew that no matter what happened to Vicksburg that he, David Rocklin, was a man with nothing inside.

CHAPTER SIX
End of a Siege

Capt. Raymond Finch stood inside the cave facing the three women. He'd come during a lull in the firing and had made his announcement in a harsh, unforgiving voice. "There's no excuse for a man like Rocklin," he said, his lips drawing tightly together and almost spitting out the words. "He ran away from the enemy in action. I tried to get him shot, but Capt. Devers wouldn't listen to it."

Leah's face was pale. "Couldn't there have been some mistake, Raymond?"

"Mistake! I saw him run myself," Finch said. It gave him some gratification to see his announcement disturbed the three women greatly. "I tried to tell you about that fellow," he said in a more moderate tone, shrugging his trim shoulders.

"Was he the only one who ran away?" Amelia asked quietly.

"Why, I suppose not," Finch said reluctantly, tugging at his mustache. "There'll always be one or two in any action who can't take it."

"Did you ask to have them shot, too?" Again Amelia's voice was gentle, but there was a harsh light in her eyes.

Finch stared at the older of the three women and shook his head impatiently. "You just don't understand how these things are, Mrs. Seaton." He turned quickly back to Leah, for it was her face he studied most carefully. He'd once entertained ideas of marrying Leah himself, at least of courting her, but she'd shown little interest in him as a serious suitor. His feelings ruffled, he'd allowed the resulting anger to fall on David Rocklin.

"Well," Claire said abruptly, "I'm sorry to hear of it. I thought he had promise, but evidently I was wrong."

"You were wrong, but you haven't known the fellow long. It's understandable." Finch again examined Leah's face, adding, "Some people look good on the outside, but when you put them under pressure, they crack."

"That's right," Claire nodded, and then she, too, turned to study Leah. "It's well that we found out about him before—" She had intended to say, "Before the courtship got too far along," but changed the subject. "What will happen now to us all?"

"Gen. Pemberton's written Grant asking for terms." The words were bitter on his thin lips and he shook his head angrily. "I think it's a mistake. We can hold out here."

"I don't see how," Leah said wearily. "Everybody's starving. More lives would be lost."

Her tone was dull as she moved away from the small group walking out of the front of the cave. She stayed away long enough to be sure Finch wouldn't be there when she returned, then made her way back. As she entered the cave, she was greeted at once by her mother who said, "We'll have to decide something, Leah."

"What do you mean, Mother?"

"Why, I mean, we can't stay in this cave for the rest of our lives."

"No, of course not. Will we rebuild the house?"

"I don't have the money," Claire said slowly. "And even if we did, I wouldn't want to live here under the rule of the Yankees. No, we'll have to leave."

"But where will we go?"

Claire Cleburne was a woman who was seldom at a loss for words, who liked to be in control. But some of that slipped from her this moment. Her cheeks grew tense and she looked down at her hands blankly. She didn't answer the question for a long time, then finally looked up, bitterness scoring her eyes. "I'll have to ask your father to help us."

"I wish you didn't have to do that, Mother."

"*You* wish it! You don't know how much *I* wish it!" Claire's voice was almost a gasp and her eyes were dull. "I've never asked him for anything—never!"

"But he's sent money all these years, hasn't he?"

"Yes, but I never asked him."

Leah sat down beside her mother. "Let's don't do it. We can think of something."

"Think of what?" Claire stared at her daughter with frustration. "What could we do? There's nothing open. What can a woman do to make a living for herself, especially with this war on?"

"Surely we can find *something.*"

But even as Leah spoke, she saw the futility of it all. There was nothing open for a woman, except perhaps teaching school, but in the throes of a losing war the South didn't put a premium on that. Children would have to be educated the best way they could. She reached over and patted her mother's hand. "We'll think of something," she said and rose to go outside again.

★ ★ ★

David was kept under arrest for only a day, and then Capt. Devers told Finch brusquely, "You might as well turn him loose. He'll go into a prison camp with the rest of us."

"I'd like to see him shot!" Capt. Finch snapped.

"Well, his chances of getting out of a prison camp aren't too good. You know what they are, Finch," Devers said with impatience. "Now, do as I tell you. We don't have time for things such as this."

Finch walked over to the house being used as a temporary stockade. Stepping inside the door, past the corporal who was serving as guard, he looked over and said, "All right, Rocklin. Capt. Devers has ordered me to release you. Get back to your unit."

85

David had been sitting on a cane-bottomed chair, staring out the window. There was no relief in his face as he stared at Finch. He said mildly, "Yes sir," and turned and left. When he got back to the unit, he found that all spirit had gone out of the group. Even Sgt. Ike Ballard stared at him listlessly and said nothing.

Lon Gere, who was sitting on a box playing solitaire, looked up and said briefly, "You got here in time to surrender, I guess. You don't have to worry about running anymore, Rocklin."

David stared at him, then shrugged, and went over to sit down and wait. "Did you hear about Ficker?" Ballard asked.

"No." David knew the truth at once. "Did he die?"

"Yep! Poor fellow. He said to tell you thank you for what you did for him. What was that, Rocklin?"

David said, "Nothing, I guess. I'm sorry—he was a good man."

A lackadaisical air settled over the trenches. The sharpshooters were not firing anymore, for both sides knew this part of the Civil War was over.

★ ★ ★

Later, David rose and made his way to the cave. He called out at the entrance, "It's me, David."

"Come in."

He stepped inside to find the three women looking at him in a most peculiar way. Instantly he knew what had happened. "I suppose," he said quietly, "you heard about me."

"Mr. Rocklin, I think it might be best if you'd not come back here anymore." Claire's voice was firm and her back stiff. "You'll be going anyway with the other soldiers to a prison camp."

"That's true, Mrs. Cleburne." David turned and said, "Leah, I want to have a word with you before I leave. Would you mind coming outside?"

"Very well."

Leah walked out of the cave and David moved to follow

but was stopped by Amelia, who put her hand out. "I'll pray for your safety, David," she said quietly, her hand firm in his. As he looked at her, he didn't see the same hardness he'd seen in Claire Cleburne's eyes.

"Thank you, Aunt Amelia," he said. "That means a lot to me. You take care of yourself now."

"Yes, I will."

Outside, David said to Leah, "Let's walk a little." She fell in wordlessly beside him, and finally he stopped and faced her. "I tried to tell you about myself the last time we talked."

"I remember." Her voice was even and her eyes cool.

"I guess I know how you feel," he said softly. "I feel the same way about myself. I can't explain it, Leah. I'm just what I am."

Leah looked at him calmly. She'd known he would come, and now she said, "I'm sorry it happened and I wish you well. I know it's hard. It'll be hard for you in the camp, you and all the others."

He knew this was a farewell, so he didn't answer for a moment. Finally he said, "Good bye. Just remember, I love you. I wish things were different." Then abruptly he walked away.

Leah sadly watched him go. Her conscience seemed to smite her, but her mother had talked to her about the matter. She'd mentioned David's weakness and had said, "If a man is weak in one way, he'll be weak in another. I'm sorry for him, but you don't need him in your life." Leah walked back to the cave. When she entered, she said nothing about their parting. Amelia stared at her for a moment, then moved away.

"I've decided we'll have to go to New York," Claire told her. "Your father has a big home there. He's often made it available, mostly to you. We'll go there—at least until we can find something better."

"All right, Mother."

"Are you all right?" Claire queried.

"Of course." Leah tried to blot out the picture of David's

face when she had turned from him. She looked up at her mother said only, "It'll be hard for you, won't it, Mother?"

"Yes, it will be, but we have to do something. Matthew always said he wanted to do something for you. Now we'll see if he's stronger than he used to be."

★ ★ ★

It was after ten now, and everything was quiet. But as a figure appeared out of the darkness, at once Corey was on guard. He had no weapon, but he doubled up his fist. He'd made himself a shack out of old boards close to the cave where the women stayed, and now he stepped quietly out of the shadows and said, "Who are you? What do you want?"

"Corey?"

"Mr. David!"

"Come on, Corey."

Corey made his way through the darkness. There was no moon at all. "What you doin', Mr. David?"

"We're getting out of here. I'm not going to spend the rest of this war in a prison camp."

"How you gonna get through?"

"Can you swim?"

"Why, yes sah!"

"We're swimming out of here. We're going down to the river and we're going to steal a boat, paddle out to the middle, and float past the Yankee guards. If they see us," he said quietly, "they'll shoot us. You may not want to go, and you don't have to. They won't keep you here. You're what they call contraband now."

Corey stood there thinking hard. "No sah," he said. "I be goin' with you."

"You heard about what I did?"

"Yes sah, I heard."

"You still want to go with a coward like me?"

Corey wanted to reach out and comfort David somehow, but he knew that wouldn't be the right thing to do. "I'm goin' with you, Mr. David. Come on. It's plenty dark. We'll get out in the middle of that river and they won't never see us."

A bit of cheer touched David—the first he'd felt since he'd run away. Although he couldn't see the slave's face clearly, here at least was one who didn't scorn him.

"Thanks, Corey," he said briefly. Then the two men faded into the murky darkness, headed toward the mighty Mississippi.

PART TWO
New York

CHAPTER SEVEN
An Uncomfortable Situation

Leah was well aware her mother was nervous as the carriage made its way through the crowded streets of New York City. A searing sun overhead poured down harsh rays, and for some reason Leah remembered today was her cousin Tom's birthday, August 10, and wondered what he was doing with himself. Glancing across the carriage, she noted that tension had caused her mother to push nervously at her hairdo, which needed no adjustment.

"You'd never know a war was on, would you?" Amelia murmured, gazing at the crowds filling the streets.

Leah noted there was a richness and a prosperity—a sense of fullness somehow—that formed a stark contrast to the scenes they'd been accustomed to in the South, especially in Vicksburg. As Amelia studied the women's dresses, she smiled. "I don't think they've been forced to do without anything, have they?"

Claire responded shortly, "No, they haven't!" She shifted restlessly in her seat and with an unusual tense note in her voice complained, "How long is it going to take us to get there I wonder? It'll cost a fortune to pay for this carriage!"

They'd been traveling for a long time. The journey had been difficult since the Southern railway systems were decimated by the war. They'd all noticed the differences as soon as they passed into the Northern areas. Even the roadbeds were better and the regular *clickety-clack* of the wheels passing over the seams sounded more solid and substantial.

All three women had been sobered by the journey, Claire most of all. *I hate having to do this—I'd rather go without, myself, but I've got to do something for Leah and Amelia,* she thought. For years she'd deliberately avoided any contact with Matthew except that which was absolutely necessary. Now she was descending upon him, asking for help. Of course, he'd helped financially through their years of separation; she had no complaint about that. But this was different.

Leah cried suddenly, "Look! Look there, Mother! Look, Aunt Amelia!" She pointed to a man and a woman who were making their way along the streets on bicycles. "That looks like such fun," Leah said, delighted. "I want to try it!"

"There are other ways of making a fool of yourself, Leah, than getting on one of those contraptions," Claire snapped.

Leah was surprised, for ordinarily her mother was a good-tempered woman. But she realized it was the situation that had made her mother tense, so Leah said only, "Well, I suppose Father doesn't keep bicycles." Leah noticed Claire's eyes grew smaller at the mention of her father, and once again she wondered, *It disturbs her so much to come here. . . . Maybe we made a mistake. We should have gone somewhere else. But we don't have to stay long if it's unbearable.*

Finally the carriage shuddered to a halt, then swayed as the driver, a thick-bodied Irishman with a shock of black hair, stepped to the ground. The door opened and he stuck his head in saying, with a gap-toothed grin, "Here it is, 900 West Twenty-Seventh Street. Can I take your baggage in, ladies?"

Claire spoke nervously. "No, let me go up and be certain someone's home." As she stepped down and looked around, she saw the street was filled with solid-looking houses, most of them three-story brownstone. Smoke curled lazily from some of the chimneys, the result of cooking fires and heating water, and nervous as she was, Claire was impressed at the dignity of the wide street. Then she moved forward and marched up the short flight of stone stairs that led to the door, giving the heavy brass knocker three sharp raps. As she stood there waiting, an impulse to turn and flee swept her. But knowing that would be ridiculous, she took a deep breath, got control of herself, and waited.

The door opened almost at once, and a tall man with black kinky hair and a light brown complexion stood before her. "Why, Miss Claire!" he exclaimed, smiling broadly. "It's you! Indeed it is!"

"Hello, Simon." The sight of the tall man brought back sharp memories, but Claire put them aside. "Is Mr. Cleburne here?"

"No, Miss Claire, he ain't, but he'll be back in 'bout two hours. Let me come out and take your bags in." He looked over his shoulder and called, "Lucy—Lucy! Miss Claire's here!"

At his call, a short plump woman with a rich chocolate complexion appeared from down the hall. She came forward quickly, moving agilely in spite of her heaviness, then stopped and nodded briefly. "Hello, Miss Claire." Claire didn't miss the lack of welcome in her tone. "Is Miss Leah with you?"

"Yes, and my Aunt Amelia. I'll go tell them to come in."

Claire returned to the carriage and paid the driver. Simon had followed her out and picked up two bags. While he waited for the ladies to go in, he smiled. "Why, this must be Miss Leah! But you're a grown-up lady now! Last time I saw you, why you was just a little thing."

Leah smiled back. "I remember you, Simon, and Lucy, too."

"You ain't forgot her good cooking, I bet. Everybody remembers that."

Claire said, "Come along," and, picking up one of the lighter suitcases, made her way back up the steps.

When they were all inside, Simon said, "Lucy, this is Miss Leah. Ain't she growed up to be a fine young lady!"

Lucy's smile was bright. "I remember the time you ate five pancakes and got sick."

Leah laughed. "So do I! They were so good! Will you make me some more, Lucy?"

"Surely I will." Lucy turned to Amelia, saying, "Hello, Miss Amelia. It's good to see you again."

Amelia smiled and said, "Hello, Lucy, you haven't changed a bit. Maybe a few more pounds."

"And looks like you done lost a few," Lucy answered, nodding vigorously. "But I'll put them back on you. You come along now and I'll show you to your rooms. Simon, you hurry up with them bags!"

Simon grinned as he winked at Leah. "You see, she ain't stopped bossing me. Mr. Matthew done give us a piece of paper years ago, said we was free, but Lucy done got another one called a marriage license—and she thinks that's just another way of saying I'm hers to boss around."

"Hush up your mouth!" Lucy said sharply. "Go get them bags." Then she turned and continued, "We'll go upstairs now and you can get all refreshed. Maybe take a nap." She moved down the spacious foyer into a hall only somewhat narrower. At the end, a wide flight of stairs led upward to a landing. When they reached the second floor, she opened the door of the first room on her right. "This here's the dressing room." She stepped aside and the women looked in. At one end, a copper bathtub was set under a large window that let light fall over the brightly colored carpet. The walls were adorned with white wainscoting three feet high, and blue and yellow wallpaper reached to the top of the high ceiling. "Mr. Matthew, he done had one of these baths put in here," Lucy said, shaking her head dourly. "I don't hold with new stuff, but you know how he is—just *had* to have it."

"Oh, it looks heavenly," Leah said. "I'm first!" She'd never had a bath in a tub such as this, and the grimy days of travel suddenly seemed worse.

They moved down the hall to the first door and Lucy said,

"This is your room, Miss Claire." To the left, another door, "This is yours, Miss Leah—and that's yours, Miss Amelia," Lucy said, pointing. There was one more door, but Lucy didn't open that.

Claire not only felt nervous, but ridiculous. She felt sure the door to that fourth bedroom was Matthew's, and it gave her a queer feeling to know he'd be sleeping so close to her. However, she said nothing. When Lucy left, saying she'd fix tea and refreshments for them if they wanted to come down, Claire responded, "We'll be down directly."

After Lucy had descended the stairs, Amelia said with admiration in her voice, "This is a fine house, isn't it? Look at the woodwork, those moldings—such fine work!"

"Yes," Claire agreed reluctantly, "it is nice." Then she added briskly, "Let's get unpacked, and then perhaps we can go down and have something to eat."

"I'm going to take a bath," Leah announced. "I think the dirt's even under my skin." As the other two began unpacking, she grabbed a change of clothes out of her suitcase and proceeded to the bathroom. Closing the door, she removed her travel-stained clothes, then turned the faucet on the bathtub. As the water rushed out, she watched it with fascination. "I wonder why someone didn't think of this a thousand years ago?" she wondered out loud. "Instead of having to carry buckets of water, just turn a handle." She waited until the tub was filled, stepped inside, then sat down with a sigh of relief. There was sweet-smelling soap in a dish beside the tub, and washcloths. For a long time she splashed and sputtered and thought about washing her hair but decided that would be too big a project. "Someday they'll figure out a way to dry hair," she said, for her tresses were so thick it took hours in the sun to achieve that.

Finally, with some reluctance, she stepped out of the tub onto a woven cotton carpet, dried off on one of the plush towels, then put on fresh underwear and a green dress with tiny white flowers on the bodice and white ribbons interwoven at the cuffs and around the neck. It was somewhat wrinkled, but at least clean. Slipping on her shoes, she looked at the dirty clothes and shrugged. *I'll see about getting them washed later.*

Going downstairs quickly, she found the others in the dining room, drinking tea from fine porcelain cups and eating cookies from a platter.

"Don't eat too much!" Lucy warned as Leah sat down. "We're fixing up a big supper tonight. I don't want you to spoil your appetite."

"I don't think I could do that if I ate this whole plate of cookies," Leah said, biting into one "They're so good, Lucy! You could always make good cookies."

The black woman sniffed, but there was pleasure in her brown eyes. "I got to tend to the cookin'."

When she left the room, Leah said at once, "You've *got* to have a bath—both of you. It's just heavenly!"

Amelia took another cookie. "I'm so hungry! That roast beef Lucy's cooking is about to drive me crazy. Maybe she'll let me help her, although she's a better cook than I could ever be."

As the three sat there, Claire was thinking of Matthew. *How will he be after all these years?* Since her childhood, Claire had been strongly determined and had had a clearly defined set of goals. Her strong code of right and wrong, with few gray areas, had ruled her life. But now she thought how empty and fragmented her life had been since she'd left Matthew, and she wondered how it would be when she faced him again.

★ ★ ★

"I'm sorry I wasn't here when you arrived."

Matthew Cleburne had come into the parlor where the three women had been waiting, all of them somewhat nervously. Cleburne stepped into the room and Leah thought instantly, *He just gets better looking all the time!* She glanced over at her mother, noting that Claire's face was fixed, allowing no emotion to show. Glancing back at her father, she analyzed him quickly—tall, lean, and, at the age of forty-three, looking much younger. He had a thin face with dark blue eyes shaded by heavy eyebrows. His brown hair was gray at the temples, and he had a closely trimmed mustache. His mouth was wide and his lips firm and fully molded. There was an English look about him, especially in the aquiline nose and the high cheekbones.

"I'm sorry to intrude on you like this, Matthew," Claire said at once. She was wearing a light tan dress that showed her figure off to good advantage. Her only jewelry was a pair of small jade earrings and a ring with a small ruby, a gift from her father. She said hurriedly, as if making an excuse, "I realize that it's inconvenient—"

"Nonsense!" Matthew interrupted. His eyes warm, he stepped forward and took Amelia's hand. "Amelia, it's good to see you again. I've missed you."

"Thank you, Matthew. You're looking so well!"

"And Leah! I don't know whether to take you up on my lap or bow from the waist." Matthew's lips curved slightly as he saw her confusion. "Perhaps I'd better not do either for a while."

Leah had forgotten how much he liked to tease. She was uncomfortable, for her feelings about her father were complicated. But she managed to say, "You're looking very well! Time has been good to you."

"Thank you, Daughter." Then something in his manner changed as he inclined his head, saying, "As always, Claire, you look beautiful. I suppose you're tired after your long trip. Well, come along. Lucy says dinner is ready."

He stepped aside, and the three women made their way out of the parlor, down the hall, and into the dining room, a spacious room with an ornate gaslight chandelier. The table was covered with a snowy-white tablecloth and pale blue china with small, darker blue figures gracing each place. The heavy silver tableware gleamed richly under the reflected light, and from a large mahogany sideboard a combination of various silver and porcelain dishes also glowed.

99

"Well, Lucy, I hope you've prepared a feast," Matthew said, winking at the servant as she came in bearing a large platter containing the roast.

"I 'spect it'll do well enough," she said, sniffing. "I ain't noticed you turning nothin' down lately."

"Ah, but our guests may be more fussy than I am." Matthew smiled, his fondness for the woman obvious. As she went back to the kitchen, he commented, "I would have starved to death if it hadn't been for Lucy." And then, as Simon entered bearing a bowl of beans in one hand and a platter of corn-on-the-cob in the other, he said, "And Simon here makes my life miserable." Simon merely smiled briefly and Matthew laughed. "I don't know what I'd do without those two. It wouldn't be easy."

"They've been with you a long time, haven't they, Matthew?" Amelia said after the two had left the dining room. "They're very fond of you, I can tell that."

"The feeling's mutual. A good argument against slavery," he said, shrugging. "I can't imagine *owning* Simon and Lucy. There'd be something terribly wrong with it." Then he stopped abruptly and glanced at Claire. "Sorry, I didn't mean to start a political argument. We'll not speak of it again."

Claire dropped her eyes and, as the meal proceeded, she said very little. Strangely enough, it was Amelia who did most of the talking. She'd always been fond of Matthew, although she said little about it. Claire especially was forced to remember how many times Amelia had spoken well of Matthew before her own attitude had put a stop to it. Now, reunited with Matthew, Amelia's eyes were bright with interest in what Matthew was doing.

Cleburne shook his head as he answered, "I'm nothing but a dull, dreary businessman. I steal all the time I can to go hunting and riding. I do that a lot. But with the war on, business is good."

As the meal proceeded, there was a strange mixture of ease and tension in the room. Amelia and Matthew were enjoying themselves, but Leah and Claire both felt strange and

100

out of place. They met each other's eyes once, each understanding the feeling of the other. Finally, when Lucy brought in the dessert, a fine apple pie, they sat nibbling at it until finally Matthew remarked, "I'm glad you got here safely. It's a dangerous time at Vicksburg, at least so I hear."

"Yes," Claire said when the other two didn't speak. "It wasn't a good time at all."

"Well, you'll have to relax and let Simon, Lucy, and me make things easy for you." He hesitated, then said quietly, "I'm glad you're here. It's good to have you."

Claire hesitated. There was an honesty in Matthew Cleburne's eyes, but then he'd always been honest with her. It was his other habits that had separated them. She said softly, "Thank you, Matthew. You were always generous to those in need." Then she rose quickly, as if she'd said too much. "If you don't mind, I think I'll go to bed early."

"Why, of course," Matthew said, rising. "We'll have time to talk later." When Claire had left the room, he said, "What about you two?"

Amelia said, "I'm a little tired myself. When you get to be my age your bones don't take the bumping around that I got on some of the railroads." She stood there for a moment, and Matthew came over and shook her hand warmly, saying, "I've missed you, Amelia. We'll have lots of time to talk, and I'll show you New York."

"That will be nice. Good night, Matthew."

Leah was not sleepy and, as soon as Amelia left the room, she said so. "I'd like to hear more about what's going on here in the North. We were pretty cooped up in Vicksburg. Will you tell me about it?" She hesitated, not knowing what to call him. She had called him *Daddy* at one point, but that was in the dim reaches of long ago. Now she couldn't call him *Matthew,* and *Father* sounded stilted. She awkwardly avoided the use of any title at all as the two went back to the parlor.

"Well," he said, "I'll tell you what I know . . ." and began to speak of the news. He was, Leah discovered, a well-informed man who understood the military situation better

101

than most. Leah noticed that he was careful not to speak of the differences over slavery.

Finally, at nine o'clock, she said with some surprise, "It's been a good evening." She'd been prepared not to like her father, since she was firmly convinced he was a wastrel and dishonorable. But he'd been courtly, mannerly, and warm, and she was confused by it all. "I think I'll go to bed."

"I think you should," he said, nodding. "That's a long trip and you've been under a strain for a long time." He stood up as she rose and came over to stand closer to her. "You're a lovely young lady. I'm very proud of you, Leah," he said. "As soon as you're able, I hope you'll allow me to show you off a little bit."

"Show me off?"

"Why, yes, go for rides and let people think, 'Who's that old codger with the beautiful young daughter?'"

Leah laughed aloud. "They wouldn't say that!"

"Well, let them say what they want. I know a great many people. I'm not much for society these days, but I get enough invitations. There's a ball coming up that I think you'd enjoy. Maybe you'd let me go with you and do some shopping . . . but of course, your mother would want to do that. In any case, I don't mean to push you. Now, go get some rest."

"Good night," Leah said.

She thought for one moment he meant to lean forward and kiss her cheek, but then he rocked back on his heels as if rebuking himself. "Good night, Leah, sleep well."

She went to her room and lay in bed, restless. In her mind was the image of Matthew Cleburne she'd had for years—a heavy drinker, a woman chaser, a man dishonorable in his marriage vows, an unsteady man.

But that wasn't the man she'd seen this night. *True enough, scoundrels often have fine manners,* she thought, *but there's something different in him. I'll have time now to know him a little bit.* Then she went off to sleep, reveling in the feather beds and the clean linen after the hard, dirty days of travel.

CHAPTER EIGHT
Flight from Vicksburg

The cottonmouth stretched his length on a decaying cypress log. Except for the long forked tongue that flickered in and out of his mouth, he was virtually invisible. A dark cavity behind his slightly upturned snout gave him the trademark of the pit viper. His eyes seemed dead, yet the mechanisms in his body designed to pick up the scent of blood or slight movements around him were all operating.

A movement stirred the water in slight ripples, and with the sinister smoothness of his kind, the snake slipped off the log, his body twisting sinuously as he swam high in the water, scarcely disturbing the glassy surface. Reaching a point of ground above the tea-colored water of the swamp, he moved onto the land, head lifted.

Two men emerged from the depths of the cypress swamp, wading knee-deep in the fetid waters, their steps stirring up the mold and decay that had settled to the bottom. Their feet made squishing sounds as they pulled them free, and as they moved up on the higher ground they stopped as if by common consent and looked back at the darkness of the forest behind them.

"This looks like better ground, Mr. David," Corey said, taking a deep breath. His chest was wet with sweat. He'd removed his shirt and tied it by the arms around his waist. His skin glistened like dark chocolate, the muscles swelling

103

with each movement. "I sho' am glad to be away from that river and through that ol' swamp!"

David didn't answer. His lips were drawn together into a thin line, and his nose was pinched with the effort that had brought him this far. He seemed preoccupied, with a distant light in his eyes, and this troubled his companion. Corey examined David closely, then said, "I expect we're gonna get away for sho' now. Them Yankees ain't gonna come through no swamp after us."

David blinked his eyes, as if stirred from some deeper thoughts, and then turned to his companion. "I guess so," he said, his voice no more than a vague mutter. There was an uncertainty in him that wasn't his usual manner. He'd made the swim with Corey down the Mississippi past the gunboats without incident. They'd half floated, letting the current carry them along until they were at least five miles downstream from the gunboats. At night they'd made their way ashore and waited in the darkness until morning. There was no shelter, no hope of a fire, and they'd shivered and suffered the discomfort silently. At dawn they'd left the river, making their way westward through the cypress swamp without having the vaguest idea of what lay ahead of them.

Now David shrugged unhappily and without a word started across the dry land. But he hadn't taken two steps when suddenly Corey struck him in the back so abruptly and with such force that he fell to the ground, catching himself partially with his hands.

He rolled over quickly in the damp soil, his eyes suddenly alert, and saw that Corey had turned to one side and was kicking at something. Scrambling to his feet he saw it was a huge, thick-bodied snake. Catching the white inside of the jaws he whispered, "Cottonmouth!" and stepped forward, looking for a weapon. But there was none. Just then Corey's foot lashed out, catching the snake and sending him flying backward.

"That'll do you, old cottonmouth!" Corey said, breathing

hard. He shook his head. "He were just waitin' for you. Lucky I saw him."

David watched for a moment as the snake swam away, leaving a V-shaped wake as he moved toward the deeper waters of the swamp. Then he turned to Corey and managed a smile. "I never could stand snakes," he said, a slight shudder running through him. "He could have gotten you, Corey. I guess you earned your keep this morning."

Corey examined David's face, pleased to see the action seemed to have picked up his spirits. "Ain't gonna let no old cottonmouth get the best of us, is we now?" He grinned, his white teeth flashing against his dark features. "Come on now, Mr. David, let's git as far away from this here swamp as we kin. I wants to see some high ground."

The two moved on quickly, and all morning long they trudged along the ground as it rose slowly. They had to fight their way through undergrowth, vines with sharp thorny spines that clawed at their legs, and once had to detour around a cane thicket that was too thick to plow through.

Just before noon they stopped and Corey said, "I got to have me a drink of water, Mr. David."

David looked down at the creek that wound languidly along the ground. It moved slowly, almost imperceptibly. He shook his head. "Could be fever in this swamp, Corey. We better hold out till we get to someplace with better water. I'm pretty thirsty myself, but that malaria's bad stuff."

"Yes sah, I reckon you right."

The two of them rested for thirty minutes, then continued their journey. Over an hour later they crossed an abandoned road overgrown with vines. Wagon tracks were fresh in it, however, and David remarked, "Not used much but some-body's there." He looked both ways and said, "Which way shall we go?"

"Well, I guess it leads to sumpin' either way." Corey's brow wrinkled and he studied the tracks. "Reckon that way probably leads back to Vicksburg. Maybe we better try this one. You got that pistol handy, Mr. David?"

"Maybe I better check it." David sat down on a fallen tree and carefully unwrapped the Navy Colt that he'd brought all the way from Richmond in oilcloth along with the powder and loads. Expertly he loaded the chambers of the Colt and then admitted, "This won't fight off an army, but I'll feel better with it." He stuck it in the waistband of his pants and looked down the road. "Let's see what we can find."

They advanced down the road alertly, not knowing what they would find. The Yankee army had passed to the west of them—David was sure of that—but he was relatively certain that except for a supply line, the bulk of the army was now engaged in besieging Vicksburg. Overhead the skies were clear and a flight of red-winged blackbirds was flying over, making their raucous calls and heading for feeding grounds somewhere to the south.

"That looks like a farm of some kind up there," David said. They halted, and the two men peered around the undergrowth where the road bent.

"Smoke comin' from it," Corey observed. "Guess it ought to be all right. Ain't likely to be no Yankees this far south."

"Let's check it out." David removed the revolver from his waistband and held it down to his side while they moved down the weed-choked road. As they rounded the bend, they saw a log cabin on a rise of high ground. It was an old place, grown gray with years of rain and the powerful sun of Southern summers. Chickens clucked around the yard, and over to the right two pigs, caked with red mud, rooted industriously in the soil. They looked up curiously as the men approached. A curly tendril of smoke rose to the sky as David said quietly, "We better give them a signal." Lifting his voice, he cried, "Hello, the house!"

A moment's silence reigned, then a tall man appeared in the front door. He had a rifle, David noticed, so he called out quickly, "Just a couple of lost travelers! Maybe you can point us in the right direction."

The man in the cabin door stepped outside, moved off the

porch, and advanced, holding the rifle. He was a lanky individual with shaggy brown hair and a pair of steady light-blue eyes that he kept fixed on the pair. "What you doing out here?" he called, his voice a high tenor.

Because David was wearing his uniform, he knew there was no point in dissembling. "Don't know if you heard, but the Yankees got Vicksburg sewed up. Me and my servant here had to swim out or get caught." He was still holding the pistol in his hand, and he waited anxiously to see what the man's reaction might be. There were Union sympathizers in Mississippi, and this might well be one of them. But the distance to the man was less than thirty feet, so he hoped it wouldn't come to a shoot-out.

"Waal now, been expecting somethin' like thet." The man slipped his hand down along the barrel and with his right thumb lowered the hammer on the musket. "You fellers was lucky to get away, I guess." He set the butt of the musket on the ground. "Pemberton was a fool to get trapped there. I said so all along."

"In that," David said, slipping the Colt back into his waistband, "I think you're right. Too late now."

"Name's Otis Sudsen. Reckon you fellers could eat some coon and a little corn pone? The pone's fresh."

"That'd go down mighty well."

Ten minutes later David was sitting at the table with the farmer eating the fried morsels of fresh-killed coon. He'd piled a tin plate high with the meat and pone and given it to Corey, who now sat in a chair close to the door, eating and listening to the two men. The talk was of the war and Sudsen said finally, "I done lost two boys in this war. One at Antietam and one at Fredericksburg. Just got one more boy. He's with Lee."

"My brother and father serve with Lee."

"Do they now? Well, I ain't got a lot of hope with the way this war's turning out. Ain't my war anyhow. Never owned a slave in my life." He looked over at Corey, then shook his

107

head. "We been led down the wrong path, I reckon. Don't see no good end to it."

David looked down at his plate. He really wasn't hungry, though he should have been. He managed to eat a little more of the coon, then said, "I'm trying to get back to Richmond, where my family is."

"That ain't gonna be no play party," Sudsen said, scratching his growth of wiry whiskers. "Railroad's cut all to pieces, Yankees everywhere you look all through here. I 'spec you'll have to go to Atlanta. Hear tell trains are still running there."

"How can we get to a train to get to Atlanta?" David inquired.

Sudsen stared at the man across the table from him as if weighing something in his mind. Finally he said, "Reckon I'm about due for a trip to town. I can take you to Kingsburg. There's a spur line there that ought to get you on your way anyhow. You'll have to go around the world, I reckon, to get there."

"Wouldn't want to put you out, Mr. Sudsen."

"Ain't nothing doing here in this place anyhow. If my boy Jimmy don't come home, ain't nothing left. My woman died two years ago. All I do is a little two-bit farming here. One place is good as another." There was a faint despair in the man's blue eyes, typical of the current Southern spirit.

"I'd be glad to pay you for your time," David said.

Sudsen, a proud Southerner, shook his head vehemently. "Don't reckon it's come to me bein' paid for doing a soldier a little favor."

Quickly David said, "That's good of you. We appreciate it."

"Reckon we might as well get on our way. Them mules I got moves like molasses, but I guess they'll get us there."

★ ★ ★

The roadbed hadn't been repaired and the cars swayed alarmingly as the coal-burning engine wound through the forest of Georgia pines. Once the cars dipped so deeply that David grabbed for the handle of the seat, thinking they were going to be overturned. "We may have to get out and walk if this gets any worse," he said to Corey.

Corey, who'd never been on a train before, was fascinated by it all. "No sah," he said with a grin. "This beats walking. Mighty nice of that farmer to take us to the train, wasn't it, Mr. David?"

When David didn't answer, Corey looked at him closely. There was a slackness in his master's jaw, and his eyes seemed fixed on something far beyond the range of the interior of the dilapidated car that clattered and rattled along the narrow gauge line. He'd noticed during the wagon trip with Otis Sudsen that, from time to time, there was a gap in David Rocklin's attention span. Now he said to himself, *Mr. David ain't right. Somethin's wrong with his mind. Sure be glad to get him home where his family can take care of him.* He tried again. "I got some of that fried coon Mr. Sudsen put up for us. Could you eat a bite, Mr. David?" But there was still no response, as if Corey hadn't even spoken. With a despairing shake of his head, Corey reached into the paper sack, pulled out a piece of the meat, and bit it in two with his strong teeth. He chewed thoughtfully, turning to watch the forest flow by like magic. But always he returned to stare at David and wonder what was going on inside his head.

★ ★ ★

"All off for Atlanta!"

The conductor, a heavy man who wore a flat-crowned hat with a narrow brim, moved down the aisle. His gold watchchain clinked against his massive stomach as he came to stand over the two men who remained on the train after all the other travelers had filed off. Looking down at David and Corey, he said, "Atlanta! This is as far as the train goes." After staring at David for a moment with his small dark eyes, he turned to the black man. "What's wrong?"

Corey cleared his throat. "Mr. David, he's a little bit

troubled, sah, but he'll be all right." He reached over, took David's arm, and shook it. Leaning forward, he said, "Mr. David—Mr. David, we're in Atlanta. Come on, let's get off the train."

The conductor watched and saw that the words didn't seem to reach the consciousness of the fine-looking young man dressed in the stained Confederate uniform. "He's been in a battle, I guess?"

"Yes sah, that's it. He's a little bit—wore out. But I'll take care of him. Come on, Mr. David."

The conductor watched as the strong-bodied servant almost pulled the white man to his feet. He gathered a small sack in one hand and, keeping the other on his master, led him off the train.

"Too bad. Looks like he's had more fighting than he can take. Hope the boy'll be all right."

Corey led David down the steps, and when they were on the cinder-covered platform said, "Come on now, Mr. David, we'll be all right." He led the man to a bench and looked around almost desperately. "Let's us set here a minute." When David obeyed him docilely, Corey sat down muttering, "Don't know what to do. What's wrong with Mr. David? We got to get *somewhere*. He got a friend here, so he said." Then he asked his companion, "Mr. David, what's your friend's name? The one here in Atlanta?"

There was no response for some time, then David blinked his eyes and coughed. "What's that, Corey?" he said, looking around. "Why, we're at the station! Is this Atlanta?"

Corey swallowed. "Yes sah, this here's Atlanta. What's your friend's name?"

"Bernard Dixon."

"I guess we better try to find him. Don't you reckon?"

Weariness tinged the face of Rocklin, and he got up slowly, almost like an old man. He looked around and murmured, "I must have gone to sleep. I don't even remember getting off the train." His voice sounded hollow and he looked, puzzled, at the black face in front of him. "How long have I been asleep?"

"Well, sah, you been mighty tired, I reckon. But you'll be all right. Let's go find Mr. Dixon."

Corey was afraid David would go off into whatever sleep he'd been in and was relieved when they found the carriage and David gave the cabdriver an address. As the two got into the carriage, David said, "I haven't seen Bernard Dixon for a couple of years. We were good friends once. I don't even know if he's still at this address."

As the cab made its way through the city, David noted that Atlanta was somewhat similar to Richmond. But there was a shabbiness about the place that hadn't been here on his last visit, six years earlier. Then it had been a busy, prosperous city, growing and filled with new construction. Now everything seemed to have stopped, and he realized it was due to some of the same genteel poverty that he was accustomed to in Richmond itself.

They reached a section of town composed mainly of white frame houses, most two stories and with fading paint, built along a wide street. The carriage stopped and the driver said, "There she is, sir."

David and Corey got out. David said, "You'd better wait. I'm not sure this is the place."

"Yes, sir, I'll wait."

David walked up to the front door, Corey following slightly behind him. When he knocked, the door opened almost at once and a white-haired woman dressed in black looked him over carefully. "Yes? May I help you?"

"My name's David Rocklin. I'm looking for Bernard Dixon."

"Why, yes, David, I didn't recognize you! Won't you come in?"

"I'd better pay the cabdriver," David said. "I wanted to be sure this was the right place."

"Bernard will be back in less than an hour, but you can wait."

After David paid the driver, the woman said, "Bernard still speaks of you often, of your days in school together. Why don't you let me take your servant to the kitchen? I'll see that he's fed. You and I can have tea in the parlor."

Corey didn't like to leave his master alone, but he had little choice. He followed the woman into the kitchen, where she said to a large black woman who turned to meet them, "Mr. Bernard has some company, Dinah. See that his man here is fed."

"Yes'm."

Corey stood there uncertainly as the woman left. Dinah examined him almost clinically. "You hongry?"

"I could eat, I reckon."

"Sot down there. I see what we got."

Back in the parlor, David waited for Mrs. Dixon. When she returned, the two had tea together. She was curious about his coming, and he explained his escape from Vicksburg and ended by saying, "I'm trying to get back to Richmond, but I wanted to see Bernard."

"He'll be so glad to see you," Mrs. Dixon said. Then she asked tentatively, "I can see you didn't have time to carry clothes from Vicksburg. You and Bernard are about the same size. Come along; you can get cleaned up and wear some of his clothes."

David went upstairs without argument. When he was alone in the high-ceilinged room he took a sponge bath, dried off, and put on a pair of Dixon's brown trousers and a clean white shirt that fit him reasonably well. Then he looked at the bed. "Just take a little nap," he said. He lay down and instantly fell into a deep sleep.

★ ★ ★

"Bernard! Your friend is here—David Rocklin."

Bernard Dixon had entered the house and stopped abruptly at his mother's words. A tall young man of twenty-three with sandy hair and blue eyes, he said with a grin, "Old Dave is here? What in the world is he doing in Atlanta?"

He listened as his mother explained and said, "I think he must have gone to sleep. His servant's out in the kitchen if you want to ask him."

"Yes, I will."

Bernard went to the kitchen, where Corey stood up at once, his eyes alertly fixed on the young white man. When he entered, Corey said, "Mr. Dixon, I'se Corey—"

Dixon, seeing that something was troubling the slave, asked, "What is it? Is something wrong?"

"Yes sah, there is. I don't know what it is, but Mr. David, ever since we left Vicksburg, he been somehow out of his mind."

"Out of his mind? What do you mean?"

"Oh, I don't mean he acting crazy. I mean he just seem like he passes out . . . like he goes to sleep and I can't wake him up."

"Was he wounded?"

"Naw sah, he didn't get hit with no bullets, but he been having some powerful bad nightmares, I knows that much."

Dixon frowned. It didn't sound like the David Rocklin he'd known. "Thank you, Corey," he said. "Have you been fed?"

"Yes sah. I want to help Mr. David get back to his family."

"We'll see what we can do."

Two hours later, David came down the stairs and Bernard Dixon greeted him warmly. "I'm glad to see you! You're lucky you didn't get tied up there in Vicksburg with the rest of Pemberton's army."

"It was kind of a miracle, I think, Bernard. I still don't know how Corey and I managed to get away."

"Well come on, I want to hear all about the battle. I'm going in the army myself next month. Maybe you can give me some pointers."

David looked at Bernard Dixon, a strange expression twisting his face. "I don't think," he said woodenly, "I'd be able to do that, Bernard."

Bernard Dixon sensed his friend was greatly troubled.

But, being a sensitive young man, he knew better than to plunge right in. *I'll have to find out what's going on in Dave's head,* he thought, then said, "While you're here, we'll get caught up. You don't have to leave right away, do you?" He waited but no answer came and he was shocked to see David appeared not to have heard him. He said quickly, "We'll talk about it later. Come along. Let's see if Mama's got any of that chocolate cake left. You always were partial to chocolate cake."

★ ★ ★

Later, David put the tip of the pen into the inkwell and then slowly began to write:

Dear Grandmother,
I know you've been worried about me, but I've been somewhat ill since I escaped from Vicksburg. Perhaps it's some form of malaria, I'm not sure. I hate to tell you this, for you have enough to worry you on the farm. God willing, I'll be well soon. Try not to worry.
  I've been here in Atlanta, staying with Bernard's family for two weeks now, and most of that time I've been merely trying to gain my strength back. I've lost considerable weight and have no appetite, which seems to be part of this sickness. Bernard and his parents have been most gracious. They wouldn't hear of my finding a room in Atlanta while I recovered. They've had their family doctor to see me, and while he hasn't yet identified what sort of fever it is, I feel sure he'll find the cure.
  I have a servant with me now, a slave I bought in Vicksburg, named Corey. He is a treasure and I intend to free him at the end of a year. He takes good care of me, fusses over me like a mother hen, and is a combination manservant and nurse.
  Please write me with any news of Pa and Dent. We hear about the awful loss of life at Gettysburg and I'm

very concerned one of them might have been wounded. I'd feel better if you could write at once. And please tell me how things are there on the farm, and how Josh is getting along with everything, especially the salt pork.

I'll stay here with Bernard until I'm recovered and can make the trip home safely. Please pray for me and write as soon as you can.

Your loving grandson, David

David put the pen down, exhausted by the weight of it. He closed his eyes abruptly, put his arms across the writing desk that sat beside his bed, and rested his head on it. He hadn't told his grandmother of the blackouts that had come to him, nor of the terrible nightmares. Both were coming more often now, and he knew that the Dixons were concerned. Corey was also worried.

For a long time he sat there, feeling himself slipping away again. Almost wildly he jerked himself upright and shook his head, gritting his teeth. "I can't go into that again!" Panic and fear tingled through his body and almost exploded in his brain.

"I can't go mad! I can't—!"

CHAPTER NINE
Very Nice—For a Yankee

"Git yo worthless self out and bring some firewood in!"

Simon had been sitting in a cane-bottomed chair reading the newspaper, but at Lucy's irritated tone, he lowered the *Tribune* and looked up, a quizzical expression in his eyes. "Why you jumpin' on me so much?" he inquired mildly without moving. "I ain't done nothin' to you, woman."

Standing in the middle of the kitchen, her forearms covered with flour, Lucy gave the tall lanky man a disgusted look. "Don't argue with me," she said firmly. "You ain't done nothin' but set around this house all mornin'. Now git busy!"

"I know what's aggrafrettin' you. You ain't been fit to live with since Miss Claire came here two weeks ago. That's a long time for a man to put up with a rebellious wife."

"Never mind about no rebellious wife!"

"The Bible say, 'Wives don't persecute an older man.'"

"Where it say dat? You tell me where!"

Simon grinned. "The book of Titus, I think. You ought to read up more on the Scripture about how to treat a husband." He creased the paper gently, his face growing more sober. Shaking his head, he added, "I know how you feel, Lucy. I ain't shore it's good for Miss Claire to come here. Just about the time Mr. Matthew gets over her, she pops up again—and down he goes."

"That's a truth," Lucy said. She picked up a wooden spoon in her right hand, cradled a huge bowl in the crook

117

of her left arm, and stared thoughtfully out the window as she stirred vigorously. It was a beautiful August afternoon with birds singing outside, but there was no contentment in her face. "I don't know what she have to come here for."

"Didn't have no place else to go."

"That ain't no excuse. Mr. Matthew always sent her and Miss Leah money." The spoon moved strong and rhythmically in the bowl, slapping the dough. "She ain't changed a bit—never will."

Slowly Simon climbed to his feet, stretched carefully, then turned toward the door. "I'll get the wood," he said. As he moved across the floor, he spread his hands out in a gesture of helplessness. "You right about it, though. Mr. Matthew, he ain't happy. She always do that to him. You reckon he still love her after all these years?"

"I don't know, but she is done made one big mess out of raising that girl. Don't even love her own pappy. That ain't *right*, Simon."

"Maybe Miss Leah can get to know Mr. Matthew better if they stay a long time. He sure is trying hard, taking her places and all."

"That ain't gonna do no good. Not with that momma of hers whispering in her ear about what a bad man Mr. Matthew is." The spoon reached a pinnacle of speed as Lucy allowed the anger in her to exit through her strong right wrist. "Now she's taken up with this Yankee soldier, Miss Leah has. That might be a good thing, though," she added thoughtfully. Looking down at the dough and testing it, she moved over to the table and set the bowl down. "She still got that Confederate mess in her mind. I surprised she even running around with that lieutenant."

"Her momma don't mind. Miss Claire maybe sees he'd be a good husband for Miss Leah. Comes from a rich-type family. I guess Miss Claire's smart enough to know there ain't gonna be nothin' left in the South when this here war's over. Anyway, I kinda like that soldier."

"You like him cause he gives you money," Lucy said, snorting. "Now, get out of here and bring that firewood in!"

Later in the afternoon, Simon encountered Leah as she was walking around the small flower garden in the backyard.

"Howdy, Miss Leah," he said, "them flowers about gone. Gonna be nothing but old dead weeds in a month or two." He stopped and looked down at the chrysanthemums. "They was real pretty when they first came on. Wish you'd been here to see 'em."

Leah was wearing a pale blue dress with yellow lace at the neck and small figures of white in the skirt, and her hair was carefully done. As Simon looked at her, he asked, "You must be steppin' out tonight, Miss Leah—all dressed up like that?"

"Yes, I am. Lt. Decatur's taking me to the theater."

"Sure 'nuff? Well, ain't that nice." Simon was insatiably curious and at once began fishing for information. "He shore is a nice gentleman. I 'spec you been out most every night since you met him at that ball?"

"That's right. He's been very insistent." Leah smiled and touched her hair in a feminine gesture. "I never thought I'd let a Yankee officer take me anywhere."

"How come you do it, Miss Leah?" Simon asked.

"Oh, I don't know. When I met him at the ball I snubbed him. I thought it would be enough to get rid of him, but . . ." A thoughtful light came into her eyes and she shook her head slightly. "He just wouldn't take no for an answer. I believe he's the stubbornest young man I've ever seen! And he is nice—for a Yankee."

"Ain't that the truth! Well, what's your momma think about you going around with a Yankee?"

"I'm sure you've asked her already, Simon," Leah said innocently.

"Who, me? Why, I don't poke around in folks's business!"

"No, so I've noticed. Well, Mama, for your information, thinks he's a very suitable young man. She approves thoroughly, at least of my going to the theater with him."

"What's yo pappy think about him?"

119

The question startled Leah. "Why . . . he hasn't said." This particular remark troubled her, and she said quickly, "I suppose he doesn't care one way or the other."

"Now that ain't so, Miss Leah," Simon spoke up quickly. He scratched his head vigorously and kicked at the clod of dirt in the flowerbed at his feet. "Mr. Matthew, he's interested in everything you do—always has been. You don't know how much he 'preciate them letters you write to him once in a while. He still got every one of 'em."

"Has he really? I wouldn't have thought that."

"'Deed he do. He read them to me over and over again. And that picture you sent two years ago, you know where it is? Right in his bedroom. He think a heap of you, Miss Leah. Never saw a pappy more attached to a young lady."

Just then a bumblebee lumbered down over a dead blossom as if perplexed. He flew haphazardly among the dying flowers, hovering in the air hopefully, then moving on hesitantly. Finally, finding nothing to satisfy him, he rose slowly, made a circle of the garden, then headed out over the fence. Leah watched him until he disappeared, then lifted her eyes to the tall, dark-skinned man. "He always wrote to me. Every time I wrote to him, a letter would come back."

"When you was just a little girl," Simon said thoughtfully, his voice almost dreamy, "he'd take you for a walk every day, when you couldn't even walk. You'd fall down and he'd pick you up." The memory was pleasant to him, and he seemed to savor it. "And he got you that dog. Miss Claire had a fit. You remember Jigger?"

"Yes, he was so sweet. I think about him all the time. Daddy gave him to me when I was just four years old." The name *Daddy* had jumped to her lips without thought, and Leah glanced quickly at Simon to see if he'd noticed. However, he merely stood there, the late-afternoon sun falling on his craggy features. Then she continued, "When he died, we had a funeral."

"Why, I remember that! It was me who got the box. It was a soapbox and Mr. Matthew—nothing would do but he'd find some satin from one of Miss Claire's old dresses and line it. Then he made a regular casket out of that."

"Yes, and we had a funeral, you remember?" Leah's eyes were misty. "We even read out of the Bible, out in the backyard by the little grave. And Daddy preached a little sermon. I still remember that," she said quietly. "I think I remember it more clearly than anything that happened in my childhood. He was so busy then, but he took time to have a funeral for Jigger."

"He give you anything you want back in them days," Simon murmured, "and I guess today, he'd do the same thing." He looked up, his wise old eyes fixed on Leah and his voice summer-soft as he said, "You miss Mr. Matthew, Miss Leah?"

Leah couldn't meet his eyes nor could she answer his question. She realized suddenly that she *had* missed her father, more than she'd known. Speaking of the funeral for the dog had brought back other memories that rushed through her. To shut them off she said, "Oh, I suppose so," then hurriedly left, saying, "I've got to get ready to go."

Simon stared after her, then turned slowly and made his way into the kitchen, where Lucy was taking a pie out of the oven. "Maybe I'd better sample that," he said.

"Keep yo' hands off it!" Lucy snapped.

"That chile still loves her pappy in spite of everything," Simon said. "It's a shame that them two ain't had no time for each other." He didn't mention Claire's name, for he knew Lucy carried a deep-seated resentment against the woman. Indeed, she blamed Claire Cleburne for bringing sorrow and distress to the Cleburne family. Simon resumed his seat in the chair, tipped it back and, as he leaned his head against the wall, inhaled the fragrant incense of the pie that hung over the kitchen. Then he sighed, thinking of what might have been.

★ ★ ★

Lt. Brian Decatur was a handsome young man, fit and trim. At five-foot-ten, his one hundred and sixty pounds was firm and solid. He moved athletically into the parlor where Claire Cleburne was sitting in a chair beside the window. "Well, hello, Mrs. Cleburne," Decatur said, smiling easily. He had curly brown hair and a mustache. He was sharp featured, and there was something unsettling about his gaze, for he had one brown eye and one blue. He moved across to bend over and kiss Claire's hand when she extended it, then said, "You really ought to be going to the ball with us, you and Mr. Cleburne."

"Oh no, I think not, Lieutenant."

Her tone was so abrupt that Decatur paid attention instantly. He'd met Leah less than two weeks ago at a ball where she'd been escorted by her father. He'd been taken by the girl's attractive manner and rather saucy ways. Escorting a Southern girl around had been a challenge to him, but Decatur liked challenges. Now he realized, however, he'd stepped into a family matter that was somewhat precarious. Being a tactful young man, he smoothed over his remark by saying, "Why, of course, maybe some other time."

As he was saying this, Leah entered and said at once, "What was it you said last time, Lieutenant—that a woman's never on time?"

"I apologize and ask your hearty forgiveness, Miss Cleburne." He advanced to where she stood, taking in the trim figure and smooth, clear complexion. "You look beautiful," he said. "No one will be able to watch the actors or actresses, not with you in the hall."

Leah laughed. "You Yankees are the romantic ones, not Southerners, as rumor has it." She turned to her mother saying, "We're going to see *Hamlet*. I've never seen it, have you?"

"Yes, I saw it with—with your father once, many years ago. Who's in the starring role?"

"I'm not sure," Brian Decatur said. "I've heard he's not the best actor in the world, but he's very popular."

"Well, try to get home before it's too late."

"Certainly. Are you ready, Miss Leah?"

Decatur and Leah left the house, and he escorted her into the carriage he'd hired for the occasion. "Capitol Theater, driver," he said, then got in beside her. As the horses *clip-clopped* along the streets, Decatur spoke cheerfully of the evening. "There won't be many more of these, I'm afraid. I'll be leaving soon."

"Where are you going, or is that a military secret?"

"Oh, not really. I suppose everybody knows that the next big battle will be somewhere around Chattanooga."

After the crisis of July 1863, both armies had reassessed their positions. The North was more optimistic and confident now that the Mississippi valley was clear and Lee back in Virginia. Lee, however, was far from beaten, and practically every expert agreed that Gen. Rosecrans, with his Union Army of the Cumberland, would be attacking Gen. Braxton Bragg somewhere around Chattanooga.

Leah sat quietly as the lieutenant spoke of the war almost lightly. She'd noted before his confidence, and now she remarked, "You seem very sure the war will go your way."

"Why, yes, I believe it will. I don't want to injure your feelings, of course, but I think it won't be long before all of this is over."

"Not everyone agrees with you in the North. Just last month, here in New York, there were draft riots."

Brian dropped his eyes, unable to answer for a moment. "I'm embarrassed about that, to think people here have so little vision!" He spoke of the crowds that had looted and actually killed during the draft riots, protesting against conscription and the war itself. "But there's always people like that," he said, shrugging his trim shoulders. "Now, let's put all this behind us and enjoy ourselves. . . ."

Leah did enjoy herself that evening. She'd never been to a first-class theatrical production, and the actors, she had to agree, put on a good show.

She looked out the window and by the gaslights saw that people were walking the street even at this late hour. "It seems so strange to see people going on with life as if there were no war," she remarked.

Decatur glanced at her quickly. It was dark in the carriage and he could only see the outline of her face. He'd found himself almost bewitched by this young woman. For some reason, the fact she was Southern and Confederate in sympathy seemed to make the attraction stronger. "It'll be over soon," he said. "Then we can put it all behind us, North and South." The horses' hooves drummed on the pavement, iron against stone, and the two sat there quietly until they finally arrived back at the Cleburne house. Then he got out and escorted her inside.

"I'd ask you in," she said, "but it's rather late."

"Of course . . . now, about tomorrow night—"

Leah laughed. "You *are* persistent, Lieutenant! No wonder you Yankees are doing so well. Don't you ever give up?"

Brian shook his head. "I've only got a few days. Now, what I propose tomorrow night—"

"I can't go out with you every night," Leah protested. "The neighbors will be talking."

"They're all in bed. Look! Almost every house is dark."

"Well, that one isn't." Leah pointed to her own house. "My mother will be waiting up for me."

"Then I'd better go in and make our excuses," Brian said quickly.

"No, I think not, Lieutenant." She put her hand out and smiled graciously at him. "I must admit, you are a charming young man—for a Yankee."

Brian laughed at her audacity. "And you are a beautiful young woman—for a Rebel."

The two stood there, speaking lightly for a moment, and then his face turned serious. "I'll be leaving soon. The army's already on the move. I'm just staying later to take my company toward Tennessee—maybe a week, no more."

"I'm sorry you have to leave. I've enjoyed our times together," she said, her voice light.

No one ever accused Brian Decatur of being a timid or

bashful young man. As the smell of her perfume wafted faintly in the air, he reached forward and saw her eyes change as his arms went around her. He expected her to pull away, but she didn't—and then he kissed her.

Leah had known, of course, that he was going to kiss her. She was experienced enough in the ways of amorous young men to know such things. She held herself slightly apart, not giving in to his embrace, but not pushing away either. This Yankee was attractive; that she couldn't deny. It couldn't be serious, of course, she told herself, but he'd been nice to her. When he had held her for a moment, she put her hand against his chest and moved back. "There," she said, "that's enough."

"For you!" Decatur said, grinning. "I'll be here tomorrow at two o'clock. Wear some clothes that aren't so fancy."

"What in the world for?"

"You'll see," Decatur said, bowing slightly. "It's been a great evening. I'll see you tomorrow, Leah."

Leah watched as he got into the carriage and rode away, then went into the house. Claire was sitting in the parlor, although it was after eleven. "You shouldn't have stayed up, Mother."

"I couldn't sleep." Claire put down the book she'd been reading and stood up. "Was it enjoyable?"

"Yes, it was different. I'd never seen anything quite like it." She sat down, and for a while the two women talked, Claire listening, a smile on her lips as Leah recounted her evening. "He's really very nice," she said finally, "but he's leaving next week, I think."

Claire nodded as if she found this reassuring. "It's just as well. He is nice—but he is a Yankee."

The two women rose and as they did Leah asked, "Has Father gone to bed?"

"Yes . . ."

There was a hesitancy in Claire's tone. Matthew had come in earlier, and for a time the two had spoken. She'd fixed him a cup of tea, and they'd sat at the dining-room table. The conversation had been mundane as he'd asked about her day and the things she'd done. Finally, he had given her an odd look and said, "I'm glad you're here, Claire, no matter what the reason."

His words had echoed in Claire's mind, disturbing her somehow. She'd gone to bed, then tossed and turned for so long that finally she'd risen, put on her robe, and come downstairs to read and wait for Leah to come in. Now, as she stood there, she looked unusually vulnerable.

"What's the matter, Mother?"

"Oh, I don't know. I feel so . . . so out of place here. I wish we could go somewhere else."

Leah sensed a rare uncertainty in her mother. "Have you and Father been quarreling?"

"Oh, no, not that. He's been . . . very nice. It's just that—" She broke off then and said abruptly, "Good night, Leah." Moving hastily out of the room, she ascended the steps and turned into her own bedroom. She put the candle down on the nightstand, then looked at the bed. She was restless, not sleepy, and she rocked in the chair a long time before finally sighing deeply and getting into bed.

★   ★   ★

The courtship went on for a week, and on Sunday, young Decatur presented himself at the door with a carriage to escort the family to church. The entire family attended the Methodist Church, where the sermon was on forgiveness.

"That was a good sermon, wasn't it, sir?" Decatur asked Matthew.

"Very good," Matthew responded. "Rev. Haws is a fine preacher."

After dinner, the two men sat out on the porch talking. The ladies joined them for a while, and the conversation drifted back to the sermon.

But Claire took no part in it, for somehow the sermon had pierced her. Finally she excused herself and left the porch. As she moved away, she thought, *I've got to get away from here. I can't bear it any longer.*

CHAPTER TEN
A Grim Picture

"I don't understand it, Mother. It's like—it's like David is a different man!"

Bernard Dixon had come to sit beside his mother, who was crocheting a doily out of light-blue thread. She looked up at him, worry in her fine gray eyes, and shook her head. "Your father says he saw men like him during the Mexican war. He said they just seem to retreat back into their own minds after their hardships."

"Yes, I know," Dixon murmured. He picked up a book lying on the table, riffled the pages impatiently, then tossed it down. "Dave just goes back into—some kind of a *cave* almost and piles rocks up until nobody can get at him. I've never seen anything like it."

"Dr. Summers says it's not physical."

"I know that. He didn't get wounded or anything. I've talked to Corey about him. He says he's changed so completely he hardly knows him."

"Has he written to his family?"

"Yes, but I don't think he's told them anything. As far as I understand, he just tells them he's got a physical sickness— a fever of one sort or another. It's not like Dave to lie like that."

"I'm not sure he's lying, at least not completely," Mrs. Dixon remarked. She put the crochet material down in her lap and clasped her hands together, easing the cramped muscles. She had the beginning of arthritis and dreaded to see it come on, for she loved to do fine work. "I don't know him well, but it seems to me he's afraid to face up to what's happening to him."

"I've noticed that, too. Every time I've tried to talk to him about it, he just shuts me off. But he's got to do *something.*"

"Dr. Summers says there's really not much he, or any doctor he knows of, can do. If it's in Dave's mind, then medicine won't help much, will it?"

"I suppose not, but I hate to see this happen to Dave! He's such a good man—and such a fine family! I think they ought to be told. I've thought of writing them myself."

"I wouldn't do that!" Mrs. Dixon said quickly. "Let David handle it. All we can do is just be available."

"I suppose so." Bernard got up and walked around the room aimlessly. "He's gone off on another of those long walks of his. What if he blacks out while he's outside? That'd be terrible."

"Usually Corey goes along with him, but he didn't go this time. He was chopping wood and David walked out of the house without saying a word to anyone." She glanced up at the clock on the mantel. "He's been gone over three hours. I didn't want to say anything, but I'm worried about him."

"I've got to do something!" Dixon exclaimed, turning to leave the room. "I'll go see if I can find him."

★ ★ ★

At that very moment David was wandering through the streets of Atlanta. He'd found his way to the center of the city and passed along the thronged streets, only vaguely aware of the conversation and activities of the large city around him. He'd left the house almost desperately, for he'd felt himself dropping off into what he'd come to recognize as a "spell." It was like falling asleep in a way, but he'd learned these periods could last as much as three or four hours. Corey had stayed close beside him during such times, and David had become very dependent upon the black man.

Now as he meandered along the streets of Atlanta, desperation swept over him. A heavyset man came out of a butcher shop, his white apron red with blood, reminding David of the fighting he'd seen in Vicksburg. Quickly he averted his eyes and walked rapidly along the street. Wagons and carriages and carts rumbled along the broad street, but he ignored them, thinking, *I've got to do something. I can't stay at the Dixons' forever—but I can't go home again either.*

He paused and waited while a six-horse team, pulling an enormous wagon loaded with barrels, went by. Then he crossed the street, returning to his train of thought. *I've got to tell my family something. They must be worried sick about me.* For another twenty minutes he walked, then made his way back to the Dixon house. *I've got to tell them,* he thought, *and I'd rather die.*

A vision of Leah's face came to him, clear as a photograph. He let the memories of their times together flow through his mind, savoring them to the fullest. There had been no woman in his life who had stirred him as this one had, and now she was as lost to him as if she were dead. *I'll never see her again,* he thought, and the sweet memories became bitter. He forced his thoughts away from her and moved down the street, his head bent and shoulders slumped.

Thoughts fluttered through his head like bats in an old barn, and he finally said aloud, "I'd rather die than lose my mind!"

This thought was both the root and effect of his problem. He was so horribly afraid of losing his mind that the very thought of it seemed to bring on the blackouts that plagued him. But as he wrenched his thoughts away from the notion of insanity, they kept swarming back. He had awful visions of what it would be like for his family, as well as for himself, if he went mad.

I don't know what to do. If it were a physical wound it would be different. But I can't stand this awful thing that's hanging over me!

★ ★ ★

As the light filtered in from the tall window in his room, David opened his eyes, then closed them quickly. He stirred carefully, turning his head away from the light. When he opened his eyes again Corey was leaning over him, his face tense, his lips drawn tightly together.

"What—what is it, Corey?"

The eyes of the black man half narrowed and he said, "You feel all right now, Mr. David?"

From the tone of the slave's voice, David instantly knew he'd had another episode. Looking down, David saw he was virtually undressed, wearing only his underwear with a sheet pulled up to his waist. Alarm jangled his nerves and he sat up abruptly, staring wildly around. He licked his lips, found them dry, and asked, "Can I have some water?"

"Yes sah!"

David sat there while Corey jumped up and poured water from a pitcher into a glass and handed it to him. He gulped it down thirstily, then handed the glass back. He watched as Corey put the glass down and sat down slowly in the chair. As the slave leaned forward, concern on his face, David asked, "Have I been—sick?"

"Yes sah!"

"How long have I been here?"

Corey swallowed hard and looked down at the woven carpet on the floor as if reluctant to answer. He moved his feet and twitched his shoulders, but finally decided there was no evading the question. "You done been here three days, Mr. David."

"Three days!"

"Yes sah. You didn't come down for breakfast and I come up to see 'bout you. You was just standing there at that window looking out. You hadn't even dressed and you didn't know me. You didn't know *nothing*, Mr. David."

A sick feeling rose in his throat, for this was the worst he'd imagined. "Tell me," he said, his voice harsh. He swung his feet out and sat on the side of the bed listening as Corey described what had happened. He'd been like a child, obedient to commands but unable to respond. Corey stumbled over the words but then said urgently, "We done had the doctor here every day."

"He's no good for what I've got."

"Maybe he is. The preacher, he wuz here, too. He pray over you every day, Mr. David. He's a good man."

But David Rocklin wasn't listening. He knew now that something terrible was wrong with him—something so awful he didn't want to say it aloud. And then he realized he had to.

"I'm losing my mind, Corey," he said quietly. He faced the slave, seeing compassion in the large eyes, then stood up and walked to the window and looked down. Outside, a red-brown, bushy-tailed squirrel was busily digging a hole in the ground with sharp erratic movements. When he'd finished, he stuffed something into the hole and covered it up. Then he scurried along the ground, scampered up a tree, and paused to look alertly around. David saw the shining glow of his quick eyes, then the squirrel twitched his tail and disappeared around the tree trunk.

David turned around slowly. Corey had risen and was watching him silently. David wanted to say something to reassure the slave, but he felt more alone, helpless, and alien from his world than he'd ever been in his life. In his hopelessness, he saw nothing ahead of him but a life of complete misery.

CHAPTER ELEVEN
The Verdict

"Lucy, can you help me a minute?"

Leah had donned her corset and now turned to Lucy, who'd just brought her dress from downstairs.

"What is it?" Lucy demanded.

"Help me lace this corset, please." Leah held onto the massive oak headboard on the bed and waited. There was a moment's pause, then the strings in the back of her corset jerked tight. Lucy's touch was so rough that Leah gasped several times until the operation was finished and the final knot was firmly tied. Then she said with a smile, "Thank you, Lucy." Taking a deep breath she shook her head, a wry expression on her lips. "I don't know why women put up with this, cutting the life out of themselves just so they can have a small waist."

Lucy didn't answer. She moved back to the dress she'd brought up and placed across the bed. Picking it up, she examined it critically.

For a moment Leah stared at the woman, thinking back to the past. When Leah had been little more than a child, Lucy had been a smiling woman, always willing to nurse Leah's bruises and to show her affection. But that warmth was entirely missing now. Ever since Leah had come back to her father's house, she'd noticed this hardness in the servant.

"Well, Lucy," she said finally, "it would appear you don't like me anymore."

"Got nothing to say about likes or dislikes."

"You don't have to say anything. It's written all over you." Leah's temper flared for a moment. "What's the matter? Why are you upset with me?"

"Nothin' was said 'bout bein' upset."

Stepping in front of the woman, Leah stood there until Lucy lifted her eyes. "What have I done? Why don't you like me?"

"No, I don't like you." Lucy's words were flat and she lifted her head defiantly to look up at the taller woman. "You don't treat Mr. Matthew right."

"That's not for you to say!" Leah replied angrily.

"I didn't say it till you asked me about it. If you don't want to know, don't ask." Lucy's lips twisted downward in a scowl. "He done everything for you that a man can do for a daughter and all you do is put him down! If you don't like him, why'd you come here?"

"We didn't have anywhere else to go."

"That's right—and all these years he been sendin' you money, ain't he, now?"

Reluctantly Leah agreed. "Yes, he's always taken care of us in that way. That's not why—" She broke off, then shook her head so violently that her hair swung up and down her back. Then she straightened with indignation; she didn't have to talk about her father with a servant. "Just help me put this dress on."

Silently Lucy assisted the young woman and when the dress was in place she asked, "You want me for anything else?"

"No—and thank you, Lucy." She waited till Lucy left the room and then when the door slammed louder than necessary, said loudly, "You're welcome!" She turned to the mirror, troubled by the encounter. She'd always had a special affection for Simon and Lucy. But although Simon was the same, Lucy had changed.

Forcing the issue from her mind, she looked at the peach dress, trimmed with emerald lace. Her father had given her the money, saying, "If you're going to a ball, you need a new dress." She'd enjoyed going with Amelia to look for it and now saw it fit extremely well. There was not a wrinkle from bosom to waist, and the skirt flared out perfectly over the hoops. Sitting down, she dressed her hair, then added a touch of rice powder and a little carmine on her lips. Taking a deep breath she stood, picked up the small reticule and the cape that really wasn't needed in such warm weather, and went downstairs.

She heard voices as she descended the staircase. Turning on the landing, she saw Brian Decatur, dressed in his blue uniform with shining brass buttons and polished black boots. His eyes lit up as he saw Leah. "So this is the new dress I've heard so much about," he said. "You look wonderful."

Leah stepped off the last stair and took in the uniform. "Not as wonderful as you look! If you drop dead," she remarked blandly, "we won't have to do anything to you—except stick a lily in your hand."

"Leah!" Claire exclaimed, as she stood beside Brian, "you say the awfullest things!"

Decatur laughed, however, saying, "I hope she's not that impudent at the ball. There's going to be some important people there, maybe even the governor."

Just as Claire started to speak, the outer door opened and Matthew stepped in. He was wearing a light-gray suit, a white shirt, and a string tie. He stopped abruptly and looked at the three. "Well, are you coming or going?"

"We're going to the ball, sir," Brian answered. He hesitated for a moment, then said, "If you and Mrs. Cleburne would like to go, I'm sure you'd be welcome."

Embarrassed silence fell over the three, and Claire said quickly, "No thank you, Brian. I'm not feeling well tonight. You two go on. Have a good time."

Matthew waited until the door was closed and said to Claire, "It might be good for you to get out. Won't you change your mind?"

Surprised, Claire looked at him strangely. "That would be rather odd, wouldn't it?"

"A husband and a wife going to a ball? What's odd about that?"

Aware of the irony of his tone, she responded, "I don't think of us as husband and wife anymore. I haven't in a long time."

Matthew clasped his hands behind his back and rocked on the balls of his feet. "Have I missed something?" he asked quietly. "Did you get a divorce and forget to mention it to me?"

Claire flushed. "You know I haven't. I never will." Then she said almost angrily, "You can have your other women, but you'll never get a divorce from me."

Matthew Cleburne's face showed no anger—and that troubled Claire. He continued softly, "I've never asked for a divorce." As she made a move to leave the room, he said, "Claire, wait a minute." When she turned to him, he asked quietly, his voice somewhat strained, "What about young Decatur?"

"Why, what about him?"

"You know what I mean. Is Leah serious about him?"

"I don't think so."

"Well, what does she say? Does she talk to you?"

"Of course she talks to me."

"Well then—?"

"I'm not sure he'd be a suitable husband."

Matthew's eyes half closed and his lips grew tight. "Doesn't meet your standards, is that it? I'm sure they're still very high."

They were on the verge of a quarrel, and Claire forced herself to say calmly, "Let's not argue about it, Matthew. I'm not sure about Brian and neither is Leah. As for my *standards,* I just want her to have a good husband."

"What you want is for her to marry your father."

Claire's face grew pale. "What do you mean by that?" she

whispered, anger rising in her. "How dare you mention my father!"

Matthew smiled bitterly and stepped closer to her, saying sharply, "That's who *you* wanted to marry—your father—or someone just like him."

"That's not fair!"

"Fair? You're an odd one to talk about fair." He reached out and grabbed her arms so quickly that she had no time to avoid him. Her eyes grew wide and she opened her mouth to protest but his words beat at her almost like blows. "You were so filled up with your father and what a glorious saint he was that no man could have pleased you. I'm not saying I was perfect. I told you then, years ago, that I was wrong. But you drove me to some of it."

"That isn't true."

"It isn't true?" His eyebrows lifted in mock surprise and his powerful hands closed more tightly on her arms. "You weren't the one who locked me out of your bedroom?"

"Only after you were seeing that woman!"

"And until then you'd been a warm, loving wife? Is that it?"

His words struck her heart, for she knew he spoke the truth. "Let me go, Matthew," she said.

But still he held her, looking down. What he saw still was the beauty that had captivated him as a young man: the lovely face and large gray eyes that had always been her best feature. Even now, at forty, her auburn hair had no gray in it, and her figure was that of a much younger woman. After a minute of silence, he loosed his grip and stepped back. "You never forget . . . and you never forgive, do you Claire? How nice it is that you've never made a mistake or done anything wrong!" He wheeled and walked stiffly down the hall without saying another word.

Claire listened as the door to his room at the end of the hall closed. Then she realized her hands were trembling. She hadn't had a scene like this for years, and now she wanted to cry out, to protest that it wasn't all her fault, that *he* was the one who had been wrong. She thought back to the time when she'd left him—how although she'd never admitted it she was filled with loneliness and despair. "I did love you, Matthew!" she whispered, staring down the hall. A longing she thought was dead and buried years ago rose in her. Now, however, as she moved blindly to the stairs, groping at the mahogany banister, she thought suddenly of the first years of their marriage, how ecstatic and happy she'd been in his arms and how much she'd loved him. As she entered her room, she stood there almost frantically possessed by a desire to run away, to leave the house because she still remembered his arms around her, his lips on hers, and the sweet way he'd treated her. Slowly she sat down on the bed, staring numbly at the rose wallpaper. Then she said so softly that her voice barely stirred the air, "I did love you once. . . !"

★ ★ ★

"I've never seen such a glutton before!"

"Glutton? I'm not a glutton." Brian Decatur sat beside Leah in the carriage and with a purpose in mind, put his arm around her shoulders. "I don't know why you'd call me that."

The two had left the ball after midnight, then Brian had insisted on taking her to a restaurant that apparently stayed open to all hours. They'd eaten fried johnnycakes and drunk strong coffee for over an hour. He'd kept her entertained with his stories of army life. Leah had never laughed so much and had enjoyed herself thoroughly. He was a clever, witty man, and now as they rode along she said, "I've had a fine time, Brian."

"Have you?" His arm closed around her shoulder and he suddenly drew her close.

"Brian! You mustn't!" she protested. But in the seclusion and darkness of the carriage, she turned to him and met his kiss halfway. His arms were strong and his hands on her back pulled her against him. His lips were firm and demanding and almost to her shock she found herself responding. She'd been curious about her feelings about Brian and thought, *This is one way to find out!*

Finally she pulled away, putting her hand on his chest. "There now!" she said. "You're as greedy for kisses as you are for johnnycakes."

But her light teasing tone didn't seem to touch Decatur. He did remove her arm but reached out and took her hand. He held it firmly, and the only sound that broke the night silence was the steady, clopping beat of the horses' hooves on the paved streets. Outside, a full moon shed its warm beams over the buildings that loomed on either side, and there was an almost holy peace about the setting.

Brian said abruptly, "I'll be leaving soon, Leah."

"I wish you didn't have to go."

His hand tightened and he turned to face her, the moonlight illuminating his sharp features. His large eyes were fixed on her carefully. "I wanted to go. I was ready to go down and whip Johnny Reb—but then you came along."

"You can't blame it on me," Leah teased, then, at the look on his face, said quickly, "I'm sorry, I didn't mean to be light. I wish you didn't have to go, really I do, Brian."

Brian seemed to struggle, then said, "Your parents, they never go anywhere together."

"No, they're separated. I thought you knew that."

"I've heard rumors, but I didn't know for sure." He hesitated, then said, "I'm asking for a reason. It's not just out of curiosity."

"A reason? What do you mean?"

"I'm going to ask one of them for permission to marry you."

At first Leah was almost amused, thinking it was another one of his light remarks. But at once she saw he was serious. "Why, you can't mean that! We haven't known each other but a few days."

"I can't help that. I wish we had a year to get to know each other, but we don't. Things happen fast in wartime."

139

Leah was troubled. "You shouldn't even think of such a thing, Brian. You can't love me. You can't fall in love with someone in a few short weeks."

"Why do you say that? You ever hear of Garibaldi, the Italian patriot? He was riding along a street, looked up, and saw a young girl in a window. He stopped his horse," Brian said and grinned slightly, "took off his hat, and said, 'I love you, I want to spend my life with you.'"

Leah waited a minute, then said, "Well, what happened?"

"Oh, he married her and they lived together for fifty years. Just one look was all it took."

"I'm not very romantic, Brian."

"That's all right," he said. He lifted her hand, kissed it, then lowered it. "I'm romantic enough for both of us." He hesitated slightly, then continued, "I love you and I want the truth. Do you feel anything for me?"

"Oh, Brian, I can't—"

"You'll love me before I'm through," he said. "I'm a very stubborn fellow." He put his arms around her again and pulled her close, whispering, "You'll get used to me. One day you'll look up and be surprised and you'll think, *Why, I've been married to this fellow for forty years and what a good husband he's been.*" Then he kissed her again, and Leah felt his urgency. She was stirred—if not by his ardor—then by some desire for order in her life.

But even as Leah was moved by his caress, a sense of shame touched her. The thought of David Rocklin coursed through her like fire: *I let him kiss me like this and I thought it meant something. . . .* She drew back, murmured a quick farewell to Brian, then hurried into the house. Once inside, she shut the door, then leaned against it, her eyes closed as troubled thoughts came almost against her will. *I thought I was in love with David, but only a few weeks later, I'm letting another man kiss me.* Disgusted with herself, she thought angrily, *I've got to forget David—it's all over.* But as she ascended the stairs, the memory of David Rocklin came even

140

more strongly and so powerfully that she was vexed with herself. *He's out of my life—that's all there is to it. . . .*

★ ★ ★

The Atlanta *Constitution* had placed a massive headline across its cover: "FORT SUMTER BOMBARDED." David Rocklin read the story as he rode along in the carriage. It recounted how eleven Federal guns on Morris Island, aided by naval armament, had fired 938 shots in the first bombardment on August 17. This was now the nineteenth, and the heavy bombardment continued.

Back to Fort Sumter, where it all started, David thought, shaking his head silently. He opened the paper and read that Rosecrans' advancing Army of the Cumberland was approaching Chattanooga in a major offensive. The editor had written almost in a frantic tone: "The Yankees must be stopped! They must not take Chattanooga or we will lose all our territory in that area!"

David folded the paper, put it down on the seat, and leaned back and closed his eyes. The war somehow seemed far away. For several days now he'd battled his own war. Four times he'd slipped off into the nightmare land where his mind ran to hide—four times that he and Corey or others had known he was out of this world. But there had been other times—times only he himself was aware of. Short times, sometimes only an hour, usually when he was preparing for bed, dreading closing his eyes in sleep. The nightmares of bayonets had returned so that every night he seemed to see a forest of bright glittering blades marching across fields all aimed for his heart. He'd either wake up fighting the bedcovers and moaning or would sink into the black oblivion, which was even worse.

The carriage stopped and the driver said, "Here we are, sir."

David got out and looked at the ancient gray building, half covered with ivy. The mortar between the dark red bricks was crumbling in places. He asked doubtfully, "This is the place?"

"Yes, sir. This is the asylum." The cabdriver, a small man with black, sharp eyes like a mouse and a thin line of mustache, asked offhandedly, "You got people in here?"

David didn't answer the question, but said, "Wait for me. I don't know how long I'll be, but I'll pay for your time." The cabdriver gave David an odd look, then shrugged and pulled his hat firmly down on his head as David walked away.

David approached the building, which was surrounded by a high wall made of wrought iron. The uprights had spearlike tips on them that looked as if they could pierce any man who fell on them. A few men were out in the yard down the way, cutting the grass without enthusiasm. The building itself loomed four stories high, a massive affair sitting by itself beside a country road.

It was simply called "The Asylum." David had come here to see Dr. Carl Steiner. After a long conference, Dr. Summers, the Dixons' family physician, had admitted frankly that David's trouble was not physical and said, "There's not much we doctors can do about cases like yours." He'd hesitated, then continued, "There is a man, Dr. Carl Steiner, out at the asylum. I don't know much about him, but I've heard he's been able to help some people with your . . . trouble."

At first David had revolted against the idea of going to a mental institution but in desperation had finally left the house and made his way to this place. As he approached, he climbed the three steps and knocked on the massive door, then waited. After a time the door opened and a man wearing a loose-fitting shirt, brown trousers, and flat-heeled shoes said, "Yes, sir?"

"I wonder if I could see Dr. Steiner?"

"Come in and I'll see if the doctor can see you now."

David followed the man down a broad hall and looked around carefully. There were no ornaments on the wall, no pictures whatsoever. It had been papered once with some sort of blue paper with small designs, but they had faded now and the paper hung in place limply, ready to give up its grasp on the wall. Beneath the peeling paper he saw nothing but ancient gray plaster.

There was a rank smell about the place, an odor partly of age and partly of decay and hopelessness.

"You wait right in here, sir."

"Thank you."

David entered the room that the man indicated and saw a rolltop desk fronted by a chair, several bookcases with large thick books, and a framed diploma. Moving to read it, he saw that it was a certificate that Dr. Carl Steiner had been awarded—his medical degree from a German university in Berlin.

Sitting down in one of the hard straight-backed chairs, David waited, his fists clenched so tightly together that they ached. Deliberately he forced himself to relax and prepared for a long wait. He was surprised when the door opened almost at once and a tall portly man, wearing a white jacket that came to his knees, entered the room. David stood and the man said, "I'm Dr. Steiner," in a heavily accented voice.

"My name is David Rocklin."

"Ah—Mr. Rocklin. Will you have a seat?" Steiner waited until David sat back down, then took his seat in the leather padded chair before the desk. He turned and put his full attention on David. His eyes were very light blue, almost as pale as the tiny wildflowers David had seen growing beside the road back in Virginia. The doctor's Germanic face had tightly drawn lips and a high dome forehead capped by a heavy mop of coarse salt-and-pepper hair. A scar traced its way down his right cheek, starting at the corner of his eye and angling back toward his earlobe. It must have been a terrible cut, for although it was old it drew his eye permanently half-closed.

"And how may I help you, Mr. Rocklin?"

David took a deep breath and began speaking. "I've been having some problems—mental problems. I go off into some sort of blackness and can't seem to come out of it. . . ."

Steiner listened without saying a word until David had finished. Then he leaned back and studied the tall young man. "How long has this been going on?" He listened as David answered, then shot questions at him for ten minutes. Finally he sat without a word, staring at the man before him.

"What is it?" David asked almost frantically. "I've never had any trouble like this."

"Tell me again about the dream, about the bayonets."

David was startled. "You think that has something to do with it?"

"The blackouts didn't come until after that. Is that not so?" Steiner inquired.

"Why, yes, that's true."

"Tell me again about the dreams—everything you can remember."

The conference went on for over an hour. At the end of that time, David felt as if he'd been put through an ordeal, which he had. His face shone with perspiration, and finally he said in an unsteady voice, "I don't want to talk about those dreams anymore."

"No, I can see that—and that is why you go off into this place you speak of . . . why you leave this world and go to another."

David started at the doctor's choice of words. "What's the matter with me?" he said hoarsely.

"There's something in your life that you cannot face up to," Steiner said slowly. "Most of us have things like that. Sometimes we hide them in some place and nobody ever knows about it." He shrugged his burly shoulders and tapped his fingertips together in an almost effeminate gesture, strangely incongruous to the massive strength of the hands. "What is it that you are hiding?"

"I'm not hiding anything," David said stiffly. "I've told you everything."

A silence fell across the room. The walls were well insulated and there was no outside sound at all. *It was like,* David thought, *being entombed.* He insisted, over and over again, that he was hiding nothing, but Steiner kept prying. Finally David grew angry. "This is not helping! Don't you have medicine or something that will stop me from whatever this thing is?"

"No."

David blinked at the harshness of the word. He stared at the physician, who stared back at him with a steadiness that was disconcerting. "I cannot help you until you're ready to help yourself."

"I'll do anything," David insisted, his hands trembling. "I can't go on living like this."

Steiner dropped his eyes and turned to his desk. Reaching up, he pulled a book down—a rather new book, David noticed. He leafed through it, found what he was looking for, then read aloud, "'If the patient refuses to discuss his problems freely, he is hiding something. As long as he hides these things he will not get better. He can only get worse. If he persists, the chances are great that he will fall into a condition of total insanity.'"

The words chilled David Rocklin. He swallowed hard and couldn't answer. He heard Steiner say, "Come along; I'll show you something."

David rose, glad to get out of the room, and followed Steiner through the door. They went down a long hall and up the stairs, their footsteps echoing hollowly. When they left the landing, there was another long hall with three doors on each side. Steiner took a key out from a chain that was attached to his belt, inserted it, and it clicked solidly. "Do not be afraid," he said quietly, "but you must see this."

Pulling the huge door back, Steiner stepped inside and motioned for David to enter. At least twenty men occupied a room that must have been at least twenty feet wide and thirty feet long. They were all wearing light gray uniforms, bulky and shapeless. Two or three of them were walking rapidly back and forth from one end of the room to the other as if their lives depended on it. One of them was talking to himself or arguing with someone who wasn't there. "I tell you," he said frantically, "it wasn't my fault. You've got to forgive me, Carol. . . ."

His voice droned on and a horror came over David as he saw that the man was speaking to someone not there. "Come this way, over here," Steiner said. He led David through the men, whose faces all seemed pasty and dead. One of them was sitting in the middle of the floor staring down at his hands, not moving, almost like a small statue of Buddha that David had once seen. He was very fat and didn't move or speak as they passed him. It was as if he were carved out of white stone.

"Here is the man I wanted you to see."

David looked at a man who was sitting on a chair. He was of medium height, and his face was pale and heavy. His eyes were brown, and as David stared into them he felt a shock: there was nothing behind the eyes—no mind, no thought, nothing!

"This is Henry Patton. He came to me three years ago," Steiner said quietly. "He had a successful business and a good family, was well thought of in society."

David stared at the man, who obviously heard none of what Steiner said. There was something eerie and frightening about a body with no mind. David's voice was unsteady as he asked, "What happened to him?"

"He started having mental problems," Steiner said softly. "I was called in before he fell into this condition." He looked over at the man and put a hand on his shoulder. "I tried my best, Henry," he said sadly, "but you wouldn't share your problem." He removed his hand and said, "This is what happens to those who hide from the truth. Come along now, it isn't good for you to see too much of this."

He led the way out of the room, then back down the stairs. "Can you come and see me on a regular basis?"

David stared at him. "I've told you all I know."

"That's what Henry Patton said, over and over again." Steiner shook his head. "It's so tragic that there was one thing in that man's heart and mind—if he'd said it he would have been free, but he couldn't bear to have anyone know what it was. Now you see what he's become." Steiner's face grew more stern. "I don't want to frighten you, but perhaps I should. These blackouts you've been having, they're very bad. One day you may go out and never come back."

The words echoed in David's mind. He muttered, "I'll come back," and put his hand out. Steiner shook it, and David left.

Steiner watched the door as it closed, then turned back and stared up at his medical degree. "What good does it do for me to see people if they won't let me help them? Nothing in that young man is so bad that it cannot be fixed—but he won't say." He'd seen many like this and a hopeless despair came to his light blue eyes. He shook his head then began reading the book before him.

David left the asylum and got into the carriage. "Take me back to town."

"Yes, sir." As the cabdriver looked at David's face, he thought to himself, *That's a bad 'un. If he's got folks in there, he didn't get no good news from them.* Aloud he said, "Git up, Babe! Come on, Nancy!" and the matched bays leaped forward. As the carriage wheeled back to the city, a plume of dust rose high in the air then settled back onto the road.

CHAPTER TWELVE
It's Never Too Late

Claire had been more disturbed than she liked to admit since the scene with Matthew. For two days she'd thought about little else and had slept fitfully, rising at dawn, her eyes puffy from lack of sleep.

"Don't you feel well, Claire?" Amelia asked as Claire came into the kitchen where Amelia was forming biscuits out of dough that she'd mixed.

"Oh, I'm all right—just didn't sleep well." She moved over to take a pan down, saying, "Suppose we make pancakes this morning?"

"All right. You always did make the best pancakes I ever saw."

Claire looked at her aunt with a faint smile. "It's the only thing I can make better than you can, and Lucy makes them better than any of us. But since she's off today, we'll have to be the cooks."

The two women worked on the meal. When they were almost finished, Matthew stepped into the kitchen. He glanced quickly at Claire and said, "Good morning," then moved over and looked down at the pancakes. "Special treat for me?" he asked pleasantly.

Amelia looked up and smiled. "You think everything's for you. I remember you used to promise me anything to get me to make you a blackberry cobbler. Do you still like them?"

"I haven't had any in a long time, not good ones like

yours," Matthew said, seeming preoccupied. "I'm going to town after breakfast. Can I bring you anything back?"

"Yes," Amelia said. "I've heard about a book called *Leaves of Grass*. I got a letter from my friend Doris Heilman, and she says there's nothing like it."

"What kind of a book is it?" Matthew inquired.

"Oh, it's a book of poetry." She smiled and said, "I'll let you read it, if it's good. It's written by a man called Walter Whitman, a New York man. Have you heard of him?"

"No, but then I don't read much poetry, not anymore."

Unexpectedly Claire said, "You used to read a lot of Longfellow and Whittier."

Unsmiling, Matthew answered, "Yes, I did," then left the room. Claire watched him go with a strange expression. Amelia noticed, but she said nothing.

Later they ate breakfast together, and afterward Amelia said, "I'll do the dishes since you made the pancakes." She began to gather the plates, and Matthew said, "It was a fine breakfast. Almost as good as Lucy's, but don't tell her I said so." He nodded as he rose and went to his study.

Claire ignored Amelia's protest and helped clear the table and, as they were doing the dishes, Amelia said, "It's amazing how Matthew keeps his good looks. He doesn't look any older than he did ten years ago. Some people are like that, I suppose."

"Yes," Claire murmured, "he's still fine looking. He always was."

Amelia glanced at her sharply and saw that Claire's face was tense. She wanted to inquire into Claire's problems but, knowing her niece well after staying with her for years, didn't feel it would be wise. "I think I'll go out and tend to the flowers. They need water," she said instead.

"All right, Amelia. Maybe I'll join you later."

It was an overcast August day with rain threatening from time to time but not quite coming. A strong wind unexpectedly kicked up, and finally raindrops, fat and thick, began to fall. Amelia hurried into the house grumbling, "Here as soon as I start watering those blasted flowers the rain comes. I think it brings it on sometimes."

Claire smiled at her but didn't answer. She was sitting on the screened-in porch reading a book, or at least holding it open. When Amelia left, she put it down on the table beside her and closed her eyes. For a long time she sat there and then got up and began to move through the house. There was little to be done, for Lucy kept the house spotless, but she was restless and created work for herself.

At noon someone knocked at the door and Claire answered it. The young delivery man who was standing there asked, "Are you Mrs. Cleburne?"

"Yes, I am."

"A letter for you. Mr. Cleburne sent it. Said it come to his office."

"Here . . ." Claire searched her pocket for a coin and passed it to the young man. "Thank you." She closed the door and stepped inside, then recognized the handwriting.

Amelia, who'd also come to answer the door, stopped as she saw Claire opening the letter. When Claire's brow furrowed, she said, "What is it?"

"It's Mother!" She looked up, trouble in her eyes. "She's very sick."

"What's wrong with her?"

"It's her heart, I think. Her old trouble." Claire stared back at the letter, which was no more than five lines long. "I think I'll have to go take care of her. There's nobody else."

"I'll go with you," Amelia said at once.

"I'm sure Matthew would be glad to keep you here."

"No, it would be awkward without you. What about Leah? Do you think she'll want to go?"

Claire's mouth tightened. "Yes, she must go. She can't stay here."

Leah received the news when Claire came to her room. She'd slept late and her hair hung about her shoulders as she listened. "Do you think it's very serious, Mother?"

151

"I'm sure it is. She's not one to complain. She says she needs help and I'm afraid it's rather critical."

"I'll go with you, of course," Leah said at once. She'd never liked it around Chattanooga at her grandmother's house, but she had a strong sense of loyalty and knew she couldn't desert her mother. "When do you think we'll be leaving?"

"I'll ask Matthew to make the arrangements," Claire said.

★ ★ ★

That night after supper Matthew waited until Amelia and Leah had gone up to their rooms to pack. Then he said, "Claire, I'd like to speak with you."

"Why—of course."

"Come into the parlor. It's quieter in there."

Puzzled, Claire moved to the parlor, and he followed her. She turned to him, expecting he'd have something to say about the arrangements for the trip. Instead he said, "Claire, I want you to consider coming back here when you're sure your mother is all right."

Claire's eyes opened with surprise. "That's very kind of you Matthew, but then you always were thoughtful of our needs."

Matthew shook his head. "I don't mean what you think." He was a tall man and she only of moderate height, so she was forced to look up at him. His blue eyes were utterly serious as he said evenly, "I still love you, Claire."

His words so shocked Claire that she couldn't think what to say for a moment. She opened her lips slightly but the words that came weren't suitable. For a flickering instant, she thought again how handsome he was. Still she said only, "That's all passed, Matthew."

"Not for me. Tell me," he said stepping closer to her, his voice low and intense, "did you ever love me, Claire?"

"You know I did." Her voice was low and she couldn't meet his eyes.

"I thought so. I thought that very few people ever had a

love like we had. I think of those times every day." He fell silent for a moment, then admitted, "I don't think there's been a day I haven't thought of our early years together. They were the best years of my life. Nothing's been right since you left."

"Oh, Matthew, we've been through all this. . . !"

"Have we? I don't think so." He thought of the bitterness and the separation, and his cheeks twitched at the sharpness of the memory. "Are you happy? If you loved me once, is there anything left of it?" He waited, looked down into her face, and saw that his words had disturbed her greatly. She had a natural control that had increased over the years so that she'd become difficult to read. Yet now her lips trembled slightly and her gray eyes masked something she didn't want revealed. "If there's anything at all left in you, any kind of love or affection for me, please tell me, Claire," he pleaded.

Knowing it took great courage for this strong man to beg her, Claire felt something akin to pity. She also thought of those early days and the sleepless nights she'd had since their last encounter. Then the old bitterness came over her. "That's all over, Matthew," she said firmly. "You can't go back to what things once were."

Standing before her, Matthew squared his shoulders and waited. He was silent so long that she wondered if he'd ever speak. Finally he sighed. "I've always hoped that somehow we would get over our difficulties. I thought that no matter how bad they were that somehow we'd find a way through them and come together again. That's been my dream," he said softly, pain and regret in his eyes. "I guess you'll never change."

"Matthew, I wish it didn't have to be like this, but we can't go back again."

He studied her carefully and then said, "I'll make arrangements for your trip."

★ ★ ★

Brian Decatur took the news with a mixture of disappointment and frustration. "Chattanooga? That's no place for

153

you to be going!" he exclaimed when Leah told him of their plans. "Why, the war is moving there! Braxton Bragg's got the Army of the Tennessee lined up, and I'm headed there right now along with Rosecrans' army. It may be the biggest battle of the war. You *can't* go there!"

"We've got to go. My grandmother's very ill."

Decatur had been shocked but then finally said, "Well, at least we'll be in the same part of the world."

"But I'll be on the Confederate side. You won't be able to come courting there," Leah said with a smile.

Brian Decatur, a self-confident young man, took her hand and kissed it. "I told you once, Leah, I'm a very stubborn fellow. Don't be surprised if you don't look up someday and see a young Union lieutenant coming up to the front door of your house."

Leah had laughed and allowed him to kiss her. Later she reported to her mother as they were packing, "The lieutenant is threatening to come calling in Tennessee—along with about forty thousand others of the Army of the Cumberland."

Claire turned, holding a dress she was packing in a trunk. "How do you feel about him? You've never really said."

"Oh, I don't know, Mother. It's not the time to think of such things. He's Union and we're Confederate. I don't see any good ending to that."

Claire stared at her daughter, suddenly swept with doubt. "These are hard times, aren't they, Leah?" The doubt and despair in her voice drew Leah's attention. She looked at her mother for a moment, studying her carefully. She was well aware that living in Matthew Cleburne's house had been a strain to all of them but especially to her mother.

Tentatively she picked up a blouse and folded it mechanically, then handed it to her mother. "Had you ever thought you and Father might . . . ?"

Claire looked up quickly. When she saw the hope in her daughter's eyes, she said at once briskly, "No, I don't think that could ever happen." As the expression in Leah's eyes faded, Claire returned to the packing, thinking, *I can't let her think like that. It would bring nothing but disappointment.*

★ ★ ★

Many days later the three women stepped out of a carriage as Claire paid the fare. "Just bring the bags in if you will," she said to the driver, then turned to look at the house. "It hasn't changed," she said as the three moved down the walk. "I grew up in this place. It has lots of memories."

Amelia said nothing, for she was depressed at the sight of the place. She had stayed here for short visits with Claire and hadn't been happy. It was not the kind of country she liked, although the mountains were beautiful. She wished they were back in New York.

As they entered the house they were greeted by a black woman who threw her arms around Claire. "I so glad you're back, Miss Claire. Yore momma needs you bad."

"How is she, Bessie?"

"She ain't no good," Bessie, a tall angular woman with white hair and chocolate-colored skin, responded. "She ain't no good at all, Miss Claire. She gonna be with the Lord purty soon."

Leah felt compressed, as if she'd been put into a box and was being squeezed. She'd spent summers at this house and they'd been bearable. Now, however, with the shadow of war hanging over Chattanooga, she knew nothing pleasant or good was going to happen. She accompanied her mother and Amelia to the sickroom, where all three were shocked with the frailness of the woman who lay in bed. Death was written on her features, and her voice was feeble. Claire said, "You're going to be all right, Mother," trying to keep her voice cheerful.

Later Leah thought, with a sharp regret, of her father's house in New York: the busyness, the activity of that city. She thought, too, of Brian Decatur and wondered if he was as stubborn as he claimed to be.

155

PART THREE
Chickamauga

CHAPTER THIRTEEN
A Rash Decision

Hearing footsteps on the back porch, Bernard Dixon set his coffee cup down, rose from his chair, and left the library. He passed through the kitchen, where Dinah, the Dixon cook, was cutting a chicken into pieces, then saw Corey enter with a cotton sack in his hand. "Hello, Corey," he said, "where have you been?"

"I been out looking for some herbs, sah."

"Oh! You're an herb master, are you?"

"Well sah, I done study it a little bit. Some folks say I was right good at it."

"I had an aunt who lived in Tennessee. I swear she knew every bush and herb in the world. Some of them did good, too. Let's see what you've got."

Dinah came over to watch as Corey unloaded his bag, laying various leaves and bunches of grass and vines on the kitchen table, explaining them carefully. "This here is saffron—good for measles, and it ain't bad for fever either. This is saxifrage—it cures infected eyes; and this one is neat stone for stomach problems. . . ."

Dixon examined the herbs skeptically, then said, "Come out to the backyard, Corey."

"Yes sah."

Corey followed the trim young man outside, stopping when Dixon turned to face him. "I really am worried about your master, Corey. He's getting worse, isn't he?"

Corey met Dixon's eyes squarely, then shrugged his muscular shoulders. "Yes sah, he is. He has bad dreams every night." Dinah had fixed Corey a pallet on the floor beside David's bed, and now as he thought of the nights that had passed he shook his head dolefully. "I 'spect these herbs ain't gonna help Mr. David. What's wrong with him ain't in the body."

"No, it's all mental. I wish it *were* a physical wound. It would have been better if he'd been shot in the leg or shoulder. Those wounds heal up." Dixon shifted his feet to watch a young mockingbird as it teetered on a clothesline. Just then a black cat with white breast and four stocking feet began slinking across the yard. Suddenly the mother mockingbird swooped down out of a pear tree and rapidly pecked the huge tom on the head. The cat blinked, shut his eyes, then fled the barrage in disgrace.

"That stupid cat will never learn," Dixon observed mildly, then turned his attention back to the slave. "Has he said anything to you about the doctor he went to see at the asylum?"

Corey shifted his weight uneasily, then shook his head. "Well sah, he did say the doctor didn't give him much hope."

"I think he ought to go home."

"That's what I told him, Mr. Dixon," Corey said energetically. He was wearing a pair of cast-off brown trousers somewhat too large for him and a blue cotton shirt open at the neck. He pushed the sleeves up nervously before continuing. "I done told him that, sah. Man in his condition needs to be with his people. From what he done told me, they a mighty fine family."

"They are. The Rocklins are the finest people I know," Dixon responded. "Look, I'll try to talk to him, Corey. I know he's mighty low, but we mustn't give up hope."

"No sah!"

Dixon left the yard and reentered the house. He ascended

the stairs, stopped before the door to David's bedroom, and knocked. "Dave? Are you up?"

"Come in."

Bernard entered to find David sitting in a straight chair, a book on his lap unopened. He was staring out the window and only slowly did he turn his head, as if it were an effort. "Hello, Bernard. Sit down."

Bernard pulled a chair away from the wall and sat down across from Rocklin. As he did so he noticed the wan, drawn expression on his friend's face. David had always been physically strong, Bernard remembered, but now he was losing weight rapidly because he had no appetite. Instead of talking about the problem, Bernard began by discussing the military situation of the two countries. "I've been reading the papers, Dave," he said. "It looks like everything's changed since Vicksburg fell and Lee was beaten at Gettysburg."

He waited a moment for a reply but David merely sat there loosely, his muscles lax, his lips drawn together tightly. Bernard hurried on, saying, "It looks like the action is going to be somewhere in Tennessee now that Grant's won at Vicksburg. Port Hudson's fallen too. The Mississippi River belongs to the Union." He frowned and despair touched his clean-cut features. "They've got the Mississippi now—cut the Confederacy right in two. Now we can expect them to hit some other targets closer to home."

David appeared not to have heard. He was staring intently out the window, and Bernard moved slightly to follow Rocklin's gaze. Across the street a young woman in a yellow dress with a white broad-brimmed hat was moving around a flower garden. Although the flowers were faded, she was trying to coax some last bit of color from the small plot of ground. Her yellow dress made a bright splash against the light-brown grass, which had died early from lack of rain, and as she looked up Bernard said, "That's Helen Raines. She was engaged to marry Tony Hardin, but Tony got killed at Antietam." He waited for a reply, but receiving none went on. "Well, I look for the Federals to hit in Tennessee—at

161

least that's what Father says. He says that Chattanooga's on the main east-west railroad line and that if the Yankees can cut that it'll leave our men there without supplies. Then too, Lincoln's always wanted to do something about Knoxville. Lots of Union folks there."

A fly moved about the room humming briskly, then lighted on Bernard's forehead. He slapped at it. "Blasted flies! I don't know why we can't keep them out of the house." He looked then at David and saw that he was getting nowhere. Leaning forward, he put his hand on David's shoulder and shook him, drawing the young man's attention. "Dave!" he said in a different tone, now totally serious. "Let's talk about this . . . problem you have."

David shook his head, and there was a dead quality in his voice as he said, "Nothing to talk about, Bernard. . . . It's not the kind of thing the doctors can do anything about."

"It may pass away like it came," Bernard insisted, his great affection for David Rocklin evident. "Look, I'm not trying to get rid of you, Dave. You know that. We'd be glad to have you stay here as long as you like." He hesitated, running a hand through his sandy hair. "But I think you ought to go home. When a fellow has trouble he needs to be with his people, and I know your family would help you."

"I can't let them see me like this." David's statement was tinged with an underlying current of despair.

"Why, they won't think less of you, Dave."

"No. I just can't do it, Bernard." David got up and moved about the room nervously, looking down at the circles containing pale pink flowers in the carpet under his feet. He lifted his eyes then and stared blankly at the pictures of dogs and cats on the wall. Then he said flatly, "If I'm in your way, I'll leave. But I can't go home, not till I get this thing whipped."

Instantly Bernard rose and clapped his arm around David's shoulders. "There's no question of that," he protested. "Stay as long as you like. I'm believing this thing will go away. You're not going back to see that doctor any-more?"

"No, there's nothing he can do."

"I tell you what. We'll go out on the town tonight. There's a new play that might be amusing."

"All right, if you like."

Bernard hesitated, then said, "We'll leave about five, go out and have a good supper. It'll take your mind off . . . your troubles."

As Dixon left David's room and descended the stairs. Corey came out of the kitchen, asking at once, "Did you talk to him, Mr. Dixon?"

"He won't go home, at least not now." Dixon's brow wrinkled. "I wish he would. It would be the best thing for him. But he's a stubborn fellow."

★ ★ ★

It was already mid-August. The trees had lost their spring greenness and were beginning to be tinged with the heat that late summer brings. The grass died slowly each day, as fall loomed somewhere beyond the horizon. Fall was a time David Rocklin usually loved—the crispness of it, the smell of the earth, the sharp bite of the wind—but now the reminder of its coming depressed him. On Sunday morning he went to church dutifully with the Dixon family. He sat in the pew and listened as the minister announced the subject: "As it is appointed unto man once to die, but after this the judgment."

It was a fine sermon, well organized, filled with Scriptures that underlined the main points, and preached with vivid illustrations. But as David sat on the hard pew, bolt upright, he heard echoes of his own mortality. Perhaps it was con-nected somehow to the approach of winter. Always he was conscious of the terrible dreams and blackouts that came to torment him.

Even as he sat there he felt himself receding and prayed, *Oh, God, don't let me pass out, not here!* He threw his will against the coming of the blackness. It was almost as if he were being sucked down into an ebony pool, and he struggled against it, not moving a muscle but with a terrible spiritual clash of his will against whatever it was that drew him into nothingness.

When the benediction was finally announced, he rose and kept his hands half concealed so Dixon wouldn't see they were trembling. He wiped his face quickly with a clean white handkerchief and shook hands with the minister, murmuring "Thank you very much" mindlessly. He sat in the carriage on the way home, listening to the family discuss the sermon. Although there were several attempts to draw him into the conversation, he said almost nothing. His presence, he knew, was a burden on the others and he thought, *I've got to get away! I can't impose any longer on these people. . . .*

The following Tuesday he was still wrestling with the problem of what to do and had begun a difficult letter home. Masking his true condition, he kept up the pretense that he was suffering with a physical affliction and would come home as soon as he could. But, filled with disgust at his own prevarication, he left the letter unfinished and went down to the main streets of Atlanta, unable to bear his own solitude. After some time he entered a small cafe where the proprietor, a short muscular man with a drooping gray mustache, took his order. He wasn't hungry, but ordered coffee and pie for the privilege of sitting at the table. It was a small restaurant, and he sipped the coffee slowly, ignoring the other customers. His mind beat inside his brain like a captive bird trapped in a box, moving from one impossibility to another. Still there was no peace nor even a glimmer of solution for him.

Slowly he became aware of a loud voice coming from his right. Turning his head slightly, he saw a tall, rawboned sergeant with a shock of black hair and a ferocious beard that bristled wildly. He was not old, not over thirty, but there was a rough-hewn quality about him that suggested a hard life. The coffee cup in his hand was dwarfed by the size of his huge paws—hands of a man who had done hard labor. David listened as one of the men beside him asked, "What was it like there at Gettysburg, Rafe?"

"Why, it was purely out of the pit."

David had heard from his grandmother that his Uncle Gideon had been captured at Gettysburg and was in a Confederate prison in Richmond. David had been tremendously relieved to discover that Clay and Dent had not been killed or even wounded, despite the terrible battle.

Rafe's loud, raspy voice continued. Here was a man who clearly enjoyed an audience. He sipped the coffee with a noisy slurping sound, then sighed in appreciation. "Aaaah! Now, I ain't had no good coffee like that for nigh on to two years 'cept that which I liberated." He winked, and a laugh ran around the civilians who listened to the soldier. "What was it like? Why, it was pure perdition. That's what it was like."

"What outfit was you with, Rafe?"

"I was in with Pickett."

One of his listeners, a smallish man wearing a neat black suit with a string tie to match, picked up on that. "I heard about that charge. I don't see how men stood up to it. Was it as bad as I heard?"

"I dunno what you heard, but it was the wust I seed—and I been in since Bull Run." Rafe slurped his coffee again, picked up a pork chop with his hand, and tore off a bite with strong white teeth. He seemed not to chew at all but swallowed it almost in its native condition. He held the bone, stared at it contemplatively, then clawed at his whiskers with his free hand. "I dunno as I'd ever want to do a thing like that again."

"Tell us about it, Sergeant," one of the onlookers, a young man not over seventeen, said. His eyes were bright and he leaned forward toward the rawboned sergeant. "That must have been something. All that advance by Pickett."

Rafe stared at the young man thoughtfully. "I reckon people got funny ideas about what war's like," he said almost roughly. "I did myself. I always thought it'd be like in a picture—some big plain somewhere and two armies marching toward each other out in the clear where you can see everything." He shook his head almost in disgust. "'Taint like that, though. Most of the times you're in the woods . . . can't see no further than ten feet away. Then after the first volley, the smoke's so thick you can't see *five* feet away. Sometimes you shoot your own fellers or they shoot you. You don't never see no battles. All you see's the ten feet away."

"But it wasn't like that at Gettysburg, was it?" the small, neatly dressed man persisted.

"No, it warn't. That was different." Rafe leaned back in his chair fingering the coffee cup, and a peculiar expression stiffened his face. His voice grew somewhat harsher as he growled, "We all lined up. There was this big field and a hill right in front of us. Right up on top of that hill was the Yankees. They must have had a thousand artillery pieces up there, probably ten thousand men, all with a loaded musket. They was behind a fence, lots of 'em were, and there we was, ready to march right into that."

"Why'd you do it? It sounds like suicide to me." A burly man with pale gray eyes and thick reddish-brown hair spoke. "Don't sound like good tactics to me."

"Looking back, I don't see that it was, mister, but Gen. Lee, he said 'Go.' I heered that Longstreet didn't want to go at all and was late gettin' up—but there we was and Gen. Pickett, he rode up and down on that fine hoss of his tellin' us that we was all Virginians. 'Course, I wasn't no Virginian but I took it all in anyhow." He hesitated, sipped his coffee once again noisily, then shook his head. "We all stepped out, started out across that field all in order, line after line. The flags was whippin', and you could hear the officers barkin' like hounds, gettin' their men to form their lines right. The grass was green that day, I remember that. Pretty farming country it was. There was a bunch of the prettiest cows I ever saw when we started across that field. They all run off scared when they saw us coming."

"How far was it from where you had to go up to the top of that hill?"

"I guess most half a mile mebbe and there was a big ditch right across in front of us. We had to break our lines, crawl across that ditch, and reform."

"Was the Yankees shootin' at ya?"

"Not hardly; they was just waitin'," Rafe said grimly, "and we knew it, too. They was just waitin' for one volley. I was right in the front of our line and I knowed whut was comin'. I heard the fellow next to me, a corporal named Patterson, say, 'Lord, for what we're about to receive, may we be duly grateful . . . !'" Rafe's eyes grew small and he continued, "He went down the first volley—throat shot plumb away. Good man . . . was from Alabama."

Rafe continued telling how the lines had advanced, and David found himself caught up in the story. He turned his chair around without pretense, listening as the soldier continued. He'd heard some stories of battles from his father and brothers, but somehow this particular incident caught his attention.

"And that's the way it was when we was no farther than fifty feet away. They opened up with the guns—they just tore huge holes in our lines—and the muskets, they all went off. As soon as they fired once, them men stepped back to reload and another line stepped in place. It wasn't no way to escape. I dunno yet how they missed me," Rafe said almost hoarsely. "On both sides of me my buddies went down—good friends. I got to where I didn't even care if I got kilt. I was so mad at the Yankees! I was screaming and hollering." He laughed almost gutturally. "I remember I was hollering, 'Come on and kill me! See if you can!' I expected it, too."

A silence fell across his listeners, and the neatly dressed man said solemnly, "I don't see how men can go in to face certain death like that. They had no chance at all."

"Me nuther," the sergeant remarked, shrugging. "I don't

167

know whut makes a man do a thing like that. I couldn't do it right now by myself. But when you're in a line like that, there's fellers on both sides of you and fellers behind you. You just can't stop even though you know you're gonna get kilt. Somehow you got to go on." He looked down at his empty cup, then ran his gaze around the small circle of men and said with a note of finality, "After all, when you're dead, all your troubles are over with. I reckon that's part of why men are able to go right up into the lion's mouth like we done at Gettysburg."

For David, the sergeant's words seemed to be framed in large black letters: *When you're dead, all your troubles are over. . . .* Over and over the words repeated themselves, like an echo coming back from a long distance that faded finally into a whisper and insistently tapped at his brain.

David never knew how long he sat there. Finally he got up, paid his bill, and walked out of the restaurant. Evening was coming on, the light in the east fading and turning to a murkiness as the sun began to sink. He walked slowly along the streets, unaware of his surroundings. Wagons bumped down the cobblestone pavement, the horses chuffing and hooves clattering against the stones. There was a murmur of talk from a group he passed, but this was all outside him. Inside he felt a strange, fatalistic peace. He reached the residential areas, then slowed his steps under the large oak trees that met overhead, forming a canopy. There was almost a cathedral atmosphere at this time of twilight, and he walked on until the light faded completely. Finally he found himself far from the Dixon house, almost at the outskirts of the city. He had no desire to return, but as the darkness closed around him he turned and made his way back.

The sable darkness brought out night birds, swifts tumbling in the sky, and then finally the shudder of black wings as bats feasted on mosquitoes and bugs.

Silence enveloped David Rocklin as he shut out the scenes that broke through his senses. He heard again the sergeant's words, this time in a gentle whisper: *When you're dead, all your troubles are over.* . . . For hours he walked. Finally, when he knew the Dixons would be in bed, he returned and went up to his room. Being as quiet as possible, he undressed and lay down on the bed. He put his head on the pillow and stared up in the stygian darkness of the room, darkness broken only by faint moonlight that filtered through his window.

With startling clarity a thought came to him with such force that he sat up on the bed and clenched his fists together as his mind reacted strongly.

"Of course!" he said softly, breaking the quietness of the room. The thought grew in his mind until it became almost palpable. A grim smile touched his lips. "I don't know why I didn't think of it before."

He felt strangely relieved after the pressures that had literally crushed him. He rose, moved to the window, and stared down on the earth across the yards and at the streets vaguely outlined by the pale moonlight. It was so simple! *All I have to do is join the army, get in a fighting outfit, and when they charge, put myself at the front of it. Maybe I'll be a color-bearer. They always go for those fellows first. If they shoot me in the leg, I'll hobble on, standing up until they finish the job.*

For a long time David Rocklin stood there, his eyes fixed on nothing, as he thought about the solution to his problem. *I've been a coward,* he thought, *afraid of bayonets. I've run away in battle, but nothing's worse than what's happening to me. I'd rather be dead anytime!*

Finally he went back and lay down on the bed, knowing what he must do. It didn't seem cowardly to him, because he would fight as best he could. Many of his friends and neighbors from home had died on the field of battle.

I can die as well as they can, he thought, *and when they kill me—why, my troubles will be over!*

CHAPTER FOURTEEN
The Army of the Tennessee

Perhaps if David's dire symptoms had left after he'd made his decision to seek death at the cannon's mouth, he might have changed his mind. However, the next day after he'd firmly decided to end his life honorably by throwing himself into the fury of battle, he suffered one of his blackouts. Fortunately, Corey was there to watch over him, and it lasted less than half a day so that the Dixons weren't even aware of it.

The result of this, however, was that David's resolve was hardened. He spent the next day writing letters to his grandmother, to his father and brothers, and to other family members and friends. His letter to his grandmother was the one that gave him the most difficulty. He made several drafts and finally in desperation wrote:

Dear Grandmother,
I know you'll be surprised to learn I'm in the army again. As you know, I have not been eager to rush into this war, but now for many reasons I feel I must do so. You might expect that I would come home and join the Army of Northern Virginia, but somehow I feel I cannot do this.

I wish I could come home and see you before I enlist for, as you know, leave is sometimes difficult to obtain. However I feel so strongly about this that I am leaving for Tennessee tomorrow. I am sending this letter back by Corey, the slave I've told you about. He has proven himself faithful and loyal beyond all my expectations. If anything should happen to me, please see he is set free at once. In any case, I have promised him that after one year he will be freed.

David went ahead to express his gratitude for the many good years that his family had provided for him, thanking them from the bottom of his heart for being the best any boy or young man ever had. He said things he'd been reluctant to express aloud and finally closed by saying:

It may not be that we shall meet again on this earth. I do not want to grieve you by speaking of this, but you both know this is a possibility for all in our army. If I do not return, do not grieve for me. I go knowing Jesus Christ as my Savior. This you taught me as a boy, and although I have not served God as faithfully as I should have liked, still I am confident I stand under God's merciful hand.

Your dutiful and loving son—David Rocklin

The best part of two days went by before he had all the letters finished and ready to mail. It was his plan to have Corey take them back to Virginia, but he encountered a stubbornness that took him unawares. It began when he took Corey aside and explained what he intended to do. Corey listened, his eyes fixed on David as he explained he'd be leaving to join the Army of the Tennessee, and that Corey was to go at once to Virginia.

"I've got everything ready, Corey." David pulled an envelope from his pocket. "Here are the papers showing you belong to me. They'll be honored by any who stop you. I have included evidence that my father and brothers are officers in the Army of Northern Virginia. I've also included plenty of money for your transportation and for food along the way. I want you to give this letter to my parents when you get there."

"No sah, I won't do it."

David blinked with surprise. "What did you say?"

"I said, Mr. David, I ain't goin' to Virginia."

"But—"

"No sah, I'm going with you to the army. You bought me and I'm gonna be with you."

A warm shock ran along David's nerves, for this kind of loyalty certainly couldn't be bought. "Why, Corey, that's fine of you," he said with a smile. He put his hand on the tall slave's shoulder, then said, "Really, it's the best thing for you to go back." He wanted to tell Corey more, but his secret couldn't be shared with anyone. However, Corey was staring at him with suspicion in his brown eyes as David said hurriedly, "I'll be all right. You go on home now and in a year you'll be free. Maybe we can help you buy a farm there. Anyhow, you'll be free."

When Corey started to argue, David snapped, "I'm telling you, you're going back to Virginia and don't argue with me!" He hardened his expression harshly. "I appreciate your offer, but it's got to be this way. Now take this and don't argue anymore." He thrust the envelopes containing the money and the letter to his parents in Corey's hand and turned and walked away.

That evening at supper he told the Dixons he'd be leaving.

"You going back to Virginia?" Bernard asked. "I think that's wise."

David avoided the question. He expressed his gratitude to all the family. "You've been so kind to me. I don't know how to thank you."

"Why, it's nothing at all," Bernard said warmly. "You tell your family when you get home that we're expecting them to take good care of you."

"Why, of course," Mrs. Dixon said. "You'll be all right when you get home among your people."

Later that night, just before bedtime, David had a farewell word for Bernard. He shook his hand, saying warmly, "You're one in a million, Bernard. Can't tell you how much you've done for me or what it means to me. I'll be leaving early, so we'll say our good-byes now."

Bernard was immensely relieved by the decision he assumed David had made. Shaking his hand, he reached around and clapped him on the shoulder. "I've been worried sick about you, David, but God's going to be with you. He's the Healer, you know, and he can heal a mind as well as a body. You'll write?"

"I'll write!" David said.

★ ★ ★

The train that left Atlanta heading north was scheduled to leave at four-fifteen in the morning. David had made arrangements to borrow a horse and leave it with the station agent, who was a special friend of the Dixons. He slept poorly but had no nightmares that night. At three o'clock, he rose, dressed, and packed his few belongings. He left the house quietly, moved to the barn, and saddled the gelding, patting him on the neck and leading him out of the small barn behind the Dixons' house. He swung into the saddle and walked the horse out into the road, then headed toward the south part of Atlanta where the train waited.

Stars were still twinkling overhead as he moved along. A quietness hung over the city, and all seemed asleep. He felt a strangeness in the air as he swayed with the movement of the gelding. He thought of many things, flashes of his time at Vicksburg . . . and of his times with Leah. She'd been driven from his mind by his mental lapses, but now as he saw his life as a book with only a few pages left to turn, his mind went back to her. He saw her face suddenly in his memory, oval, with alert greenish eyes and the red hair that always shone gold in the sun. He thought of the faint odor of lilacs that always hung about her and the firmness of her body as he'd held her and kissed her.

Then he shook his head, murmuring, "I've got to put all that behind me now."

He'd gone approximately halfway through town when he was aware of soft noises behind him. It was still dark, and only a faint light from the sky touched the earth, for the moon was hidden behind skeins of clouds that scudded across the velvet blackness. Here and there a star or two put its feeble light over the city streets and only rarely did a gaslight offer a pale gleam.

David's hearing was better than most, and he was sure he heard something or someone behind him. He thought of a thief and slipped his hand into the saddlebag where he kept the Navy Colt. Pulling it out, he tried to remember if it was fully loaded but could not. He rolled the cylinder, feeling it with his hand, and the heft of it told him there were loads. Suddenly he wheeled the horse around and drove his heels into its sides. The gelding snorted wildly, then half reared. David kicked him again and leaned over his neck as the horse thundered back at a dead run. He hadn't gone more than fifty yards when he saw a form ducking to one side.

"Hold it!" he said, throwing the Colt down and pulling the horse to a shuddering halt. "Don't move or I'll shoot!"

The shadowy figure made no answer. David gathered the reins more firmly, then moved the horse closer to the man who stood waiting for him. He was a tall man, but that was all David could see as he held the pistol on half-cock. "Why are you following me?" he said.

"It's me, sah . . . Corey!"

David's teeth clicked together. "What are you doing here?" he demanded.

"I told you, I'm goin' with you, Mr. David."

David slipped off the horse, took the pistol off half-cock, and shoved it back into the saddlebag. Then he turned to Corey, coming close enough to see the slave's face in the dim starlight. "You fool!" he said angrily. "I told you what to do. You're not free yet. You go on back to the house."

"No sah, I ain't goin'." Corey's voice was so calm and

even that David knew any argument was useless. "I'm goin' with you, Mr. David. You done bought me and you done promised me my freedom. Until that time comes, I'm your man."

"But I'm going to join the army. You can't go with me."

"I don't know much 'bout no army, but I know some of the men take their body servants with 'em, and that's what I'm gonna be. I'm gonna do your cookin' and take care of your uniform and your gun, and if you get hurt, I'm gonna take care of you. And if you get kilt I'm gonna take your body back to Virginia to your family."

David stood there transfixed. Finally he pulled off his hat, ran his fingers through his hair, wildly trying to think of a better argument. Then the last remark Corey had made, "If you get kilt I'm gonna take your body back to Virginia to your family," caught him.

He thought swiftly, *Pa and Grandmother would like that. It won't mean anything to me, but it'd mean a lot to them.* He jammed his hat back on his head, settled it firmly, then muttered with a smile, "You're the stubbornest man I ever saw."

Corey saw the smile and knew he'd won. "I guess we'd better get goin', Mr. David. It's a long way to Tennessee, ain't it?"

"Pretty far. Well, if you've got to do it, let's go." He moved to the horse, swung on, and kicked his foot free. "Put your foot in there and get on behind me."

Instantly Corey was behind him. He was carrying a sack containing his possessions in his left hand, and with his right he held on to David's waist.

"You're a stubborn fool, Corey," David said again. "Don't you know that people besides soldiers get killed in battles?"

"Ain't nothin' gonna happen to me," Corey said. "Now, let's get goin', Mr. David."

David, for the first time since his illness, laughed. It was a soft sound on the air, and he was amazed to find he had any laughter left in him. But Corey's gesture had disarmed him. He'd been so concerned with his own problems that he hadn't thought of anything else. Now, as the horse moved along at a fast walk, he thought, *This man is what we've been trying to own in the South. It'll be a good thing when it all stops. I won't see it, but men like Corey will be free someday.*

The two men swayed with the movement of the gelding and soon saw the lights of the station far down the road. An aureole circled the gaslights outside, and David commented, "There it is, Corey. It won't be long till we'll be in Tennessee."

"Yes sah, I guess that's right."

CHAPTER FIFTEEN
Shock of Battle

After the trying times at Vicksburg and the bustle of activity in New York City, life on a farm outside of Chattanooga was placid and almost dull to Leah. She spent a great deal of time strolling through the woods as September came and all the battles seemed far away. She heard with regularity from Brian Decatur, who informed her that the Army of the Cumberland was on the move at last and headed for Tennessee. "I told you I was a stubborn fellow," he said in his letter, and she smiled as he insisted, "I'm going to be hard for you to get rid of, Leah. You might as well get used to having me around, for I intend to be with you for a lifetime!"

Leah read his letters, for the most part, to Claire, who listened with mild interest. Once she asked, "Do you feel anything for him, Leah?"

"He's entertaining and a fine young man," Leah said. "I don't know if it will ever go past that."

She said as much to Amelia, who shook her head, saying, "I doubt if you'll ever think of marrying a Yankee. They're different from us, Leah."

Claire spent a great deal of time nursing her mother. Martha Rayborn had been ill before, but this time Claire had seen almost at once that her mother was in worse condition than she'd imagined. Martha's face was drawn and sunken and the dullness in her eyes frightened Claire. She spent long hours sitting beside her mother's bed and was surprised when her mother, whose habit was not to dwell on the past, wanted to speak of those days long ago. Somewhat to Claire's surprise, her mother didn't speak a great deal of her husband, Thaddeus.

Finally, late one afternoon, Claire asked her, "Tell me some more about Father." As the sun streamed down in golden bars through the window, it fell upon her mother's face, emphasizing the gauntness of the stricken features and making the sunken eyes even more cavernous. At Claire's question, the pale lips drew more tightly together. "What do you want to know about him, Claire?" Martha Rayborn asked, her voice flat and unemotional.

"Why, I think about him so much . . . how he used to take me places and how he was always so good to me. I remember how people would come to the house," Claire said dreamily, "famous people, anxious to meet him. I thought there was nobody like him. I still think that."

A fly buzzed in the room with an insistent drone, landing on the sick woman's forehead, but Martha Rayborn didn't have the strength to brush it away. As Claire fanned it away with a folded newspaper, she seemed deep in thought but finally murmured, "He was admired by everyone. I've kept all the letters from the president and the senators. He even received a letter from Henry Ward Beecher, the famous preacher, commending him for his work." Claire leaned forward, her face intent and still. "Tell me about your courtship. You've never said much about it, Mother. Was he romantic?"

"No, not really. There was a—a magnetism to your father. When he came into a room, nobody could look at anyone else and I was the same. I was so young, and I was shocked when he began to court me. I couldn't believe that of all the women in the world he'd be interested in me. There were others more beautiful, more charming, and certainly more rich. Some of the most prominent young women in the land practically threw themselves at him."

"When did you fall in love with him?"

Martha's eyes half shut and she didn't speak for a moment. Finally she said slowly, "I don't know as I would call it that. It wasn't like in the romances. I admired him and thought he was a great man . . . and he *was* great in his way."

Something in her mother's voice caught Claire's attention. "What do you mean, Mother? Didn't you have a good marriage? I thought it was wonderful."

"You only saw it from a child's eyes. Your father was gone a lot of the time. He was very busy, very popular, with everyone seeking his attention. . . ." Martha talked for a while, and then her eyes opened and she examined her daughter with a strange curiosity. "You've always been enamored of your father, Claire—too much so, I think sometimes."

"Why, Mother! How can you say that?"

"He wasn't a saint. He had his faults."

"Why, we all have our faults. But he was good to us."

Martha Rayborn hesitated, then said slowly, "I may have done you an injustice, daughter." Seeing a look of incomprehension on Claire's face, she breathed heavily as if drawing on some inner resources. A spasm of pain took her and she closed her eyes for a moment, clasping at the coverlet with her skeletal fingers. She waited until it passed, then breathed carefully. These spasms always left her with the feeling her heart was made of fragile crystal and the slightest shock could destroy it in a moment. When she'd regained her strength, she said, "My time is short—oh, don't bother, Claire, we both know I can't live long in this condition. I've had a lot of time to think, and there's something I want to tell you."

Claire loved her mother and hated to see her suffer so. "What is it?" she asked quietly, picking up her mother's hand.

"It's about your father. I have to tell you something . . . something you won't like and may not even believe."

A cold wind blew through Claire. She'd never been able to listen to criticism of her father from anyone, and now, with it coming from her mother, she had a sudden urge to turn and leave the room. But she knew that she mustn't. "Go ahead, tell me," she said, holding her mother's cold hand tightly as if to ward off a blow.

"Your father was one man in the public eye and quite another in his private life. He was unkind to me. He never loved me as I wanted to be loved—"

"What do you mean 'unkind'? What did he do?" Claire asked, bewildered. She'd never seen this in her parents. Their relationship had been formal, but she'd assumed that was merely their public appearance.

"He was cruel in many ways. Some of them were of the mind. He verbally abused me, taunted me with not being what a woman should be. He said I was cold, and that was why he . . . why he went—" Martha's voice broke and tears appeared in her eyes. Her voice grew husky. "That was why he had other women."

Claire Cleburne couldn't have been more shocked if the roof had suddenly collapsed. *No!* something inside her screamed. *It can't be true, it can't be! Not Father!* As she sat there trying to assimilate what she'd heard, she couldn't speak to save her life. She released her mother's hands and clasped her own hands tightly together, for they were trembling. Her eyes were fixed on her mother's face as if searching to refute the words.

"I know—this is terrible for you, Claire. I never wanted to come between you two, so I never told you any of this. And I always hoped he would change," Martha whispered. "He never abused me physically. That would have been easier." She lay there exhausted, her eyes closed, her lips barely moving. "I'm sorry to destroy the dream you've had, but you needed to know." She opened her eyes briefly and said, "I saw how you compared Matthew to your father and I knew I should have said something. You tried to make your husband live up to a man who never existed. It was unfair, but I was a coward and afraid to speak." And then, in the way of the very ill, without warning she abruptly closed her eyes, her breathing deepened in a ragged fashion, and she was asleep.

Claire Cleburne rose and walked blindly from the room. Her world had been shattered in a few minutes, and she couldn't think clearly. Visions of the past appeared before her, her father's face smiling and laughing. But then she thought, *I never saw him kiss my mother, not once!* She went to her room, shut the door, and fell across the bed, her body wracked with sobs.

★ ★ ★

"What's the matter with Mother?" Leah asked Amelia, a puzzled tone in her voice. She was putting the finishing touches on her hair, preparing to go to a rally held in Chattanooga to encourage the soldiers. She looked over and saw that Amelia's face was noncommittal. "She hasn't said ten words in the past two days. Is it Grandmother's illness, do you think?"

Amelia, as a matter of fact, didn't think that was the case. She knew Claire too well and besides, she'd had her own talks with Martha and knew of the scene that had taken place. "That may be so," she said guardedly. Then, preferring not to talk about it, she continued, "We'd better get all these eatables in the wagon if the soldiers are going to get any of them."

Bessie and Amelia had been cooking pies, cakes, and cookies all the previous day, and now Pax, Martha's manservant, came to load them into the wagon. When everything was safely loaded, Amelia and Leah got onto the seat beside Pax. As they pulled out, Pax said, "Them soldier boys sho' is gonna enjoy them goodies you been makin', ladies. I wouldn't mind a bite myself."

Leah laughed, reached back, pulled a large box from the pile, and opened it. "Here! Try some of these cookies. I made them myself so they're probably not as good as Bessie's or Aunt Amelia's. But you're welcome to them."

Pax opened his hand happily and bit into one of the

cookies she'd put on his pink palm. "Gingersnap!" he said. "That sho' is fine, Miss Leah, and they ever bit as good as Bessie could make. But don't you tell her I said so. . . . Giddup now, hosses, we got to go to the doin's."

When they reached Chattanooga just before noon, the city was humming with activity. Military bands played martial airs, and people from the outlying areas packed the streets.

When Leah asked a short, fat private the way to where the food would be served, he looked up and answered with a roguish grin, "I'd better 'scort you there. All these soldiers ain't the gentlemens they appear." He scrambled into the wagon, stood behind them, and pointed the way. When they arrived, he jumped down and helped Leah and Amelia, holding to Leah's hand a little longer than was absolutely necessary.

"You deserve an award, Private," Leah said and reached into a box and removed a thick slice of chocolate cake. "Sorry, no lemonade to go with it."

The soldier plopped half the cake into his mouth and mumbled, "I'll help you unload this stuff, Miss. There's the tables right over there."

Leah and Amelia joined the women who were laying the refreshments out on long tables made of planks placed across sawhorses. Leah enjoyed the frivolity of the day, and for over an hour she was besieged with soldiers hungry for female company as well as for cookies.

Later there was a speech by Gen. Braxton Bragg. The crowd gathered down at the far end of the street to hear him, but Leah stayed at the table so she could get a clear view. "He doesn't look like much," she observed aloud, "and his speechmaking isn't very inspiring. I wish we had Robert E. Lee here or Stonewall were still alive. We'd show those Yankees!"

"Hello, Leah."

Startled, Leah whirled to see David Rocklin standing before her, dressed in the butternut uniform of a private. For one moment she thought she was mistaken. *He can't be here!* she thought wildly, *and not in uniform!* She was so confused she couldn't speak, and David smiled at her, his face more thin than she remembered.

"It's me all right. I didn't mean to startle you."

"David . . . what are you doing here?"

He looked down at his uniform and in a wry tone said, "I'm defending the Confederacy, can't you tell?" The scene flashed before her eyes of the time when she'd said good-bye to him so coldly and rebuked him for his cowardice. But somehow the face of the man who stood before her now was changed. He looked as if he'd been ill, but he was somehow more calm than she remembered him.

"I am surprised to see you—and in uniform."

"You've got a right to be surprised. After I ran away, no one would expect me to put myself back into a uniform again."

Leah was baffled and intrigued. She had, in her mind, blotted David Rocklin out, never wanting to see him again. Indeed, she never thought she would. But now, as he stood before her with his hat removed, his black hair moving slightly in the fall breeze, she suddenly said, "Come along. While they're listening to the speech we can visit a little." Turning, she went back, put a piece of cake on a plate, and handed it to him. Then she poured a glass of lemonade saying, "Come on, there's a space back here where we can have a little privacy." She made her way behind the tables and around a corner to a large open space. It was vacant now, and after they sat down she asked at once, "What have you been doing, David?"

David entertained the idea of telling her the truth but had purposed never to let anyone know of his illness. As he looked at her, admiring the clearness of her eyes, the smoothness of her skin, the youthful beauty of her face, the love he'd felt for her at Vicksburg surged through him. "You haven't changed," he said slowly. "I've thought about you a great deal." Then, when she didn't speak, he realized he'd embarrassed her. "Oh, don't worry. I'm not here to pursue you. We won't be here that long. The Yankees will be here probably within a week." He bit into the cake, nodded his approval, then asked, "Where are you staying? I didn't expect to see you here at all. I thought you went to New York."

"My grandmother's very ill. She has a place just outside of the city here. Mother, Aunt Amelia, and I are staying with her. I don't expect she can live long, so we had to come."

"I'm sorry to hear that."

"But you—what are you doing in Chattanooga? And in the army?"

David shook his head. "It's not a very interesting story, Leah. I never thought I'd see you again, so let's not talk about the past."

Leah couldn't put it all together. She had put David Rocklin out of her mind, but here he was now, sitting relaxed before her. True, there was a shadow in his eyes that hadn't been there before. She wondered if he hadn't been able to live with his cowardly behavior and if the shame accounted for the change in him. He'd also lost weight. "How long have you been in the army?" she asked.

"Not long," he said briefly, then changed the subject abruptly. "I would like to see Aunt Amelia. I don't suppose your mother would like to see me, though."

"Why, Amelia's gone to hear Braxton Bragg, the general, speak. You'll see her when she comes back."

As Leah talked to David, she grew more amazed at how much he'd changed. Some time later Amelia came back. Her eyes brightened and she cried out, "David," coming at once to put her arms around him.

David, who had stood up, was somewhat surprised at her display of emotion, but he embraced her and looked down at the petite woman saying, "Bad penny turned up again, Aunt Amelia."

"Never that, my boy!" She reached up to touch his cheek

fondly, then sat him down and insisted on feeding him cookies and cakes as Leah watched.

Later on, the crowds came back and Leah said, "Come and see us, David, if you can get away." She read his thoughts and responded, "Mother will be glad to see you and so would we."

"All right. I'll come if I can, but I doubt there'll be time. The Yankees are coming with three hundred thousand men, so they say." He stood and left abruptly, his back straight as he made his way through the crowd.

After he left, the two women talked of his strange appearance and of his decision to join the army. "I don't understand it," Leah murmured, her brow furrowed. "He's different, isn't he?"

"Yes, he is. I can't explain it, but he's changed somehow. He's more serious than he was, but it's more than that. He looks troubled—and yet he's somehow more of a man than he was. He's been through a hard time. We've got to help him all we can."

"Yes," Leah agreed, thinking it even more strange that David Rocklin, who she thought was forever out of her life, could walk back into it on one sunny afternoon and be an even stronger presence in her life than ever.

★ ★ ★

The Union Army of the Cumberland, led by Gen. Rosecrans, had begun moving toward Chattanooga in August. By August 21 Gen. Bragg, the Confederate commander, received reports that the bulk of the Federal army was moving toward him. His own army now totaled only thirty thousand men. Bragg was justly nervous, for he knew he didn't have a large enough force to combat the Federals. On August 31 the Army of the Cumberland started to cross the river at Stevenson and poured into the mountains that were south of Chattanooga. Three times during that week, Gen. Bragg started to pull his men away from Chattanooga, each time reversing his decision. At last, however, he made his decision: On September 7, Bragg and his Confederate army gave up Chattanooga and moved south over dusty roads. They hadn't fired a single shot.

Bragg's retreat from Chattanooga led Gen. Rosecrans into a serious mistake. Assuming the Confederates were in a full-scale retreat, Bragg thought he had a once-in-a-lifetime opportunity to destroy the Army of the Tennessee. But Bragg wasn't fleeing for his life; his withdrawal from Chattanooga had been orderly. On September 9 he stopped close to La Fayette and reorganized his infantry units, preparing for battle. He was also being reinforced with new troops. Gen. Thomas and his twenty thousand Federals were marching into a trap.

On the evening of September 9, Bragg gave orders for the trap to be sprung the next morning, and all along the Confederate line excitement was generated. At last they were to have their chance at the Yankees and this time on their own terms! But, due to disorganization in Confederate ranks, nothing came of the promised battle with the Federals.

It wasn't until the morning of the thirteenth that David found himself moving forward with Company H, with Sam Watkins on his right. "Looks like it's gonna be a good 'un," Sam declared almost blithely. "Don't reckon they gonna be countin' how many cartridges we shoot off this morning long as we get a Yankee with 'em."

They were advancing over rough terrain studded with second-growth timber, making progress difficult. It was a weird scene in a way, but picturesque. As David stumbled through the dark wilderness of woods, vines, and overhanging limbs, somehow everything looked very solemn: the trees, men, and even the horses. He thought about the nights he'd passed since leaving Atlanta. To his shock (and relief) he'd not had dreams of bayonets, nor had there been any reoccurrence of the black pit into which he'd fallen so often before. That morning Corey had wakened him early with breakfast already cooked. The slave had bent over and looked into David's eyes, and what he saw in his owner reassured him. "You all right, Mr. David," he had said, grinning. "Your eyes is just as clear as a mountain stream! Here, come and get some of this breakfus'."

Now as David marched along, conscious of being in the first line of battle and of men on his right and his left, he felt he wasn't a single individual, but part of some complicated machinery. *I couldn't run if I wanted to!* he thought grimly, glancing down the lines of infantrymen. But he didn't have time to think further, for Lt. Archie Biers suddenly shouted, "There's the Bluebellies! Get ready! They're coming our way!"

"We'll give 'em the best we've got in the house, Lieutenant!" Sam Watkins called out. He turned and flashed a wild grin at David. "Let's get more of them than they get of us, David. What do you say?"

"All right," David promptly replied.

He felt a calmness he couldn't explain, even when he suddenly saw a line of blue ahead of him. He also saw bayonets, glinting in the morning sunlight, but amazingly he felt no fear. *I'll be shot before they get to me with those bayonets*. . . . he thought. Then the colonel came galloping down the line on a fine bay stallion, waving his sword and screaming, "Charge! Charge! For the Southern Cause and the Confederacy! Men, protect your homes and your wives!"

The whole Confederate line surged forward, and David began to run at full speed. He was conscious of the humming of bullets about his ears and felt a tug as one of them touched his slouch hat, but he didn't slow his pace. As the din of battle increased in pitch, men around him began to fall and gaps opened in the blue line ahead. Black smoke obscured the scene and finally the blue line retreated. Wild screams came up from the Confederates, and Lt. Biers, his face blackened by powder and yelling like a demon, cried out, "Come on, we've got 'em on the go!"

Again the line charged. There were fewer of them this

time, and the fire became more intense. Artillery pieces and shells fell in the midst of the Confederate lines, lifting men into the air and then down, still, on the leaves beneath their feet. The Confederates wavered, then just ahead David saw the color-bearer go down. Without conscious thought he ran forward, grabbed the colors, lifted them high, yelling, "Come on!" and ran straight into the terrible fire.

Col. Bleeker, seeing this, called out to his aide, "Who is that man?"

"I don't know him, but look at him go! Right into those guns! He'll never make it, though," the lieutenant said, shaking his head regretfully. "That fire's too hot."

Somehow, however, David did make it, and as he ran directly into the fire his courage inspired others. Sam Watkins yelled, "Come on, don't let that rookie show us up!" and threw himself forward. The Confederate line charged once again, and David was the first man to reach the blue line. The Federals were, however, not waiting; they'd turned and fled, throwing their rifles down and running wildly as if in a race.

A cheer rang out as the Confederates overran the Union lines, and men pounded David on the back. Lt. Archie Biers came to him soon, grabbing him by the arm. "I never saw anything like that!"

Col. Bleeker had ridden up also, his face wreathed in smiles. He looked down from his horse and said, "What's your name, Private?"

"David Rocklin, Colonel."

"Have you got room for another sergeant in your company, Lt. Biers?"

"Yes sir!"

"Well then, Sgt. Rocklin, you're now promoted."

That night David was amused at the warm admiration that came his way. Corey insisted on hearing the story over again from as many men as would tell it and was as proud of his master as a man could be. His black face glowed and he said finally to David, "I guess you showed 'em, sah, what a real soldier's like!"

David Rocklin was seized by a grim amusement as Company H extolled him that night. He listened to it all, smiled, and took the teasing that came with his sudden promotion well. Later, when the camp had gone to sleep, he lay on his blankets, thinking of the strangeness of it all. Here he'd sought death—and hadn't found it. Instead he'd found something far different, something he thought he'd never have: the approval of brave men!

If they only knew what a coward I am, he mused, *it would be different.* Then he thought of the next day. *There'll be another line of battle and I'll rush right into it just like I did today. A man only has so many chances, so much luck. So many good fellows went down today, better men than I am.*

He was exhausted, but the sleep he fell into was a healthful sleep. Corey came once to stand over him, his black face filled with admiration. As he pulled David's blanket up, he whispered, "You is some soldier, Mr. David! Your family gonna be downright proud of you!"

CHAPTER SIXTEEN
Leah Has a Visitor

The abrupt knock on the door startled Leah. Glancing up at Bessie, who was standing across the kitchen from her cutting up a chicken, she asked, "Who can that be? I'll go get it." She made her way through the house's central hallway and opened the door, expecting to find one of the neighbors. Instead, however, David Rocklin was standing there, smiling at her surprise.

"I took you at your word, Leah."

"Why, David! Come in!" Leah was conscious of how pleased she was to see him. She'd thought of him almost constantly since their encounter a week ago and had finally decided he wouldn't come to visit. Now she took him by the arm, drawing him inside. "I didn't expect you. What are you doing away from the army?"

David followed her into the front parlor, where he took a seat in a rocking chair and explained, "Neither army's doing much. There's a big battle coming up, but it looks like both generals are afraid to make the first move." He was wearing his uniform and had gained a little weight, but he still wore the same look of relaxation and ease that Leah had noted before. He continued, "I still feel odd about coming here. I know your mother doesn't have much use for me."

"I think you'll find her different now. I told her all about you joining the Army of the Tennessee, and we had a visitor from your regiment who passed through. He's a neighbor boy who lives down the way. He told us how you'd showed such courage that you were promoted to sergeant." She looked at the chevrons on his sleeve and saw his flush of embarrassment. "I'm so proud of you, David—and Mother is, too. She wants to see you. Now, tell me all about it."

"Why, it wasn't all that much . . . ," David protested, feeling like a fraud, but at her insistence he gave a quick sketch of the battle.

Leah listened to him relate the tale then said, smiling, "Jed Thompson tells it a lot different. He said none of the officers had ever seen a man run head-on into fire like you did. It was almost," she said, a fleeting frown crossing her face, "as if you didn't care if you were killed or not."

David looked down at the carpet, unable to speak for a moment. *If she knew how close to the truth she is!* Then he shook his head, saying, "I didn't come here to talk about the war. What about you and your mother and your grandmother? Is she well?"

"No, she lives from day to day, I think sometimes. She's in a shadowland, David, but she's ready to go—anxious actually." She saw that her words had struck some sort of response in David, for he nodded slightly as if he read a meaning into her words that she herself had missed. "Why do you look like that?"

"Oh, I don't know. It seems a good thing to be ready to go, I suppose. I've thought about it a lot lately."

The two of them sat there talking, and when Claire came in, she fulfilled Leah's words by smiling warmly and coming over to offer her hand to David. "I'm so glad you're here," she said. "We've heard all about your promotion and how well you performed. You're staying for supper?"

"Just dinner, if it's not too much trouble."

"Of course not! You stay here and talk with David, Leah. Bessie and I'll see what we can do about dinner for this young soldier."

It was a pleasant day for David. He and Leah took a long walk through the fields, once stopping to watch a white-tailed deer go bounding across in effortless flight. Later, before they got back to the house, she stopped him, saying, "David, I'm glad you came." Once again David was aware of the richness of her complexion and her inner excitement that seemed ready to bubble over. As the cool winds flushed her cheeks, blowing her red-gold hair in tendrils down her back and over her simple light-blue dress, her vibrant figure spoke to David of life, youth, and hope.

"Leah, I—" He hesitated, then said, "I've got to go back." He wanted to say more, but he was walking now in the shadow of what he knew must come. True enough he'd had no more blackouts, but it was a menace that was always with him. He was frightened, not of death, but of losing his mind—and now this honorable way of avoiding madness had become a way of life to him.

"David, be careful!" Leah whispered, disturbed again to find that his return into her life stirred her so strongly. As she reached up suddenly to touch his cheek in a half caress, she saw a clearness and purpose in his eyes that she hadn't seen before. "I don't want anything to happen to you," she murmured.

David felt helpless, for in his own mind he was already a dead man. *This is the last time I'll ever see her,* he thought, and reaching forward he took her in his arms. "I shouldn't do this," he whispered, "but I want to tell you something. Of all the women I've ever known, you're the loveliest and sweetest and dearest." He leaned down, hesitating, and gave her time to pull away. But she didn't draw back. Instead, she lifted her arms, pulled his head down, and he felt the sweetness of her lips under his. For that one moment he forgot the war, forgot his madness, forgot everything except Leah and the richness of her as she held him tightly. There was a rushing in his veins, and his ears tingled as he inhaled her fragrance—partly lilac, partly rich young womanhood. He'd never experienced anything like this, and he held her for a long time. But finally, drawing back, he said huskily,

"Good-bye, Leah." Then he pulled himself away abruptly and walked away, not turning around.

Leah stood and watched him until he disappeared down the dusty road, then walked slowly into the house. Her mother was in the kitchen cleaning up. Bessie had gone and the house was silent. "Is he gone?" Claire asked.

"Yes, he's gone."

Claire looked up suddenly, then put down the glass she'd been drying and came over to stand beside her daughter. "He's different, isn't he, Leah? I could see something in him that wasn't there before."

"Yes, and I don't know what it is. It's strange, but I wish he didn't have to go." She turned suddenly to her mother, misery in her eyes. "This war is awful," she said bitterly. "It tears people apart, ruins families; it's nothing but death! I think sometimes I can't bear it."

Claire put her hand on Leah's shoulder. "You're a grown woman now," she said, "but there's something about you that reminds me of when you were just a little girl." Her voice grew soft and her face tender. "You used to come to me when you'd stubbed your toe or put a splinter in your finger or cut yourself. I'd take you in my lap and hold you . . . and I think at times," she said with a half smile, "you'd hurt yourself on purpose."

"I did," Leah confessed. "I didn't think you knew it, though. I needed that." Her eyes brimmed with tears. "I guess I still do."

"Leah—" Claire pulled her daughter close and held her as she hadn't in a long time.

As the two women stood there, Leah said, "I'm so afraid for him, Mother!"

"I know." Claire wanted to offer words of comfort, thinking of herself when she'd been Leah's age. It was about then that she'd married Matthew, and the thoughts that came of that time were sweet, strong, and poignant, as always. They'd become even more so lately, especially since she'd discovered the truth about her father. She felt sharp remorse, for now she'd accepted her mother's words as truth.

Finally Claire stepped back and said, "A woman needs a strong man, Leah. That's the way we are. No woman is complete by herself, and I suppose no man is either without a woman to love."

Leah stared at her mother in surprise. She'd never heard her talk like this. She said slowly, "Do you still feel that way? That you need a man after all these years?"

"I didn't think I'd ever need anybody or want anybody. But I'm not as strong as I thought I was, Leah."

Claire turned and walked away, saying no more. For a while Leah simply stared at the door through which her mother had disappeared, the meaning of what she'd heard sinking into her.

Startled, Leah realized, *She still loves him! After all these years, she still loves him. I never knew that!*

★　★　★

The Battle of Chickamauga was almost a reenactment of a famous line of poetry where the poet spoke of "ignorant armies that clash by night."

On September 19 Union forces moved forward through the densely wooded areas. They had marched over unfamiliar territory where landmarks were practically nonexistent and every tree looked just like the last one. The front line stretched about six miles through the woods. As the battle began on the morning of the nineteenth, brigade after brigade, both Union and Confederate, entered the fray all along the line. First one side, then the other would attack. Before the day ended almost every unit of both armies had been engaged, yet neither side had made any substantial progress. That night Lt. Gen. James Longstreet arrived to reinforce Bragg with two Virginia brigades. Other units also filtered in. For the attack the next day Bragg organized the Confederate forces into two parts: The right half of his army he put under Lt. Gen. Polk; the left under Longstreet.

When the Confederates advanced the next day, however, they found out that the Union forces were not where they had been. David marched along with Company H in this part of the battle, and Gen. Polk ran up against such terrific fire that the Confederates went reeling backward.

Longstreet did his best and found a large gap in the Union line. Through this hole he poured his army. In this attack, Gen. Hood, who'd been severely wounded at Gettysburg, lost a leg.

It was the great opportunity for the Confederates, but Bragg failed to understand the situation. Instead of following through the line with Longstreet, he insisted on sticking with the original plan, which simply threw brigade after brigade against Union commander Maj. Gen. George H. Thomas. Thomas had been a former lieutenant in Bragg's battery in the Mexican War. He was a man slow to act, methodical, careful. It was here on this field that he gained his nickname, "Rock of Chickamauga." And it was against Thomas's men that David and the remains of the already thinning brigade were thrown. "I ain't never seen such fire!" Sam Watkins complained. He was lying down behind a small fallen tree with other members of his squad to his right and left. He glanced over at David and grunted. "We done lost some mighty good fellers, Dave."

David's heart was pounding. He knew there was no way they could live through the fire if they were commanded to charge. Somehow he'd forgotten or put in the back of his mind his purpose in coming here. He'd thrown himself into the battle, determined to do his part. He owed that to his commanders and to his squad. He was watching down the line where Lt. Biers was speaking to the colonel. The pair were sheltered by a large oak tree, but chunks of iron from artillery still flew through the air. Explosions from the Union guns punctuated the afternoon with mighty bursts of sound, and muskets popped all along the line like firecrackers going off.

After studying the colonel and the lieutenant, David

turned to say, "Sam, I think we're gonna have to charge. It looks like that's what the colonel's telling Lt. Biers."

Sam lifted his head over the tree and immediately a bullet took his hat off. He ducked back, scrambled after his hat, and pulled it down almost to his ears. "Why, Dave, we can't make no headway against that! We'd all get killed!"

David heard Watkins' remark but had turned again to watch the lieutenant. Biers suddenly dropped down and came wriggling on his stomach behind a slight hummock. Dave watched as he came closer and turned to meet him. "What is it, Lieutenant?"

Biers replied, "There's a nest of sharpshooters right over there. If we can wipe them out, we can get out of this artillery fire. But they're dead shots and I believe they've got some of them seven-shooting Spenser rifles. Get your squad together, and we'll go see if we can knock 'em out."

"Yes sir!" David looked up and down the line and called out, "All right, Company H. Let's go get 'em!"

Sam Watkins complained, "Why do we always have to be the heroes and pull the chestnuts of them generals out of the fire?" But he followed, nevertheless, as did the rest of the squad.

As they moved out of the line of artillery fire, David could see what the lieutenant meant. There, on the crest of a hill, was the rifle fire that was decimating the Confederate lines. "We've got to get those Yankees out of there!" Biers exclaimed.

"We can't get across that open field, Lieutenant," Sam said. "At least I don't see how."

Biers' face was pale. "We've got to try. Are you with me?"

Seeing the fear on the men's faces, David responded, "We can do it. You stay here, Lieutenant."

But Biers rose, pulled his pistol, and said, "They're not looking this way. Let's work around a little bit more, then we'll charge across that open field."

David followed the lieutenant and, glancing back, saw that at least thirty of the company were creeping along, keeping down to avoid the fire. When they reached the end of the timberline, Biers gasped, "All right. We've got 'em flanked."

"They'll spot us before we get across that open field," Watkins warned.

Biers shook his head. "We've got to stop 'em. Come on!" He jumped out of the timber and started across the open field. David followed, finding himself yelling. Somehow all fear had left him. All that mattered was taking that small hummock where the enemy was killing his fellow soldiers.

They were halfway across the field when a cry rang out and suddenly musket balls began to whistle and men began to drop. They hadn't gone more than another ten steps when Lt. Biers suddenly fell, his face bloodied by a musket ball. He lay still and there was no question he was dead. David reached down, picked up Biers' pistol, and yelled, "Come on, we've got 'em!"

From across the field, Col. Bleeker saw what had happened. "They're going to make it!" he exclaimed. "Look, they are! Rocklin's leading them in!" There was more musket fire, and then David stood up and waved.

"They've flanked them! Come on! We can get around through that gap!" Bleeker led the remnants of the company around the edge of the timber and, when he got to David, said, "Somebody's got to take the men on in. It'll have to be you. Right now I'm appointing you a lieutenant—brevet, of course."

"Brevet!" David said. "That means I get to be a lieutenant until I get killed!" Amazed at his own ability to joke under such circumstances, he continued more soberly, "Yes sir, I'll do it."

He turned back to the company and grinned at Sam. "You can now address me as Lt. Rocklin, Sam. At least for the next ten minutes." He looked around at the men who had gathered and said, "The colonel says for us to keep going and flank these Yankees—get behind that artillery. I hear the

Bluebellies brought some candy with them. I'm going to get some of it. Any of you boys got a sweet tooth?"

Surrounded by laughter from the men, Sam Watkins said, winking at the squad, "I can always stand a little of that. Any of you fellows feel like following Lt. 'Candy' Rocklin?'"

That was how David got his nickname: Lt. "Candy" Rocklin. Some later would think it was his real name on first meeting him. That day Rocklin led the men in a flanking maneuver, and by the time night fell, the battle was over. The union general, Thomas, held his position for a time, then marched back to Chattanooga.

Chickamauga was merely a tactical victory for the Confederates, who captured thousands of small arms and fifty-one guns. Coming less than three months after bitter defeats at Vicksburg and Gettysburg, this small gain gave new hope to the people of the South.

The Union army retreated to Chattanooga, and Gen. Bragg followed, laying siege to the city. That night David and Corey sat before a campfire and celebrated the victory. The colonel came by and said, "Well, Rocklin, you can be a lieutenant—brevet, of course—for another few weeks at least."

David was still shocked at being alive since he'd fully expected to be killed, and now he said sadly, "That should have been me instead of Lt. Biers. He's worth a lot more to you than I am."

The colonel looked at David, his eyes filled with compassion, and laid his hand on David's shoulder. "He *was* a good man, but so are you. I hear they're calling you Lt. 'Candy' now. Well, they can call you what they want. We've got a lot of hard fighting ahead, my boy, and I'll be depending on you."

David talked to Corey later on when all the rest of the men were asleep. "Corey," he said quietly, "do you know why I joined the army?"

"No sah."

David said abruptly, "I joined to get killed. I couldn't stand the thought of going crazy."

Corey's ebony face glistened in the firelight as he nodded slowly. "Yes sah. I can see how that might be better—but you ain't gone crazy, Mr. David. And you ain't been killed either. You reckon the good Lord's got something else on his mind for you?"

"Well, if I don't go crazy and I don't get killed," David said simply, "maybe he has."

CHAPTER SEVENTEEN
"I Was All Wrong . . . !"

After retreating from Chickamauga, the Federals attempted to reform their broken lines on Missionary Ridge. David was in the force that moved on them at once, but there was little action, and the shattered Union army fell back to Chattanooga.

"We ain't never gonna blast them out of Chattanooga," Sam Watkins said mournfully to David. It was almost noon, and they'd had nothing but a little salt meat for breakfast. Sam gnawed on the last bit that he'd saved, shaking his head. "We built them breastworks and forts, and I know whereof I speak."

David looked down on the city from Missionary Ridge, where his company was stationed, and saw a beautiful panoramic view. The whole city of Chattanooga, with the Tennessee River curling around it, lay at his feet. The position the company had taken seemed to be on a precipice, and as David looked down he commented, "We may not be able to take Chattanooga, but the Yankees sure can't take *us*. Why, it would take a mountain goat to climb up to this place!"

Sam swallowed the bite of salt meat, took a swig of water out of his wooden canteen, then shrugged his thin shoulders. "Well, time for preaching. We might as well go get it over with."

Amused, David asked, "Don't you like preaching, Sam?"

"Yeah, I like preaching, *good* preaching, but what we're gonna hear this morning ain't gonna be much."

"Who's the preacher?"

"Reverend P. D. Holmes." Sam made a face. "One of our fellers used to hear him when he was a young man and said he knew how to turn his wolf loose. But he went off to school somewhere and learned to read Greek . . . and that just about ruint him! And then he's bought a dictionary somewhere along the way and studies how he can get the biggest, longest, most highfalutin words he can into every sermon."

"Doesn't sound like much of a treat," David offered, getting up and brushing off his clothes. "But we might as well go."

As they made their way toward the opening where the company had gathered for the Sunday service, Sam Watkins said grumpily, "I think Rev. Holmes is scared to death that somebody's going to understand what he's talking about, but he don't have to worry about that."

The two men settled themselves along with the other members of the company. Soldiers of the other brigades began filtering in, and soon a large crowd had gathered. P. D. Holmes got up on a small knoll formed by an outcropping of gray rock spotted by lichen and began by saying a prayer the like of which David had never heard in all his life!

"O thou immaculate, invisible, eternal, and holy Being, the exudations of whose effulgence illuminates this terrestrial sphere, we approach Thy presence, being covered all over with wounds and bruises and putrifying sores, from the crowns of our heads to the soles of our feet. And Thou, O Lord, art our dernier resort. The whole world is one great machine, managed by Thy puissance. The beatific splendors of Thy face irradiate the celestial region and felicitate the saints. There are the most exuberant profusions of Thy grace, and the sempiternal effux of Thy glory. God is an abyss of light, a circle whose center is everywhere and His circumference nowhere. Hell is the dark world made up of spiritual sulphur and other ignited ingredients, disunited and unharmonized, and without that pure balsamic oil that flows from the heart of God . . ."

David was highly amused by Holmes' prayer and the sermon that followed in the same vein. It contained little spiritual food, for indeed Holmes seemed to be enamored with the sound of his own voice—which was smooth and of sufficient volume to reach almost to the city of Chattanooga.

But at the end of the sermon Holmes seemed to change. It was as if now that the prayer and the sermon were out of the way he could be himself again. He looked over the men who were watching him and said earnestly, "Men, you have fought bravely for our Cause. There's much hard fighting ahead. Some of you may not be at the next service. We are that close to eternity. I want to simply say that if you do not have Jesus Christ as your Lord and Savior, this is the hour for you to make that decision."

He went on in a simple manner, and something about the earnestness of the plea brought tears to David's eyes. When Holmes asked those who wanted prayer to come forward, at least a dozen men made their way to the front. David turned away and, as they left, Sam said, "Are you a Christian, David?"

"Yes, I am. Not much of one though. How about you, Sam?"

Sam hesitated. "No, I ain't."

David gave him an astonished look. "Why, I thought you were! You never miss a service."

Sam Watkins was an engaging young man, full of fun. He was courageous, David knew, to an extreme degree. He'd seen many of his friends shot to death, others maimed beyond belief, and yet he was always in the forefront whenever the call was made for dangerous work. "What's wrong, Sam? Why aren't you a Christian?"

Watkins shook his head. "Don't rightly know, Dave. Who knows about things like that? I do know one thing. That last

205

little bit of talking the preacher done, that was preaching! That other stuff, he was just tickling his fancy."

David marched along silently and finally, when the two were clear of the crowds and settled down alone looking down at the city, he said, "Sam, you ought not to put it off. I'm no preacher, but I know all of us are in poor condition here. No longer than I've been in the army, I've seen that we live on a tightrope. Why, that young man, Jed Hotchkiss . . ." David spoke a minute about one of the young men in his company that he'd met the day he entered service, then continued, "I'd grown close to that fellow. He was going home to be married. His girl was named Sylvia. Now he's dead and in the presence of God. He was a Christian, he told me. I'm glad of that."

Watkins picked up his musket and began running his hand along the barrel. "I reckon he was, Dave. A real one, too—not like some of the imitations I've seen. I thought a heap of that young feller." He let the silence run on for a while, then said, "I know the Bible is true. Just can't understand why I've let it go."

"Be a good time right now to call on the Lord," David prodded gently.

Watkins looked at him carefully. "I been watching you, Dave. You shore ain't afraid to die! Matter of fact, sometimes you skeered me half to death the way you charge into them guns! I think maybe there's such a thing as being a little bit *too* brash. I know you're ready to meet God, but, shoot, I wouldn't be in no hurry about it if I was you."

David continued to talk with Watkins for some time. He had a real affection for the young man and was sincere in his desire to see him come to know God. But Sam's last words stayed with him after he left the young man: "Don't be in too big a hurry to meet God."

As he walked along the ridge, noting the usual activities of the soldiers who were playing cards, digging latrines, patching their clothes, and reading books, he thought, *You haven't had a single blackout since you decided* . . . For a moment he couldn't frame the rest of the words. Then they came to him: *to die*. Somehow he hadn't put this together in his mind. Now he wondered, *What's happened? Maybe just giving up on the idea of life has made a difference in my head.* He'd had several fleeting bad dreams of bayonets, but they had been mild compared to the awful nightmares that had blackened his life before. Now as he walked along, he tried to puzzle out the confusion in his mind.

"Lt. Rocklin!"

Turning, David saw Col. Bleeker walking rapidly out of the grove of trees where the officers had pitched their tents. David hurried forward. "Yes sir? What is it, Colonel?"

"Come along with me. Got some special duty for you." Bleeker gave him an odd look, then grinned. "You're always ready for hard, difficult tasks, aren't you?"

"Why, I'm always ready to do what you order, Colonel."

"That's fine. Come along." Bleeker moved away down the winding path that led to the officers' tent. The Confederates had commandeered some Sibley tents captured from the Yankees, and Bleeker had made one of them his own command post here.

"Here we are," he said abruptly, his bulky form blocking Dave's view. Then he suddenly turned aside, and a shock ran through David. Leah was standing there, wearing a plum-colored dress, and a broad-brimmed hat with flowers on top was tied under her chin with a green ribbon. David thought she looked somewhat subdued.

Bleeker grinned at David's surprise. "This young lady tells me she's a friend of yours. I don't usually let my officers receive ladies, but for 'Candy' Rocklin, I suppose all things will go. You two have a good visit."

As Bleeker moved into his tent, Leah stepped forward, her face somewhat pale. "I know you're surprised to see me, David."

David had seldom been more surprised, but he said quickly, "It's always good to see you, Leah." Looking around, he noticed that several of his fellow officers and the

207

corporal who served as the colonel's personal servant were grinning at him. He mumbled, "Come along. I'll show you the view of Chattanooga." He swung around, and she moved forward and took his arm lightly.

They moved back down the path and were shortly standing on the brink looking down once again at the city. Leah said, "I've never been this high before. It's beautiful, isn't it?"

"Yes, it is." David couldn't think clearly. He'd been thrown off guard by her coming. Then he asked, "How is your grandmother?"

"Not well at all," Leah answered slowly. "Could we go somewhere and sit down, David? I feel rather foolish coming this way."

"Of course. Look, there's a big old tree that's down. No chairs, but it's a little more private than most places."

He led her to a small glade set back from the brow of the hill. The rocks had been scoured out by geologic action, making a flat surface across which an uprooted oak tree three feet in diameter lay. The spot was sheltered by undergrowth, but there was still a partial view of the city below. Leah sat down and when David joined her, she said seriously, "I have to congratulate you on your promotion." Then, thinking of the colonel's words, she asked, "Lt. 'Candy' Rocklin . . . how do you like that name?"

David made a face and shrugged. "Oh, it's a bit of foolishness."

"Why did he call you that?"

David repeated the incident where he'd incited the soldiers to take some candy away from the Yankees.

"Was it a hard battle, David?"

"I suppose they're all hard. I lost some good friends. Hadn't known them long, but it's hard to see men go down, shot to pieces."

"What's happened to you, David?" Leah said suddenly, her clear greenish eyes fixed on him appealingly. The sun, past the meridian, touched her reddish hair, bringing out the gold glints and making her look very feminine—and somehow vulnerable—as she sat there. What David didn't know was that Leah had been going over her relationship with him almost constantly. All the affection she'd felt for him at first—that which had been driven away by his cowardice—had come back. Now she said quietly, "Something is different about you. I can't explain it, but I want to know . . . that is, if you'd like to tell me."

David sat on the log, suddenly desiring to share what had gone on in his life. He'd kept it bottled up so that, except for Corey, no one really knew what had happened. Still in his mind was the knowledge that he had been a coward, that he had run away. He still felt shame over that and thought he'd never get over it. Even his way of fleeing from it—to deliberately throw himself into battle, to seek death as a release from what he'd become—seemed cowardly now in the light of day.

And then as he sat there a determination swept over him. His jaw set tensely, he began to speak. "You saw what I was at Vicksburg—nothing but a coward." He spoke for some time of how he'd never been afraid of being killed by a musket or by artillery fire but that the sight of bare naked steel somehow drained his manhood from him. It was difficult to speak, and he clasped his hands tightly together and looked down at his boots, avoiding her eyes. Several times he thought he couldn't go on as he spoke of what it was like to endure those nightmares. And then, when he spoke of running away, he said, "All my people have been courageous, Leah—all of them. The Rocklins may have been many things, but if they were cowards nobody ever found out about it. I'm the only one. Do you know what that means?" He looked at her, his eyes almost wild. "I couldn't stand to have my father and brothers know they had a coward in their family."

A great wave of compassion rose in Leah. She'd never seen David like this before, and somehow as he spoke she knew she loved him no matter what he'd done. She didn't tell him this, however, for he continued to narrate what had happened. He told her then of the blackouts that had occurred, and his hands trembled as he buried his face in them. "I couldn't stand the idea of going mad. Anything would be better than that . . . anything." He straightened his shoulders. A wry expression on his lips, he said, "The doctor told me that that was where I was headed, more or less. I couldn't face a lifetime of madness. I wouldn't put my family through that. So, I decided—"

He broke off, and Leah waited quietly. Around her echoed the sounds of a soldier singing and a woodpecker rattling a tattoo on a dead tree. The sweet smell of evergreens and the smoke of a wood fire surrounded her. But she was unaware of all this, focused on the torment in David Rocklin's face. Then suddenly she knew!

"You joined the army to get yourself killed, didn't you, David?"

Astonished, David turned to her, his eyes widening. "Yes," he whispered. "You see that?"

"I don't think it's as unusual as you think."

David shook his head. "It's a coward's way out, but I'd rather be dead than insane. I couldn't stand the thought of that, Leah! I decided to join the army, and when the call to action came I'd just throw myself in and . . . get killed, as you say."

Leah reached over and put her small, well-shaped hand on his. When he took it in his strong hands, he squeezed it so tightly that it pained her. But she said only, "I'm so sorry, David. If I'd shown more understanding, it might not have come to this."

"I don't think it would have mattered," he answered slowly, aware of the warmth of her hand, and of the strength it held despite its size. He reached over with his left hand, stroked it, then looked up. "Something has happened. I didn't think I could ever speak of this to anyone." A look of surprise came into his eyes and he said quietly, "The doctor tried to get me to tell him what was in me. I couldn't even tell him how I felt about being a coward."

"You are *not* a coward, David!"

He stared at her. "Why, of course I am!"

"You are not a coward! Everyone in your company knows it, and the colonel is as proud of you as if you were his own son. He said he'd never seen such courage."

"He didn't see me at Vicksburg."

"You've got to put that behind you," Leah said firmly. "It was a fault, but you were caught off guard. Have you seen bayonets since?"

David realized, *Why, I have seen them, but I guess I was so intent on getting myself killed that I didn't pay any attention.* Some of the Union soldiers he'd charged had had bayonets, but the fear that had paralyzed him before hadn't taken him.

"You see," she said, reading his thoughts, "that's the way it is, I think, with fear. If we face it honestly and earnestly, with God's help we can overcome it."

David sat there, her hand still in his. Suddenly he raised it to his lips and kissed it. "Thank you, Leah," he whispered. Then, in the quietness of the glade, with her face turned toward him, he leaned over and kissed her lips. They were sweet and innocent, but there was also a warmth and a passion in them as he put his arms around her and drew her close.

Leah surrendered herself to his embrace, and when he lifted his head, she said, "Be careful, David. I know you have to fight, but don't throw yourself away."

David looked at her tenderly. She was soft and yielding in his arms and yet she had the same strength in her face that first attracted him. She was a daring girl and yet she had a sweet femininity. David had never found this mixture in any other young woman. "I love you, Leah. No matter what happens, I want you to always remember that."

Leah reached up and laid her hand on his cheek. She was about to speak when voices approached and David stood up.

A squad of soldiers marched by the opening of the small

glade where they were sequestered, and David said, "We'll talk later."

"All right, David."

The two left the glade and spent an hour walking along the ramparts, David speaking of the men in the company and introducing her to Sam Watkins.

"This is a particular friend of mine, Miss Cleburne," he said, "Sam Watkins."

"Proud to know you, Ma'am. Won't you come and have dinner with us?"

Leah, liking the look of the cheerful young fellow, said, "Why, I'd be glad to."

"Right this way," Sam said. He led the two to where the rest of the squad were gathered and introduced Leah as "Lt. Rocklin's lady friend."

Leah was treated with respect, as well as astonishment. When the meal was set out, it turned out to be parched corn. "Is this all you've got to eat?" Leah exclaimed.

"Rations are a might shy right now," Sam admitted, "but I'll go out and liberate some if the Yankees give us a little breathing room."

"We've got a pig at home that's about half grown," Leah said abruptly. She turned to David and said, "Lieutenant, if you'll prevail upon Col. Bleeker to allow you to escort me home, I think you could bring back that porker."

"Do it, Lieutenant!" Sam said, "and let me go along. I'll dress that there hog out, and we'll have cracklin' bread and pig's feet."

David grinned. "You can have the feet," he said, "but some pork chops would go mighty good. I'll go ask the colonel for a pass."

Col. Bleeker was pleased to grant his request but added, "I'll expect some ribs. I'm mighty partial to barbecued ribs, Lieutenant."

"Yes sir. I'll see that you get them."

David and Leah made their way through the lines. The Rayborn place lay east of Chattanooga, sufficiently far from the Yankee lines so that there was little danger. When they arrived, Amelia and Claire greeted David with smiles. "I'm glad to see you, Lieutenant," Claire said, and David noticed there was something different about her.

Later, as Sam Watkins took over the butchering of the hog, David walked with Leah among the trees.

"There's so little time," Leah said as they paused under the shade of pecan trees that towered overhead. "It seems that's the way it's always been."

David looked out over the farm. "This reminds me a little of our place in Virginia." He ran his hand down the hair that hung freely down her back. "Maybe you'll see it after the war."

Leah wanted to say, "David, be careful," but she knew there was no way for an officer in the Confederate army to be careful. So she said aloud instead, "Have you had any more of those black spells, David?"

"Not a one."

"Maybe they've gone away," she said hopefully.

The thought had been in David's mind. "Maybe they have. Maybe when a man meets fear in its worst form, there's nothing else that can happen worse than that. I think I gave up when I decided to join and let the Yankees kill me."

Leah took his arm and said what she'd planned to say. "David, I—I think I love you. I don't know much about love, but I was all wrong to turn away from you as I did. Love shouldn't be like that."

David stared down at her, touched by her admission. "We're all wrong, I guess, from time to time, and maybe you're right. Love is forgiving as much as it is anything else." He touched her hair gently, then the two moved toward the house.

CHAPTER EIGHTEEN
Love Never Changes

After the battle of Chickamauga, the Federal general, Rosecrans, attempted to shift the blame of the loss to his subordinates. Nonetheless, Lincoln was well aware of Rosecrans's shortcoming. Lincoln did what he could to support Rosecrans; however, it was becoming clear to everyone that Rosecrans was unable to handle the situation. He was, Lincoln said, "Stunned and confused, like a duck hit on the head." The solution came with the decision to send Maj. Gen. Ulysses S. Grant to assume command. After a frustrating summer in Vicksburg, Grant had suffered a fall from a horse and his leg was swollen from the knee to the thigh.

Some suggested that Grant was drinking, but he was firmly supported by Gen. Sherman. Sherman had had mental problems at one time, and Grant had stood by him firmly. Now he said with a flash of wit, "Grant stood by me when I was crazy—so now I'll stand by him when he's drunk."

Chickamauga was not a clear-cut victory for either side, the Confederate capture of Union equipment being the only real gain. And so the Confederate command was also in turmoil. Braxton Bragg blamed Gen. Polk for the loss and relieved the general. He also sacked Gen. Thomas Hindman and in general tried to avoid all blame.

However, on October 4, a group of corp commanders, including Longstreet, D. H. Hill, Polk, and Simon Buckner, sent a formal petition to President Davis. They accused

215

Bragg of being incapable of command and unfit physically to lead the army.

Since Bragg was a personal friend of Jefferson Davis, the president interceded as best he could. When his efforts failed, he took a train to Bragg's headquarters outside Chattanooga and gave a speech, rebuking the soldiers for their poor opinion of Bragg. However, that night he presided over a council of war consisting of Bragg's staff. Davis begged the commanders to support Bragg, but in response Longstreet declared, "Our commander could be of greater service elsewhere."

Unfortunately, Jefferson Davis was perhaps the only man in the Confederate government who liked Bragg. In addition, he couldn't find anyone capable to replace Bragg. Therefore, when Davis departed a few days later, he left the unpopular Gen. Bragg in command. This pleased no one— possibly not even Bragg himself—and the entire army fell into a depression over the president's choice.

★ ★ ★

A knock at the door startled Leah, who was sitting in the parlor reading *Ivanhoe*. She'd buried herself in the romantic novel, wishing life itself were as romantic and idealistic as the world the writer had created. Rising to her feet, she called out, "I'll get it, Aunt Amelia . . ." and made her way to the front door. When she opened it, she exclaimed, "Why, Father—!"

Matthew swept his hat from his head and smiled at Leah. "I should have let you know I was coming," he said briefly, "but the mail to this part of the world seems to have broken down."

"Why, come in," Leah said, stepping back. "How did you get here?"

"By train. Some of the lines are still intact, even in this area—the Union lines, that is." Matthew was wearing light-brown trousers, a frock coat of darker brown, and a shirt of fine quality that was somewhat wilted. His brown hair had been pressed down by the soft felt hat he wore and, as he handed it to Leah, he asked, "Is your mother here?"

"No, she's gone over to a neighbor's. But I'll send Pax over to fetch her. Come into the kitchen. We've got some lemonade."

"That sounds good."

The two of them went to the kitchen, and after seating her father and giving him a glass of lemonade she went out the back door to where Pax was chopping wood in slow motion. "Pax, go down to Mrs. Jamison's. Tell Mother that Mr. Cleburne is here."

"Yes'm, I'll do that."

Moving back inside, Leah sat down and questioned her father about his journey. She didn't want to ask outright about his purpose, but she was intensely curious.

As Matthew talked quietly, Leah noticed he looked tired. There were lines about his eyes that she hadn't seen before. Finally he said, "I've come to try to get your mother to come back to New York. We can take your grandmother with us. This place is a powder keg, Leah. The battle could go right over this farm. It's just not safe."

"I don't think Grandmother can be moved," Leah said.

"Is she that bad?"

"I'm afraid so. Would you like to see her?"

"Yes, I would." Draining the rest of the lemonade from his glass, Matthew stood up, then followed Leah through the house to the bedroom. When he stepped inside, he found Martha Rayborn much changed, but he'd been prepared for this. The last time he'd seen her she'd been in good health. Now, however, her face was pasty and drawn and there wasn't an excess ounce of flesh on her body. However, her eyes still had a brightness and she whispered, "Matthew—," as he came across the room.

Taking her hand, he kissed it and held it as he sat down. "I'm sorry to find you so ill, Martha." Matthew had always liked his mother-in-law and she him.

The separation had hurt her, he knew, and she'd told him

once, "Claire is making a terrible mistake; she'll never find a man like you."

Matthew thought of this as he sat beside her, speaking quietly for fifteen minutes. She was interested in his life, and Matthew noticed that Leah had seated herself in a chair across the room and was listening. Finally Martha looked at him directly and asked, "How is it that you never sought a divorce? A man like you wants a wife and a family."

Leah studied her father's youthful-looking face. Now that her grandmother had asked the question she herself had wondered about, she leaned forward unconsciously and waited.

"I can't really answer that," Matthew said slowly. Then, realizing Martha Rayborn wanted an honest answer, he continued quietly, "I think love never changes."

His simple reply surprised Leah. She drew a sharp breath and her eyes flew to her grandmother, whose eyes met hers. *Why, that's not what I thought he'd say!* Again she remembered those few precious times she'd had with him as a child. Finally she heard her grandmother say, "You always had strong feelings, Matthew. I've always respected you for that. Still, a man needs people and you've had no one."

Matthew Cleburne shifted his weight uncomfortably. He hadn't spoken of these things to anyone. During the long separation, he'd struggled with loneliness. There had been many women anxious to share his time, for he was handsome, strong, virile, and had enough money to satisfy most. More than once he'd been tempted to throw himself into clandestine affairs, but he never had. Now, in the silent room, he said quietly, "A man's word is about all he has in this world, and when he breaks that he doesn't have much left. When a man gives his word, it's like he took water in his hands and held it there. If he opens his fingers and lets the water go to the ground, he needn't expect to gather it back again. I've done some things I'm not proud of in my life, but I like to think I'm a man who knows how to keep his word."

"You mean your marriage vows?" Martha whispered.

"Of course."

"Most men wouldn't have felt that way."

"Well, they must do as they see fit." Matthew once again moved his shoulders uncomfortably. "Now then, what can I get you to make you more comfortable, Martha?"

A slight smile tugged the corners of Martha Rayborn's thin lips. "I'll be very comfortable shortly, Matthew," she said, humor touching her fine eyes. "There have been times I've wondered about Christianity, about death, about judgment, but now that it's upon me, I find it most comforting to look back and remember that always, even with my doubts, I've been convinced of the truth of the Lord Jesus."

He held her hand gently and glanced over at Leah. "Your grandmother was responsible for leading me to the Lord, Leah, did you know that?"

"No, I didn't."

"I was fairly wild, I suppose, and some had given up on me, but you never did, did you, Martha?"

"I saw something in you the first time you came to our house that I admired and liked. I wish it—" Martha broke off her words, giving a slight gesture of despair. "Why did you come, Matthew? Just to see an old woman make her exit from this earth?"

"I came to take you back to New York, Martha. You'll be safe there and we can take better care of you. There are fine doctors and it would be a comfort to have you."

"That's like you, Son-in-law," Martha said. It was what she'd always called him, and Matthew was touched by hearing the old phrase. Then she shook her head. "But I'd never live to see New York. I wish you would take Leah and Claire. I'd feel better if they were safe."

"I won't leave," Leah insisted. She rose, came over and took her grandmother's free hand, and smiled down. "You're not getting rid of me that easy." Then she looked at her father. "I'll go down and start fixing something to eat. You and Grandmother visit." She left the room and found

219

Bessie, saying, "Bessie, I want us to fix a good meal for my father tonight."

"Yes'm. What you want?"

"His favorite food was always steak. Do we have any of that?"

"Yes'm. Paxton killed that yearling and we can have 'bout anything you want."

"Let's have T-bones then and potatoes and carrots if there's any left." She was still planning the meal when her mother walked in. "Mother," Leah said, "Father is with Grandmother."

"Did he say why he came?"

"Yes—he said he came to take us all back to New York."

Claire bit her lip. "She'd never stand the trip, I'm afraid."

"That's what she said. She said she wants you and me to go back to New York with Father."

"We can't do that."

"Of course not, but it was nice of him to come, wasn't it?"

"Yes." Claire hesitated. "Your father is always a thoughtful man in things like this. How long will he stay?"

"He hasn't said, but I'm fixing a good dinner tonight. Why don't you go and sit with him?"

"I'll let them have their visit. Your grandmother always thought the world of Matthew. From the very first time he came to the house, she liked him. But my father didn't care for him."

"Why not?" Leah was intensely curious. "Why didn't Grandfather like him?"

It was a question Claire had often asked herself, and now that she was faced with it, she spoke impulsively, "He was too strong a man, I think, and—he'd come to take me away."

"Well, it should have pleased him to give his daughter to a strong man," Leah said, astonished. "I don't understand."

Claire shook her head. "I didn't either for a long time. Perhaps I still don't." She walked out of the room and Leah followed her to the parlor. "I thought about it so often," she said quietly, her eyes troubled. "I fell so in love with Matthew. He was everything I wanted, everything I'd dreamed of as a young girl. I thought Father'd receive him with open arms. He always liked strong men and Matthew was that. But he didn't."

"Did he ever say why he didn't like him?"

"No, but he tried to persuade me not to marry him."

"I didn't know that."

"Oh yes, and Grandmother, for once in her life, stood up to him. They had an awful argument about it and I guess for once she won." Claire smoothed her dress over her knees and sat looking at the figures in the carpet. "I think now about those times and I see that Father was very possessive, most of all of me. I was his little girl and he didn't want to turn me loose."

Leah watched her mother's face quietly. "Do you think he was wrong?"

Startled, Claire looked up. She'd never once admitted that anything was wrong with her father, but now she said finally, "I think in this case he may have been." She would have said more, but at that moment Matthew walked in the door. Claire got to her feet at once and said nervously, "Hello, Matthew."

"Hello, Claire." There was a hiatus of silence, and feeling somehow out of place, Leah said, "I'll go help Bessie with the dinner."

When Leah left, Claire felt awkward and couldn't put into words what she was feeling. "I'm glad you've come, but you shouldn't have."

Matthew moved closer to her. "Claire," he said quietly, "I need to talk to you."

Surprised, Claire looked at him. "Why—certainly. Shall we sit here?"

"No, let's go outside for a walk. The air's cool out there."

"I'll get my cape." Claire put on a lightweight cotton cape and a bonnet, and the two left the house. As they walked along, the leaves that were falling from the trees rustled dryly at their feet. "I always liked the fall," Matthew said. "My favorite time of the year."

"I remember you couldn't wait until the hot summers were over and the coolness would come." She smiled as she looked up at him. "I always like spring best, but you like fall." They moved to the deserted road that led to the north. Far-off fires from the fireplaces of houses scored the sky, the breeze driving the smoke out of tight spirals into long skeins as they left the chimneys. Overhead a flight of red-winged blackbirds argued noisily in the crisp, invigorating air.

Finally they came to a bridge over a small creek and stopped to look down at the clear water. "Look at that!" Matthew said abruptly. "See him? That's a bass. I wouldn't mind catching one that size."

"Do you still fish sometimes? You always loved it so."

"I did for a while. It's not so easy in New York City. You have to go out of town. I miss the country. Remember how you used to go with me? You'd never fish though."

"I didn't like to bait the hook," Claire said, smiling. Then she asked quietly, "Do you still think of those days, Matthew?"

He turned to her at once. "I've never stopped thinking of them, Claire. That was the happiest time of my life. I think of it all the time, those days we had together."

There was a silence in which they occasionally met one another's eyes. Finally Matthew said, "Claire, let me take you back to New York."

"Mother would never stand the journey," Claire said simply.

He looked at her quickly. "If it weren't for that, would you come back?"

"I—oh, I can't say, Matthew. It's impossible anyway." She turned from him, the wind blowing her auburn hair about her face. She pushed it back under her bonnet, her heart too full to speak.

He put his hands on her shoulders and leaned down, his

cheek against her hair. He felt her stiffen but he whispered, "Claire, I still love you. I always have—I guess I always will."

Startled by his touch, Claire felt a sudden rush of emotion. As Matthew pulled her back to lean against him, she felt the strength of his body, felt his lips kissing her hair. A sudden thickness in her throat prevented her from speaking, and tears rose in her eyes. She was a woman who needed love, who needed a man's warmth and presence, and she knew she'd stripped this from herself. The years had been long and cold and lonely—and now, as he held her, his strong hands on her shoulders, she knew she had missed so much. For a moment, she wanted to turn to him, to throw her arms around him. She couldn't trace the exact moment it had happened, but somehow she had gradually come to understand that she'd made a terrible mistake in her life. But she was a proud woman and now, as she struggled with her feelings, she realized she couldn't give him what he was asking for. So, with large, wide eyes, she moved away and turned to face him. "I—I can't come back to you, but I want you to have all of the time you can with Leah." She dropped her head and bit her lip. "I've been unfair about Leah. I've robbed her of her time with a father and I ask you to forgive me, Matthew."

Matthew Cleburne knew her pride. It was keen and sharp—and sometimes too hard. But now he saw she was vulnerable in a way he'd never seen before. He said instantly, "Of course. I'd like that very much."

They stood there for a moment, Matthew wanting to say more. But he saw that Claire had drawn inward, and though there was a sadness he couldn't quite identify about her mood, he knew this wasn't the time to speak of it. "Come along," he said. "We can talk about some of the good things. Do you remember the time that . . . ?"

★ ★ ★

Late in October, the Army of the Tennessee prepared for the onslaughts that were coming. For weeks they'd watched

Grant's army build itself down below. Chattanooga, they knew from the spies who came almost freely back and forth, was bristling with soldiers from the Army of the Cumberland. Grant, Sherman, and Gen. Thomas were there, ready to launch the well-fed, well-clothed, and well-armed Union soldiers against the thin, ragged line of Confederates that lay rank along Lookout Mountain and Missionary Ridge.

David was standing at twilight one Monday, looking down at the city. It was almost invisible now except for the lights that twinkled through the falling darkness. He almost fancied he could hear the Union army as it hustled, pulling itself together for a massive strike against the mountains where their Confederate adversaries lay.

A sound caught David's attention and he turned to find Corey bearing a cup in his hand. "Coffee for you, Mr. David. 'Bout the last there is. You better enjoy it."

David took it gladly. "Did you get some for yourself, Corey?"

"Yes sah! The cook, he always eat good." Corey's white teeth flashed in the darkness as he stood there, looking down on the city with David. "Lots of them soldiers down there in them blue uniforms, ain't they, sah?"

"Yes, there are. Quite a few." David sipped the coffee, which was bitter but hot and welcome. "Corey, I've talked about this before, but I'd like it if you'd go on to Virginia."

"Ain't no use, Mr. David," Corey said quietly. "I belongs to you and I'll do anything you says—'cept leave you."

David again felt a warm surge of affection for this tall young man. He'd understood for some time that slavery was the basic flaw in Southern culture—a cancer eating away at civilization. He knew his father and the rest of his family felt the same way. But although he'd been around slaves all his life, he'd never understood what it meant to accept a black man as an equal until he'd met Corey. He knew it had something to do with the fact that Corey had seen his weakness and had accepted him in spite of it. Now he looked at Corey and asked, "Why do you insist on staying with me, Corey?"

"Because," Corey said, his voice slow and strong and rich, "you the first one ever treat me like a man, Mr. David. To ever'body else I was no more than a mule or dog—but not you. I ain't never gonna forget that, and I ain't never gonna leave you!"

"You'll be free sooner or later, Corey."

"Well, then you and me'll be partners—on a farm, maybe." Corey smiled at Rocklin. "Wouldn't that be sumpin'? I 'spect you and me'd be about the best farmers there was."

"I like farming."

"I knows you do. You talk about that farm, Gracefield, all the time. I'm anxious to see it, sah, but I ain't going back without you."

"One day, Corey, all your people will be free. It'll be a better world then," David finally said.

"It'll still be hard, Mr. David. No piece of paper's gonna make black folks and white folks love and trust each other."

"No, that's true, but you and I love and trust each other. So we know it can happen, don't we?"

Corey Jones looked at the man who owned him—at least on paper—and smiled. "Yes sah, I guess it do prove that."

225

PART FOUR
Chattanooga

CHAPTER NINETEEN
Two Women

The decision to send Gen. Ulysses S. Grant to assume command in Tennessee was quickly made, but not so easily implemented. Grant's rough fall from his horse caused him severe physical problems. His score of critics insisted his fall was the result of his being drunk. In any case, Grant spent fourteen days in bed, but on October 16 received orders to report to Louisville, Kentucky. He was also ordered to take his staff with him for immediate duties.

Grant was met in Indianapolis by none other than Edwin Stanton, the irascible secretary of war for the United States. Stanton had never met Grant, and when he moved into the railroad car he ignored the small, unimpressive man in the shabby uniform. He at once shook hands with Dr. Edward Kittoe, Grant's staff surgeon, saying, "How are you, Gen. Grant? I knew you at sight from your pictures."

A smile crossed Grant's face; he was accustomed to such things. When he identified himself, Stanton, in some confusion, gave Grant command of the armies and called upon him to make a decision. "Do you want to retain Gen. Rosecrans as commander of the Army of the Cumberland— or would you prefer Gen. George H. Thomas?"

Instantly Grant chose Thomas. He regarded the man as too slow, but a vast improvement over Rosecrans. The two men talked strategy for the rest of the day, but they were both shaken when the secretary received alarming news that

Rosecrans intended to abandon Chattanooga! Stanton at once commanded Grant that under no circumstances could the Union afford to lose that city.

Grant at once left for the Tennessee, stopping in Alabama, where he met Rosecrans, then proceeding to Chattanooga over a long Federal supply route. This trip showed Grant how difficult the problems he faced were, for the narrow and steep stone road was, in Grant's words, "strewn with the debris of broken wagons and the carcasses of thousands of starved mules and horses."

"If we don't find some way to supply our troops," Gen. Grant told his staff, "we may very well lose Chattanooga to the Confederates."

★ ★ ★

Brian Decatur had come earlier to Tennessee and now was informed that the first priority on the commanding general's list was to see that the supply line was open. The Confederates were solidly entrenched on Missionary Ridge and Lookout Mountain to the south of the city, and there seemed no hope of rooting them out. It was not the kind of war Decatur had envisioned, and he grew restive. Finally, in late October, he obtained permission from his colonel to be gone for a short leave.

"I don't know where you'll be going," Col. Smith said, grumbling. "There's nothing ahead of us but Rebels, and nothing behind us but mountains. But go on! Young men will find adventure in anything, I suppose."

Taking Col. Smith at his word, Decatur managed to liberate a thin horse well past his prime from the quartermaster. Following rather vague instructions in a letter he'd received from Leah, he left the city, moving to the west. Actually he had little trouble finding the Rayborn house. He stopped at two farmhouses, but the inhabitants slammed the door in his face. However, at the third house he found an elderly woman who had, he discovered, been born in Michigan and was staunchly Union despite the disapproval of her neighbors. "Who you looking for?" she demanded, cupping her hand over her ear. Then, without waiting for an answer, she said, "When's the Union army going to run those Rebels off those ridges?"

Brian grinned at the old woman's fiery spirit. "I was talking with Gen. Grant about that this morning, Auntie," he said. "I figure it won't be long now." Then, leaning forward, he continued, "Do you know of a family named Rayborn?"

"Rayborn—Rayborn?" The old woman stared at him with eyes bright as a crow's. "Why, I know four Rayborns in this valley. Been here most of my life," she said, nodding firmly. "Which Rayborns would you be wanting?"

"Mrs. Martha Rayborn—her husband's name was Thaddeus Rayborn."

"Why, everybody knows Thad Rayborn's place. I'm surprised you had to stop and ask."

"I'm a stranger here, Auntie. Which way is it?"

The old woman gave him complete instructions and would have welcomed more talk about the Union invasion. Decatur stood talking with her for a time, then finally made his apologies and galloped away. She cried out in a surprisingly strong voice, "Get them Rebels out of Tennessee! Tell Mr. Lincoln we're ready to see the end of this thing!"

The incident had amused Decatur, and he was happy at his luck. He followed the old woman's instructions and two hours later pulled his weary horse up in front of a large two-storied frame house set in the midst of a grove of pecan trees. He was somewhat apprehensive for, naturally, Rebel sympathies were strong in this part of the world. Sharpshooters and even plain citizens had picked off more than one lonely Union officer who wandered from the city. However, he tied the horse to the fence, walked up to the front porch, and was delighted when Leah herself stepped out of the house. "Why, Brian!" she said with a smile. "I never expected to see you here."

Swooping off his hat, Decatur ran up the steps. He

reached out and took the hand she offered and kissed it. "Why, I told you I was a stubborn fellow, Leah!" All the weariness from the tedious days of siege faded from him, and he pulled her toward him, intending to kiss her.

Leah, however, put her hand on his chest. "Now," she said, "come inside. Mother and Amelia will be glad to see you."

Decatur wanted to say, "I didn't come to see your relatives . . . ," but had more judgment than that. He entered the house and was quickly surrounded by the three women. Amelia and Claire seemed glad enough to see him, and as they sat down for a while in the parlor, he accepted tea and a slice of cake that Leah had made.

"Nothing this good to eat in Chattanooga." He grinned, shoving a huge chunk of the cake in his mouth. Washing it down with a cup of tea, he added, "We're mighty hungry back there."

"What's going to happen, Brian?" Leah asked. Then she instantly added, "But I suppose you can't tell us that since we're the enemy."

"Well, I don't think I'd be shot for mentioning that things are picking up. Everybody in this area knows that Gen. Grant's come and new forces are moving into Chattanooga. Sooner or later there'll be a battle."

Claire leaned forward, her eyes curious. "Have you ever met Gen. Grant?"

"Of course. I've been in on several staff meetings," Decatur said. "I'm just a lowly lieutenant, but I'm Col. Smith's aide. I was there waiting on him mostly. Naturally I wouldn't dare to open my mouth in that sort of company."

"What's the general like, Brian?" Amelia asked. "We've heard so many things about him."

"He's not much to look at," Decatur admitted. "Small and almost insignificant. When he first got here, he wore a private's uniform with only his stars on his shoulders to show that he was a general. Take those stars off and you'd walk right by him—never even notice him. But evidently Lincoln

and Stanton think a lot of him. Made him overall com-
mander of the Union armies."

The talk went on for some time about the war, but there
was a stiffness to it all. Finally Leah said, "Come along and
I'll show you around the farm. We've got a litter of pigs. I'm
sure you're interested in that," she said, smiling slyly.

Brian rose at once. "Nothing I like better than looking at
a litter of new pigs! If you ladies will excuse us . . ."

The two left the house, and Brian followed Leah around
to the back to a pigpen that held nine squealing pigs that
sounded the alarm as they came close.

Brian leaned on the fence, looking at them with interest,
then turned his eyes on her. Leah was watching him curi-
ously. She found his gaze disconcerting, partly because of his
one brown eye and one blue eye, but even more by his
expression that she couldn't quite identify. "I didn't really
come down to look at pigs. Are you a farm girl, Leah?"

"Not really. We spent some time here at my grand-
mother's when I was younger and I loved it. But I'm always
glad to get back to the city."

This answer pleased Decatur and he nodded. "I'm glad
about that. I love you, but I don't think I'd make much of
a farmhand."

"You don't love me, Brian."

Leah was practical in many ways and she'd thought a great
deal about Brian's proposal. Now looking at him as he
leaned negligently against the fence, she remarked quietly,
"I don't think a marriage between a Yankee and a Rebel will
ever work."

Decatur examined her thoughtfully. He looked up in the
sky, where a red-tailed hawk was circling silently, then gazed
back at her. "You may be right about that. But when this war
is over we can't be Rebel and Yankee anymore. We'll have to
be one people again."

"After all that's happened?" Leah shook her head. "Al-
most every family I know in the South has lost sons or
brothers or sweethearts, and so many women are without

husbands. We've been stripped of the finest of our men. How could the women of the South forget that—or the men either, for that matter?"

"There are lots of empty places at tables in the North, too, Leah. I believe in this country." Decatur was totally serious now. "We've been torn in two by this terrible war. I feel it had to come because slavery isn't right. That may not have been the only quarrel between the North and the South, but it's the issue at the heart of this war. But when that's gone, after a time we'll have to learn to forgive each other."

"I don't know if that's possible, Brian." Leah thought of her own mother, who had harbored unforgiveness for her father as long as she could remember. Her mother was a good woman, Leah knew, and if she couldn't forgive one she'd loved, how could the South and the North become one people again?

The pigs crowded against the fence, squealing and grunting. Leah picked up an ear of corn and held it down, watching as they fought to get at it. "I sometimes bring the leftovers down here," she said, more to take her mind off the way the conversation was going than anything else. Looking down at the pigs, she said, "I doubt they'd love me so much if they knew what we had planned for them. They'll all end up as pork chops one day not too far off."

They talked for a time, then she took him on a quick tour of the farm. When they returned to the house, Claire asked, "Can you stay for the night, Brian?"

"As a matter of fact, my pass *is* overnight—but I don't want to intrude."

"Nonsense!" Claire said briskly. "We'll be happy to have you. Come along, I'll show you to your room."

That night Decatur had a fine time. He learned that Amelia had a fine wit and enjoyed teasing him. However, Claire Cleburne's behavior puzzled him. When he and Leah were alone, he asked, "Is your mother depressed about your grandmother?"

"Well—yes, she is. She's very fond of Grandmother."

Then Leah hesitated. "My father was here for a visit. He wanted us to go back to New York with him."

"I think you should have gone, but I suppose you couldn't leave your grandmother."

"No, that would be impossible."

"Your parents . . . they've been separated for a long time, you said. Is there any chance they'll ever be reconciled?"

"I don't think so."

Her answer was so bleak that Decatur didn't pursue it. "It's a bad situation," he said. "Your mother's such a lovely woman. I haven't met your father. What's he like?"

The question troubled Leah. "I haven't been around him very much because Mother took me away when they separated. But I do remember things about him that I like very much." She went on for some time speaking of her father, and Decatur saw the longing in her eyes. *She's been robbed of part of her life. Everyone should have a good home to grow up in, and Leah's missed out on all that. . . .* he thought sadly.

Even as the two were speaking downstairs, Claire, who had gone to sit beside her mother, was thinking of her past life with Matthew. She'd given her mother some painkiller, but it hadn't taken effect yet. Suddenly her mother asked, "Claire, did you talk to Matthew while he was here?"

Claire looked at her mother with surprise, wondering if she was falling under the drug's power. "Of course I talked to him, Mother."

"No, I don't mean that. I mean, did you talk to him about . . . about you and him?"

Instantly Claire realized her mother was not wandering in her mind. The eyes sunken back in the sick woman's head were clear enough, and she seemed to be resting easier. Very uncomfortable beneath her mother's steady gaze, Claire finally said, "There's nothing to talk about, really."

The room was almost silent, except for the rhythmic ticking of the Dutch clock that had been placed on the mantle over the fireplace so Martha could know the time without asking. The clock made a rhythmic ticking sound, sharp and clear, as it broke the silence.

"Mother," Claire said suddenly, "I've been thinking about what you said about Father."

Martha Rayborn's lips tightened, as if she'd been expecting this. "I should have talked to you long before. I made a mistake, Claire, about your father and about you."

"A mistake? What kind of a mistake?"

"I thought it would be unsuitable to tell you about your father when you were a child. And then after you grew up to be a young woman, somehow it was too late," she replied, her face shaded with a pain that came from deep within.

Claire clasped the frail hand and said quietly, "I'm *glad* you told me, Mother. I made a mistake about Father, too, but it's too late to go back and fix things."

"It's not too late for you to fix your marriage."

"I could never do that!"

"Most of your trouble with Matthew stemmed from your love for your father. I saw it. I tried to talk to you more than once, but I couldn't do it without destroying your father's reputation in your sight, and I didn't want to do that." Bitterly she added in a whisper, "I wish I had now. You're a woman made for love, Claire."

Soon afterward Martha dropped off to sleep. Claire sat there, her face highlighted by the amber light of the table lamp, and studied her mother's face. She thought back over the years since she'd left Matthew and realized there had always been something missing from her life. Now she felt she knew what it was, but the past couldn't be reclaimed.

Finally, with a heavy heart, she rose and left Martha. As she went to her own room, she was aware that Leah and Brian Decatur were talking in the parlor. Her daughter's voice brought a fresh pain to her and she breathed an urgent prayer: *Oh, God, don't let her marry the wrong man. Give her a good home. Don't let her make the mistake I've made!*

CHAPTER TWENTY
A Startling Discovery

For the most part life went on with great difficulty for the Confederates perched on Missionary Ridge and Lookout Mountain. The supply lines were thin and usually broken. In a book of recollections, Sam Watkins wrote about that time:

> In all the history of the war I cannot remember of more privations and hardships than we went through at Missionary Ridge. When in the very acme of our privations and hunger, when the army was most dissatisfied and unhappy, we were ordered into line of battle to be reviewed by the Honorable Jefferson Davis. When he passed by us with his great retinue of staff officers at full gallop the cries went up from the troops, "Send us something to eat, Massah Jeff. Give us something to eat, Massah Jeff. I'm hungry! I'm hungry!"

David Rocklin spent most of his time learning how to be an officer. Much to his surprise, he learned more from Pvt. Sam Watkins than the higher-ranking officers. The wiry young man was full of native wisdom. He was "country smart," as they called such men back in Virginia.

David quickly discovered there was considerable communication between the two armies. He was out once checking on a detail, talking quietly with Sgt. John Tucker and Sam Watkins, when the three heard the pickets calling from across the river. Sam began hollering at the top of his voice across the river, which was about three hundred yards wide at this point. Sam said, "Look, Lieutenant, there's an island out there!"

About that time a Yankee voice cried out, "Oh, Johnny! Johnny! Meet me halfway in the river on the island."

Sgt. Tucker said at once, "Is it all right if I go, Lieutenant?"

"Go ahead, Sergeant. Maybe you can find out something about our friends over there."

Tucker immediately undressed, wearing only his underwear and a hat in which he carried tobacco, the Chattanooga *Rebel,* and some other Southern newspapers. He swam across to the island and stayed for quite a while. When he got back David said, "What did you find out?"

"Well, we swapped a few lies and some tobacco for some coffee. You know what, Lieutenant? That wasn't no private out there—that was Gen. Wilder his own self!"

David stared at him in disbelief. "That can't be right!" Gen. Wilder commanded the Federal cavalry and was known as the best at his job in the whole Union army. "A general wouldn't be out on an island talking to a Rebel."

"Oh, it was him all right," Tucker insisted, his head bobbing up and down. "I seen his picture in the Chattanooga paper. And besides that, he had an aide with him. The general wasn't wearing no uniform, but his aide whispered something and he called him Gen. Wilder. That was him all right!"

David laughed aloud. "We should have captured him— but I guess that wouldn't have been fair, seeing as how he'd just come to swap for tobacco."

Although David wasn't aware of it, Gen. Grant himself had become involved in a similar action. He'd ridden down to water his horse one day when a Federal picket had called out, "Turn out the guard for the commanding general." Grant said, "Never mind the guard," and the men went back to their tents. At the same time he heard from across the river, "Turn out the guard for the commanding general!" and Grant thought they mentioned his name. Later he wrote, "Their line at a moment fronted to the north facing me and gave me a salute which I relished."

David had one brush with the high and the mighty. He was very low down on the chain of command—as officers were counted he was the lowest of the low, being a mere second lieutenant and a brevet at that—but he was witness to a scene that he was never to forget. It concerned Gen. Nathan Bedford Forrest, probably the best cavalry commander on either side of the Civil War.

Lt. Rupert Allen had become interested in Rocklin, and the two had become friends. He called him one day saying, "Come along if you want to see an explosion."

"What's going on, Rupert?" David asked curiously.

"Bragg's decided to send Joe Wheeler to attack the Yanks, and he's commanded Gen. Nathan Bedford Forrest to turn over his entire command to Wheeler, except for a single regiment and one battery."

David whistled and lifted his eyebrows. "From what I've heard about Gen. Forrest, he's not likely to take that sitting down."

"Not him! He's coming over, we've heard. Come on, let's just mosey over to Gen. Bragg's headquarters. Maybe we'll get to see some of the fireworks."

The two men made their way to Bragg's headquarters, where they made themselves as unobtrusive as possible. They hadn't been there long when Gen. Forrest, accompanied by Dr. J. B. Cowan, his chief surgeon, rode into camp. Forrest was a tall, strong man with handsome features and a well-cared-for beard. There was a power that emanated from him, and it was known that he'd killed more men personally than any staff officer on either side of the forces of the Civil War. David tried to make himself invisible, as Bragg, looking sickly as he always did, stepped out of his tent. There was fear in his eyes as well as he met Forrest.

Bragg put his hand out, but Forrest ignored it. "I'm not

here to pass civilities or compliments with you, but on other business," he said brusquely. He drew himself up to his full height and stared down at the commanding general. There was a harsh ring in his voice as he said, "You commenced your cowardly and contemptible persecution of me soon after the Battle of Shiloh, and you've kept it up ever since. You did it because I reported to Richmond the facts, which you reported to be lies." Forrest spoke loudly, not caring who heard. His voice carried over the clearing so that Bragg's entire staff of officers, as well as many of the enlisted men, heard his voice clearly. He used such epithets as *scoundrel* and *coward* and finally shouted, "You may as well not issue any more orders to me, for I will not obey them." Then he hunched his shoulders, looking absolutely deadly. His piercing eyes fastened on Gen. Braxton Bragg. "If you ever try again to interfere with me or cross my path it will be at the peril of your life."

There was a silence in the glade as Forrest waited for the general to speak. Every officer there, David included, expected Bragg to take up the challenge, but he didn't. He sputtered, growing pale, and finally said, "Now, now, Gen. Forrest, let's not lose our heads."

Forrest stared at the man with disgust, turned away without a word, and mounted his horse. He and his companions rode away at a dead run and Braxton Bragg ducked into his tent.

As Allen and David made their way back to their own campsite David said, "And *that's* the man who's supposed to lead us while we whip the Yankees? He's not much, is he?"

"Nobody can explain Braxton Bragg," Rupert said, shrugging. "I don't think there's a man in the army who likes him—except Jefferson Davis." A dark shadow crossed his face and he shook his head in disgust. "Nobody can explain that either. Of all the men Davis might admire, such as Gen. Forrest, he has to form a friendship with a weakling like Bragg."

David later learned the outcome of Forrest's challenge.

Gen. Forrest took his complaints straight to the president. Jefferson Davis, instead of punishing him, gave him an independent command in western Tennessee far from Bragg.

★ ★ ★

Despite David's feverish activities to learn the rudiments of military procedure, his own problem was never far out of his mind. He spoke of it to no one except once to Corey. Late one evening Corey was preparing a meager meal out of what could be scraped together. David was slumped on a nearby log reading a book on tactics.

"What you readin', Mr. David?"

"How to be an officer and fight a war." David looked up and gave the book a disgusted slap with his free hand. "It's all about how to march men across fields, make them all turn together—forward march, about face, oblique right." He glanced down at the steep drop-off of the mountain and smiled at the foolishness of his words. "I'd like to see someone march men right up that mountain, or down it either for that matter!" He went back to the book as Corey came over and sat down on a cracker box across from him. He studied the young man's face carefully. David had become the single most important thing in Corey's life. He'd given David a devotion that had been withheld from other men, and he knew that it was returned. He waited quietly, then finally said what had been on his mind for some time.

"You ain't had no spells lately, Mr. David."

Looking up quickly, David saw Corey's eyes fixed on him steadily. "No, I haven't," David said briefly.

"I think that's a good thing. Maybe your troubles be over."

"The doctor said it wasn't. He said it'd come back."

"Well, doctors don't know ever'thing."

David didn't answer. He got up and walked away, leaving Corey to look after him with a strange expression in his eyes. "You sho' is in a mess, Mr. David," he commented sadly, then went back to the meal he was cooking.

None of David's unit knew his background. Only Leah, her mother, and Amelia knew of his cowardice back in Vicksburg—and only Leah and Corey knew why he had joined the army in desperation, hoping for death.

He walked for a long time, then finally went back to his tent and pulled out an encouraging letter he'd received from Bernard Dixon a few days earlier:

> Dave, there's a medical officer, Maj. Tom Dillard, who's a friend of mine. He did a lot of work with people before the war who had mental problems. He resigned to serve in the army. He's got a lot of sense— knows a lot about such problems. Why don't you see if you can find him? Maybe he'd help.

David put the letter back in the box where he kept his personal effects and tried to analyze what was happening to him. The likelihood that Maj. Dillard was anywhere close by was small indeed. Still . . . At last he sighed deeply and murmured, "It won't hurt to try."

Surprisingly, finding the physician wasn't difficult. David went to Rupert, who said, "I never heard of the doctor, but our own medical officer knows them all. I'll find out for you." He disappeared and came back shortly, saying, "Maj. Dillard is serving with Joe Wheeler's cavalry. They're camped out beyond Missionary Ridge right now, but Wheeler's leaving to go on a raid. He'll probably take the doctor with him, so you'd better get over if you want to see him." He gave David a sharp look, asking, "Feeling poorly?"

"No, I wanted to make an inquiry, something about a friend," David said quickly.

Fortunately there was little to occupy him that day. He made his way behind the lines and found out where Wheeler's cavalry was stationed. He saw great activity going on and discovered without much difficulty that the cavalry was going to be sent to attack the Federal supply line.

"Can you tell me where I can find Maj. Dillard?"

The tall private he had stopped nodded. "Yes sir, he's right down over that way behind the horse pen. I seen him not thirty minutes ago."

"Thank you, Private." David made his way past the milling horses, noting that they all looked lean and hungry. The cavalrymen themselves, for the most part, were undersized. Most of them had only parts of regular uniforms, but there was pride and a cocky spirit about them. Joe Wheeler was one of the Confederacy's best cavalry commanders, known for his aggressiveness and innovation in combat. Finding a line of tents, David asked a lieutenant, "Is Maj. Dillard about, Lieutenant?"

"There he is, right over there."

David looked up to see a powerful man with a full black beard smoking a long cigar. He advanced and saluted saying, "Maj. Dillard?"

"Yes, what is it, Lieutenant?"

Now that he was here David felt insecure. "Sir—" He hesitated, wondering how to put it and knew he was making a poor show of it. "You're probably busy. I'll come back later."

"Wait a minute, Lieutenant." Dillard took the cigar from his lips and stood there studying the tall man before him. "Is it a private matter?"

"Yes sir, it is."

"Come along. I've got some time on my hands just now." Maj. Dillard turned and led the way to one of the tents, stepped inside, and waved to one of the two camp chairs. "Have a seat. What's your name?"

"David Rocklin, First Tennessee up on the Ridge. I know you're busy. This is a very personal matter." He took a deep breath and said, "Sir, I've been losing my mind. I don't know any other way to put it."

Dillard leaned back and puffed on the cigar, sending purplish smoke rising to the top of the tent. He had large hands, more like the hands of a blacksmith than a physician, but there was a keenness in his dark blue eyes that revealed a great intelligence and discernment. "Tell me about it if you can."

David halted at the words *if you can*. "Why, I think I can, sir."

"Not many can who are going mad. Most of the time they want to cover it up. What makes you think you're losing your mind?"

David replied, "It goes back to Vicksburg. I was in the army there and I ran away. . . ."

The physician listened carefully as David spoke, his eyes never leaving the young man's face. Finally when he'd heard it all he said, "Have you had any nightmares lately?"

"No sir."

"What about blacking out? Have you done that?"

"Why, no sir. It's been a few weeks, but—"

"Have you ever told anybody about this? About your running away, about your fear of disgracing your family— the things you've just told me?"

"Yes sir, after I ran away and I felt pretty much alone. But I have a servant who's with me. He's very faithful, stayed with me when most would have left. Matter of fact, he saw me through those black spells. I told him what I intended to do, join the army and get killed and be done with all of it."

"Tell anybody else, Lieutenant?"

David dropped his head and couldn't answer for a moment. "Yes sir," he said finally, lifting his eyes. "A young lady I'm very fond of."

"I see. Tell me about her."

"About her, Major?"

"Yes, about her. Why'd you tell her?"

David couldn't speak for a moment, then he looked the physician firmly in the eyes. "Because I love her. I'd failed her, and I wanted her to know that she was right to have nothing to do with a coward like me."

Maj. Dillard sat so still he might have been carved out of stone. The quietness filled the tent and mounted, although outside men were dashing about, noisily getting ready to leave. Finally Maj. Dillard said, "You know why many people lose their minds, as you put it, Lieutenant?"

"No sir. I don't know much about things like this. We never had any of it in our family."

"They lose their minds because they bottle everything up. Finally it doesn't have any outlet and the mind just blanks out. You were very ashamed of running away, weren't you?"

"Of course I was, sir! Who wouldn't be?"

"You'd be surprised how many men wouldn't be," Dillard said dryly. "But you're of a different sort. From what you tell me your family has an honorable tradition, men of courage and honor."

"Yes sir, that's right."

"That would make it all the worse for you. You couldn't face being the one coward in your family, so that's why you started blacking out. You didn't like this world, in other words, so you just went into one of your own where there wasn't any shame, because there was nothing there. . . ." Dillard went on explaining the reasons for David's blackouts. His voice was low, but his eyes were steady and they pierced David constantly. "I've studied this for years, Lt. Rocklin, and as best as I can tell you, it's a very simple matter. All of us do things we're ashamed of. When we do, there are only two things to do with them: We either bury them or else we confess them. If we bury them, they begin to stink just like a dead body. Later they'll fill the whole house, the whole world, the whole mind. And that's when we can't stand it, Lieutenant—that's when we lose our minds."

"And what's the other way?" David asked, although he felt he knew.

"Why, I think you've already done it. If we confess what we've done, just *say* the thing, why, we're rid of it. It may be hard to take the consequences from those around us, and it's hard to confess that we've been wrong." The major paused for a moment. "There's a lot of this in the Bible. Are you a Christian, Mr. Rocklin?"

"Yes sir, I am."

"Then you know what the Scripture teaches. If we confess our sins he is faithful and just to forgive us our sins. The Bible also says that he who covereth his sins shall not prosper." He leaned back and puffed again on the cigar. "I've thought about that a lot—covering up our sins. God knew what he was talking about when he said that." Maj. Dillard smiled suddenly. "But he always does, doesn't he?"

"Yes sir, I believe so." David was stunned by what he was hearing. Hope had begun to rise in him. "Are you telling me, Maj. Dillard, that I'm cured?"

"I think you have the answer to that. You were afraid of bayonets, but who wouldn't be? The bayonets weren't your problem. Oh, they caused you to run away, but the bravest men run away when situations are just right. As for your being cured, I think you began the process when you confessed what was going on inside you to your manservant, then to the young woman, and now to me. There's only one more step, and I believe you'll be completely recovered."

"Yes? And that step is . . . ?"

"I think you need to tell your family all of this."

David seemed to shrivel. "I'd hate to do that." When the major didn't answer, he grinned suddenly. "But I've known all the time that I'd have to."

"Now, there's just one more thing," the major said. "I just recognized you. You're 'Candy' Rocklin, aren't you?"

"That's just a foolish name that got attached to me."

"Yes, and the word is you're fond of leading charges straight into the center of the hornet's nest. Everyone says you're like a man trying to get killed—and they're right. But that's got to stop, Lt. Rocklin!"

David suddenly blinked. A thought occurred to him, a rather appalling thought, which he spoke at once: "I was anxious to die before, because I was losing my mind, but now that I'm not will I run away again—dodge the fight?"

"That's what I want you to face up to." The heavy officer leaned forward, the cigar between his teeth. He puffed on it for a moment, then removed it. "You're back where you were at Richmond. You're facing battle, you're afraid to die, and it may be you'll face some more bayonets. Whatever it is, your courage will be tested. You had an automatic out before—just get killed and you wouldn't have to worry about anything. But you can't lean on that anymore, can you?"

David shook his head slowly. "No sir, I can't." He thought again about the bayonets that had come at him and had driven him to flight and wondered, *Can I stand up to that again?* Aloud he said, "Thank you, Major, for helping me. But I guess no one can help me when the battle starts."

"I'm glad you see that, Lieutenant," Dillard replied. "It's one thing to talk about courage and theorize about it. I think a wonderful thing's happened to you; you've been given another chance. But when the firing starts it'll be whatever's within you that'll keep you in place with the rest of your men."

David rose, saying, "I've got to get back to my unit, Maj. Dillard."

Dillard rose with him and shook his hand. "Write to your parents, my boy, and your brothers. Tell them how you feel, what's in your heart." There was an urgency in his grip and in his eyes. "Don't put it off. Word has it that we're going to be attacked. Grant won't wait long."

"Yes sir. That's what everyone says. Thank you again, sir." He turned and left the tent, then made his way back through the lines until he got to his own unit. Corey was feeding the men, so David sat down, taking his plate of parched corn and a small piece of meat. When he didn't join in the conversation around the campfire, Corey noticed instantly. Moving over to David, he whispered, "You all right, Mr. David?"

David saw Corey's concerned expression. "Yes, Corey, I think I am—and I think you ought to hear what the doctor said." He explained the essence of the doctor's words and ended by saying, "So you see, I'm not going to lose my mind, and there's no need of getting killed on purpose."

"You see! I done told you that, Mr. David!" Corey exclaimed with delight. "We're gonna make it all right, jus' fine!"

David smiled. "All we have to do is stand up to about a million Yankees."

"You can do whatever you has to do. You got yo' mind, and we're gonna see great things, you and me." Corey's face was wreathed in smiles. He half laughed and said, "You know what, Mr. David? I almos' put my arm around you and gave you a hug just like you was black just like me. Too bad you white or I'd a'done it."

Instantly David moved over and put his arm around Corey's shoulders. He felt the muscles tighten, for no white man had ever touched Corey—except to hurt him. "Someday, Corey, you'll be able to do that without any fear. In the meantime, I guess I'll have to tell you, you're a mighty good friend."

Corey dropped his eyes. The warmth of his owner's hand and arm burned into his shoulder. When he looked up there were tears in his eyes. "You take good care of yourself, Mr. David. I can't afford to lose you!"

CHAPTER TWENTY-ONE
Fall of an Idol

As October passed and November brought colder weather, the siege wore on in Chattanooga. It became almost impossible to feed the mules. Half-starved, the poor beasts chewed on anything that was vaguely edible—trees, bushes, fences—anything they could reach. During that period over ten thousand draft animals died.

Those trapped in Chattanooga were scarcely better off. Men stole corn from the horses or hunted for it on the ground. W. F. G. Shanks of the New York *Herald* reported, "I have often seen hundreds of soldiers following behind the wagon trains which had just arrived picking out of the mud the crumbs of bread, coffee, and rice which were wasted from the boxes and sacks by the rattling of the wagons over the stones."

But if the army suffered greatly, the population suffered even more. They had no one to help them, and they lived in squalor in what had once been a prosperous town. The thirty-five thousand army men were jammed together in an area of about one square mile. The civilians, their houses having been demolished for the sake of firewood, were crowded together with the army. "Their shacks," Shanks reported, "surpassed in filth, number of occupants and general destitution, the worst tenements in New York City."

The Confederate army suffered just as badly, as did their counterparts living in Chattanooga. Capt. Fitzgerald Ross, an Austrian army officer and visitor to Bragg's camp, wrote, "The army is in a bad way. Insufficiently sheltered and continually drenched with rain, the men are seldom able to dry their clothes and a great deal of sickness is the natural consequence."

One of Longstreet's officers observed sourly, "There is a tradition among these flats that there has been a time in the past when it wasn't raining."

As winter approached, both sides were aware that a conflict was building. There was no turning back for either side. The Confederates couldn't afford to lose the area around Chattanooga, and the Union army couldn't afford to let them keep it. Thus, as the skies overhead darkened with the oncoming winter, darkness also fell upon the spirits of the men of both armies.

★ ★ ★

The civilians on the farms outside of Chattanooga didn't suffer as greatly as those in the city itself. The harvest had been good. Since both armies were guilty of allowing their men to steal from civilians, most farmers grew wary and learned to hide their livestock and keep their smoked food and preserves under careful guard.

Pax and Bessie had taken over that particular task, and together they formed a formidable pair. Pax slept lightly and more than once had let off his shotgun when stirrings in the brush around the house told of pilferers. It was a game that delighted Pax, and he told Leah, "Miss Leah, I'm just as good as an army around here, ain't I now?"

"Would you really shoot someone stealing our pigs, Pax?" Leah asked with a smile.

"Why sholey I would! The Bible say so, don't it?"

"That you ought to kill anyone stealing pigs? I don't remember that particular verse."

"Well, I don't remember it either, but if it ain't in there it *ought* to be!" Pax, carrying the shotgun proudly, said adamantly, "I don't care whether they is Union or Confederate, they gonna leave our pigs and our chickens alone or I'll fill their legs so full of buckshot they won't be able to walk!"

Amused, Leah went into the house and said, "Amelia, I think Pax has found his true calling. I'm afraid he's going to hurt someone though."

"I think he's just loaded with bird shot," Amelia said placidly, knitting as usual. She looked up to study her niece's face. "Claire tells me that Martha had a bad night."

"I know. I think Mother was up with her all night, Aunt Amelia. I'll go up and give her a rest." She left the parlor and mounted the stairs to the second floor, where her mother was sitting beside the sick woman. Going over to stand beside Claire, she put her hand on her shoulder and said, "Mother, you go rest awhile. I'll sit with Grandmother."

"I'm not really tired."

"You need the rest. Go on, don't argue."

Claire got up, stretched, and looked down at her mother, who was breathing shallowly, obviously in a fitful sleep. "She gets weaker every day, doesn't she?"

"I'm afraid so, Mother."

"There's only one end to that." Pain touched Claire's eyes and she left the room without speaking again. Leah sat down, picked up the Bible that lay on the table, and began reading it. She had spent many hours reading this book to her grandmother, who could no longer hold the book nor see clearly enough to read it. Her grandmother's favorite had been the Gospels, and Leah had been surprised at how much she herself had learned simply by reading for hour after hour. She opened it now and began reading in the book of John. After a few minutes she heard her name called. Looking up quickly she saw that her grandmother was awake and struggling to move. Quickly putting the Bible down, Leah stood and said, "What is it, Grandmother?"

"Can't . . . breathe." Martha's face was ashen and Leah was alarmed. "Let me help you sit up," Leah said, knowing this posture often helped. She leaned over and pulled her grandmother into a sitting position, putting the pillows

251

behind her. She was relieved to see some color come back into the thin face. "Thank the Lord! That frightens me so when you do that."

Martha was breathing rapidly. She turned now and said, "I'm such a bother, Leah."

"You're no such thing!"

"I always hated to be a burden on anyone, and now that's all I am."

Leah leaned over, fluffed her pillows up a little more, then kissed her on the cheek. Sitting down, she said, "You're not a burden. I'll read to you some more."

She opened the book to the Gospels but her grandmother said, "Read in Revelation, the last chapters."

"In Revelation? All right, Grandmother." Leah found the last book in the Bible and at her grandmother's instruction began reading. She herself had never found this part of the Scripture a favorite, but when she finished, her grandmother said, "That's a marvelous chapter, isn't it? I've always loved it."

"I never read much in Revelation," Leah said quietly.

"It's always been one of my favorites. Life down here's been so tiresome sometimes. It changes so much and usually not for the best." Her eyes half closed. "I've had a good life but some of it has been hard. When I read about that scene in heaven, it makes me yearn to be there."

Leah was somewhat disturbed. "You're going to be with us a long time yet, Grandmother."

Martha turned her head and smiled. "I should have taught you better than that, Leah, to face up to the truth. I won't live long and I wouldn't want to. I'm ready to go—anxious really." She looked at her granddaughter with a mildness in her fine eyes. "You can't understand that now because you're young and strong, but the day will come when you'll feel like someone on a long, hard journey. The closer you get to the end of it, the closer you'll be to what's most precious. To me, the most precious thing has been the

Lord Jesus. Soon I'll be seeing him. How could earth itself or anything in it compare with that?"

"That's beautiful, Grandmother," Leah whispered. She reached out and took the thin hand and said, "You love the Lord, don't you? You always talk so much about Jesus. My father always saw that in you. You helped him become a Christian."

"Your father was ready to become a Christian. He was hungry for the things of God. I never saw anyone hungrier."

Leah hesitated. "I haven't treated him fairly, Grandmother. I should have been kinder to him."

"Yes, you should, and so should we all. We've all failed Matthew, but it's not too late. He's a young man and has a long time to live if the Lord is willing. Do you want him back as your father?"

"Why—it's too late for that!"

"Don't say that." Martha's lips grew stern. "It's never too late for God." Martha plucked at the yellow, red, and blue-checkered quilt with her fingers, then looked up at Leah. "I made this quilt the first month after you were born. Every day Amelia and I, along with all the women from around here, would work on it together. Those were good times. We sat together and talked while we quilted and then embroidered the lambs and birds in each square. When you came to this house as a baby, I thought you were the sweetest child I'd ever seen."

Leah looked out the window at the sun falling in golden bars on the yard. "This house . . . I remember it so well. We moved often, but always when we'd come here, it felt like home."

"I never knew you felt that way."

"You were always so kind. You spent so much time with me, especially when I was a little girl. I was very lonely."

"I know you missed your father."

Leah dropped her head. "Yes, I did." It was the first time she'd admitted this aloud to anyone, and now she looked up, her eyes sad and poignant. She was a sensitive woman—

strong, yet at the same time full of hunger for the things of life. "I always felt incomplete somehow because I had no father . . . or at least he wasn't there. And I blamed him for it. I've seen lately how wrong I was to do that."

"Then you should tell him so, Leah."

Leah bit her lips uncertainly, then said with fierce determination, "I will, Grandmother! I'll go back to New York, and I'll ask him to forgive me for the way I've felt and acted."

Happiness lighted Martha Rayborn's pale face. "That will mean a great deal to him. And I'm praying your mother will come to see she needs to do the same thing."

"Do you think that's possible?"

"With God," Martha Rayborn said softly, "all things are possible."

★ ★ ★

David had grown quite adept at persuading Col. Bleeker to grant him leaves. Bleeker was amused by his fledgling lieutenant. It was quite an honor to have "Candy" Rocklin in his troop, for the word of Rocklin's daring exploits had spread through the Army of the Tennessee. When David had asked for a day off, Col. Bleeker had said indulgently, "I believe you've earned it. Lt. Allen tells me you've learned quite a bit about how to be a soldier, and Sgt. Hickman, whose recommendation I find invaluable, tells me the same." He smiled then and asked, "You're going to see that young woman of yours?"

David flushed. "Sir, she's not exactly *my* young woman—but yes, I'd like to go calling on her."

"Go on then. Have Capt. Davidson write you out a pass. Bring me back some of that cake your young woman baked for you last time."

"Yes sir, I'll see what I can do."

As David made his way across the country he was highly alert. There had been reports of Yankee cavalry in this area, and the *last* thing he wanted was to be captured and spend the rest of the war in a prison camp. So he traveled under cover of darkness and waited until dawn before approaching the house. He had just passed the front steps when somebody called out, "Hold it right there!" David looked around, startled, as Pax appeared around the corner of the house peering at him suspiciously.

"Hello, Pax. You're not going to shoot me, are you?"

Pax blinked with surprise. "Mr. David! I didn't know it was you. We been having trouble with some chicken thieves."

"I'm glad you ask questions and shoot later." The door opened and Leah stepped out. David said quickly, "Pax is about to gun me down, Leah. Put in a good word for me, will you?"

Leah laughed and said, "Get away from here, Pax. Nobody's gonna steal chickens in broad daylight." Then she took David's arm. "Come inside. You're just in time to help me cook breakfast."

The two went into the kitchen, where he sat and drank imitation coffee made of roasted acorns. It tasted terrible, and they both laughed at the faces they made trying to drink it. She cooked bacon and fried ham and a large portion of grits. When Amelia came in, the three of them ate together. Afterward Claire entered and when David rose she said, "My mother said last week that she'd like to see you if you came back. Would you go up and visit with her?"

"Of course, Mrs. Cleburne."

"I'll take him up, Mother," Leah offered. "You sit down and eat." David followed Leah out of the room and up to the sick woman's room. As they entered, Leah said, "Look Grandmother, David's here."

David sat on the chair on one side of the bed and Leah took the other. "How are you feeling, Mrs. Rayborn?" he queried.

"Very close to heaven," was her simple answer. Martha, noting his look of confusion, put out her hand, saying,

"That startles people, but I'm more in the other world than I am in this one. It's very real to me."

"I think that's a wonderful thing," David said quietly. "You know, you remind me of the women in my family, especially my grandmother."

"Tell me about her."

David talked about his family for some time, Leah listening with interest. Finally he said ruefully, "I've become a regular chatterbox!"

Martha shook her head. "No, it's good to hear such things."

Sensing that Martha Rayborn wouldn't live long, David said gently, when it was time for him to go, "I'll be going into battle soon, Mrs. Rayborn. I may not see you again."

Martha Rayborn looked at him steadily. "We live from day to day, David. You're a young man and I'm an old woman, but you may be in heaven before I am."

"That's very true. I've thought about that a great deal lately."

"Do you know the Lord Jesus?"

"Yes, ma'am, I do."

A smile wreathed Martha's face. "I'm so glad." She turned her head toward Leah. "You have good taste in young men, Granddaughter."

Leah flushed, then smiled almost roguishly at David. "Yes, I do. I demand the best."

Looking at the pair, Martha said, "I have no time for subtleties. Do you love my granddaughter, David?"

"Yes, I do," David responded. "I've told her so."

Then Martha turned to Leah. "Do you love David, Leah?" As confusion washed over her granddaughter's face, Martha continued, "I have no tact or manners, but when a man loves you, you should at least have *some* idea how you feel. But I won't embarrass you anymore. Go along now."

"I'll visit you again before I leave, Mrs. Rayborn."

When Leah and David were outside, David said thoughtfully, "She's a very beautiful woman. Her spirit, like I said, is much like my grandmother's."

"Yes. I'm just now realizing how wonderful she is. Why can't we learn to value pepole while they're still with us?"

They were alone in the hall, so he paused uncertainly, then turned her toward him. "I'm sorry she embarrassed you. I know I love you, but that's never enough." She started to speak, but he shook his head. "Perhaps it's just as well you don't love me, Leah. The battle that's coming is going to be pretty bad. But I've got some things to tell you about myself."

"What things?"

"Not here. Later. Now, let's go."

The two enjoyed their day together. Amelia and Claire watched them leave the house, Leah heavily bundled in a red and green coat with a bright red hat over her red hair. As they disappeared across the road and entered into a woods, Amelia sighed. "They make a beautiful couple."

"Yes, they do," Claire said quietly. "He's a fine young man."

Amelia asked, "Would you approve of him if he came asking for Leah's hand?"

"I can't imagine he'd ask, not with this war going on. But then people do fall in love and get married even in a war."

"*Especially* during a war." Amelia looked down at the garment in her hands and then asked herself aloud, "Why am I constantly knitting these things?"

"Why, you always give them to people who need them. I think it's a noble deed," Claire said with a smile. "What do you think of him? David, I mean."

"I think he's the finest young man I've seen since Matthew Cleburne came to our house."

Startled, Claire stared at her aunt. Amelia's face flushed, then turned pale. Amelia had said almost nothing about Matthew during recent years, but Claire knew he had been a favorite of hers. "You haven't talked about Matthew in a long time," she said quietly.

"No, because I knew how you felt. Every time I mentioned his name you added a brick to that wall you'd built around yourself. I hated to see you bury yourself alive, Claire, but that's what you've done."

Claire looked down at her hands, unable to speak. Finally she lifted her eyes and whispered, "Mother's been talking to me. Was my father really like that? He was your brother. You'd known him all of his life."

Amelia thought for a few moments, then shook her head. "He was a strange boy and he became a strange man. There was greatness in him—you saw that. So did everyone. But there was another side to him, a dark side that he kept concealed. I found out about it, of course, when he was very young, but he could charm almost anyone. I don't suppose you remember, Claire, but I tried to tell you about it before you married Matthew. It was at our house when you'd just announced your engagement.

"I *do* remember," Claire said softly. "I got upset, even angry. For a long time I didn't like you because of what you'd said."

"I should have said more," Amelia responded, "but you wouldn't have believed me."

"No, I wouldn't have. I wouldn't have believed anyone."

Amelia said abruptly, "I hope they *do* get married. It might be short. He might not outlive the war, but then people die every day. Leah needs a man like that, I think. I think she loves him, although for some reason she's afraid to say so. She's been very choosy about men."

"So have I," Claire admitted bitterly. "As I look back over my life, I've made almost every mistake a woman could make!"

Her admission surprised Amelia and she said quickly, "It's not too late for you. Matthew loves you and he always has."

"No." Claire's voice was almost harsh. "I can't go back. Not after all this time!"

"That's your pride speaking, Claire, but pride is a cold and lonely thing. A woman like you needs the warmth of a man's love and the touch of his hands. Go back, Claire!"

Claire got up and left the room at once, her face stiff. But Amelia wasn't discouraged. "I think she still loves him," she whispered to herself. "When love is there, no matter how small, it can work miracles."

Outside, Leah and David walked along a pathway that led through the woods. "This is an old logging trail," Leah said. "It goes way deep into the woods."

"I'd like to go to the end of it," David said, "so far back that there wouldn't be any war, any killing . . . but that can't be." He turned to her suddenly. "I've found out something about myself."

"What is it, David?" Looking up in his face, Leah saw an utter seriousness there. "Is something wrong?"

"No, although I'm not quite sure that's an honest answer." He caressed her cheek, which was smoother than anything he'd felt in his life. He let his hand rest there for a moment, then touched her hair. "You're so beautiful, Leah!" he said, his voice quiet and gentle. "But I would love you even if you weren't."

"What's the matter, David? What did you want to tell me?"

"It's about myself," he said, seeing she was troubled. He related his conversation with Maj. Dillard as she listened intently. Finally he concluded, "So, I really believe I'm cured." He laughed lightly. "I cured myself, according to the doctor, by confessing what a rotten scoundrel I was. Somehow that makes it all right. But I don't think it can be that simple. It can't be!"

"You haven't had any bad dreams, nightmares about bayonets?" Leah queried softly.

"No, not a one."

"And you haven't blacked out anymore?"

"No, I haven't, and that's what gives me hope. Those things frightened me to death, but as I think back it's only after I confessed it to Corey and to you and then finally to the doctor that I've been freed. The doctor's a Christian man, and he said confession of our wrongs frees us from bondage."

"I think he's right." Thinking of her father, Leah hesitated, not wanting to speak. "Something's been wrong in my life for a long time. I've never told anyone about it, but I'd like to tell you."

"What is it, Leah?" He asked, not being able to imagine what was making a shadow in her greenish eyes.

"I've been terribly unfair to my father. I've just found it out by talking to Grandmother. And Mother—she's changed too." She went on speaking almost feverishly and finally said, "I wish you could meet my father, David. You'd like him."

"I'm sure I would." David took her arm, and they began walking slowly through the woods. "Tell me about it. Maybe it will help. It surely helped me."

As they moved along under the trees that were shedding their orange and red leaves, making a multicolored carpet on the forest floor, Leah spoke of her father. She related that somehow she had hated him for leaving them, even though now she realized it wasn't his fault. She also told of how she'd held herself back from him when he tried to do things for her, to be with her.

"I was so *unfair*, David, so cruel! I've got to go to New York and ask him to forgive me . . . and that's going to be so hard." Her lips trembled. "I don't know if I can do it."

"I think you can." As he pulled her close, she rested her head on his chest and began to weep. David said nothing for a long time, knowing this release of tears was something she needed. After a while she lifted her head. Her lips were soft and vulnerable as he kissed her. "I think that doctor was right," David said, still holding her tightly. "We have to *say* things to make them right. You need to tell your father, and I've got to go to my people too. Or write them. I've already started and it's very hard."

They walked through the woods for a long time until she finally said, "We'd better go home." As they retraced their footsteps, a rabbit started up right at their feet, startling them both for a moment. They laughed, relieving the tension of their talk, as he ran away, ears wildly flopping. But before they got home, David said seriously, "I may not have a chance to say good-bye properly, but I want you to know I'm a one-woman man, Leah." He kissed her again. "If I live through this battle, I'll find out whether I'm going to be able to be a man. I may run away at the first shot—just like that cottontail."

"You won't," Leah said firmly. "I know you won't. Your doctor friend *was* right. We have to face the thing we fear most. If we turn and run from it, it will pursue us and destroy us."

Now back at the house, they stepped up on the front porch. Instantly a hard voice startled them both. "Hold it right there."

David whirled to see a Union officer, a lieutenant, holding a gun on him.

"Brian!" Leah cried. "What are you doing?"

Brian Decatur had come, obviously, to call on Leah. He'd seen the two of them go into the woods and had waited. Now he held the gun steady saying, "Don't move, Lieutenant. I'm taking you prisoner."

David, not carrying a gun, felt a moment's helplessness. Then he said, his voice steady, "I think this is neutral ground, isn't it, Lieutenant?"

"What are you doing here?" Brian asked, as if barking an order.

"He came to see me. He's an old friend." David's eyes turned toward Leah, but she ignored them. "Brian, this isn't right."

Decatur looked at her with surprise. "This is war, Leah. If he'd caught me, he would have taken me prisoner. Wouldn't you?"

David shook his head, not answering. The despairing thought foremost in his mind was, *Now I'll never know whether I'm a coward or not. I'll be rotting in some prison. That'll be worse than some battle.* But he wouldn't beg. Leah

261

put her hand on his arm as she said, "I won't let you take him, Brian. Please let him go for my sake."

Decatur stared at her, an unreadable expression on his face. "You're you asking this of me? You know I'm a soldier bound to be true to my oath!"

"This isn't a battle," Leah insisted, "and I'm asking it of you—as a friend."

This wasn't something Brian Decatur wanted to hear. Nevertheless, he lowered the revolver. Staring across at David he said almost bitterly, "You're a lucky fellow, Lieutenant." Then he holstered the pistol. "I feel in the way here," he said briefly.

Knowing Brian was dreadfully hurt, Leah stepped toward him. "Please, my grandmother's ill. This is our home. We've tried to keep the war out of it. That's all I mean by this, Brian. I'd ask the same of David if he'd captured you."

"You would? Really?"

"Of course I would."

Decatur took a deep breath, then eyeballed the taller man. "I think I'll have to honor Miss Leah's request, Lieutenant."

"Thank you, Lieutenant," David said, studying the sharp features of the other. "I'd like to think I'd do the same thing." He turned to Leah and said, "Good day. I can't speak before my opponent here, but it seems unlikely I'll be back anytime soon. So good-bye for a while. Tell your grandmother I'll be praying for her." He nodded at Decatur, saying, "Your servant, sir," then walked away.

Decatur watched him go. "Quite a fellow there," he said softly to Leah.

Disturbed, Leah offered immediately, "Come inside, Brian. I'm a little upset, but I'll be better." She led the way into the house.

★ ★ ★

When David got back to the camp, Corey asked, "How was the ladies, sah?"

"They were fine."

"Sure would like to see them again. They mighty fine, all of 'em."

"Yes, they are," David said briefly. He glanced in the direction of Chattanooga, where the enemy lay, then toward Leah's home. After the encounter with his enemy, he wondered what Decatur's relationship with Leah was.

"Well, old boy. We'll be tasting battle smoke soon," said a voice beside him, interrupting his thoughts. Startled, David turned to find Lt. Rupert Allen standing beside him.

"Did you hear something, Rupert?" David queried.

"I think the Yankees are moving into position. They'll hit us pretty soon. I'm glad we've got you, Lt. 'Candy' Rocklin, the famous fighting Virginian, on our side!"

David summoned a smile, accustomed to being teased by the use of this nickname. But as he turned to go with Rupert to headquarters, his thoughts were with Leah.

CHAPTER TWENTY-TWO
The Battle above the Clouds

At the Battle of Gettysburg the Union army had occupied the top of a series of ridges. Perched there above their enemy, they could plainly see the Confederates as they approached across open ground and made their way up the hill.

Now, just outside of Chattanooga, Tennessee, the situation was almost completely reversed. Up above Chattanooga and the bend where it's nestled in the Tennessee River, the Army of the Tennessee stretched itself along a long ridge called Missionary Ridge. The left flank of this army was planted on top of Lookout Mountain, the right flank at the end of Missionary Ridge. The officers in charge of defending Missionary Ridge were Breckenridge, Hardy, and Cleburne on the right flank. Rarely has it been so easy to diagram a battle. The Confederates were stretched in a thin line across Missionary Ridge. Approaching them was Grant's army, with Hooker on the right, Gen. Thomas in the center, and Sherman on the left flank.

The chronology of the battle is equally simple. It took place on three separate days. The first day, November 23, 1863, was little more than a skirmish, known later as the Battle of Orchard Knob. This involved Gen. Hooker striking the Confederate force on the left and driving them back to Lookout Mountain. This proved to be the outpost from which on the following day, the twenty-fourth, the battle for

Lookout Mountain was launched. This battle has become known by the poetic name "The Battle above the Clouds," but in fact, the battle wasn't fought on top of the mountain, but in a heavy mist on a rocky slope about five hundred feet below the crest. Hooker's force outnumbered the Confederates about six to one, and the outcome was never in doubt. The next day a detachment planted the Stars and Stripes on top of Lookout Mountain.

Brian Decatur found himself temporarily detached to Sherman's army. That unit, instead of attacking directly, moved around north of Chattanooga itself, shielding its movements, and came to attack the right flank of the Confederate army. The army had to cross the river, and did so on pontoon bridges. Decatur was on one of these bridges, which were over 1,350 feet long.

"I don't think we'll ever get across. This bridge won't hold," Decatur complained.

The bridge rose and fell with the current of the river, seeming to be more of a toy than a real bridge. His fellow lieutenant Gerald Colvin agreed with him. "I'd rather fight the Rebs than cross a thing like this! I can't swim."

Decatur grinned at him. "Well, if you drown you won't have to put up with these bad rations anymore."

Colvin gave him a sour look. "That's not much of a comfort," he said, grunting. Then he looked ahead, saying, "Come on, let's get off this bridge." They stepped off the bridge and joined the troops that were hurrying about. Colvin said suddenly, "Look, there's Gen. Sherman over there." They moved forward, expecting some sort of orders. Instead they found Sherman, livid with rage.

"What's the matter with the old man?" Decatur asked.

"Don't know. Let's find out." As they moved closer Colvin asked the colonel of their brigade, "What's Gen. Sherman so mad about?"

Col. Jones stared at him. "We're on the wrong hill. That's what's the matter."

"The wrong hill, sir?"

"Yes. We did all this sneaking around Chattanooga to get on the foot of Missionary Ridge. Now look at that." He pointed forward and they saw a valley. At the top of the hill across from them Confederate troops were plainly evident, digging in with artillery and lining up along the top looking down on the Union.

"That's where we're supposed to be, but the general had the wrong map, I guess."

Sherman called a brief council of war. "We'll fortify this mound, but tomorrow morning we'll take that hill over there, gentlemen." He looked up at the right flank of the Confederate army. "I understand Gen. Cleburne's up there. If he is," Sherman said, his mouth stubborn and intense, "—if Pat Cleburne's up there, we'll pay for every foot of ground we take!" Then he kicked at a rock, running his hand through his wild red hair. "But we'll take it. Yes, we'll do it if we have to crawl our way up with our fingernails!"

The next morning both Union and Confederate troops stared at the heights of Lookout Mountain, but Grant downplayed the mythology that surrounded the battle. He later said that reports of an incredible victory at Lookout Mountain were "one of the romances of the war . . . it is all poetry."

At first light they looked up at the heights of the ridge where two Confederate divisions under Patrick Cleburne had arrived during the night, shifted from Lookout Mountain. The fact that the defending Confederates knew the rugged terrain helped to compensate for their deficit in numbers.

Standing on top of that line, David stood shoulder to shoulder beside Sam Watkins and Sgt. Baker Hickman.

"There sure is a heap of 'em, ain't there now?" Sgt. Hickman murmured.

"There's a passel," Sam agreed. "But they got to climb that hill."

David looked down, seeing that Sherman's troops would have to climb down the hill they occupied, cross a valley and an open field under fire, then ascend a steep slope—all against troops who were protected by log-and-earth breast-works. "If we just keep our heads," he said, "they'll never make it. I just wish we had more ammunition."

Even as he spoke, down below, Sherman, the Union general, signaled the advance by saying to his brother-in-law, Brig. Gen. Hugh Ewing, "I guess, Ewing, if you're ready, you might as well go ahead."

As the movement toward the top of Missionary Ridge began, Col. Bleeker moved up and down the line of the First Tennessee Infantry, encouraging the men. "Don't fire till you've got a good target, men, and remember, you're shoot-ing downhill, so fire low."

The Federal advance began, and at once three Confeder-ate batteries opened fire on the blue line.

"Hold your fire! Hold your fire!" the officers were crying, David among them. Already he could see the sun glinting on the bayonets that the attackers had attached. Then they disappeared from his view as they climbed up the six-hundred-foot incline.

As David Rocklin stood there, he thought of his past and of Vicksburg and how the bayonets had driven him from the field. Stiffening his back he pledged to himself, *I won't run this time. If they run me through a hundred times, I'll stand right here on this spot.*

Soon the battle began to rage all along the line. As the Federals attacked in the center, directly in front of David, hissing lead flew between the two armies.

All morning long the fighting raged with intensity. About three o'clock that afternoon David, his face blackened like everyone else's in the line, was still clinging to his ground desperately. Line after line of the Union troops had been thrown forward, and Sam Watkins said, "Them Yankees got nerve, I'll say that. They just keep on a-comin'!"

Even as he spoke David said, "Look! There's the general." His companions watched with him as Patrick Cleburne leaped on top of the Confederate breastworks. Then, flourishing his sword, he led a Texas brigade in a charge on the Yankees.

Instantly Col. Bleeker stood up. "Come on, men. Let's give the Texans a hand."

David ran his eyes down the Confederate line. "Come on!" he cried at the top of his lungs and plunged forward.

At first the Union troops were shadows, dodging behind rocks and scrub trees; then they were separated into individuals. He felt the hiss of musket balls close to his ear, humming like angry bees. Beside him a man stumbled and fell, but David never turned. He was still determined to stop the oncoming blue line. "You won't get this hill!" he cried. "Come on, men!"

Beside him Watkins yelled, "Lt. Candy'll show us the way!"

They hadn't moved forward more than twenty yards when a Union private, a large man with wild eyes and a ruddy face, suddenly appeared in front of David. He'd evidently fired his musket, but his bayonet gleamed in the sunlight. He came straight for David, the bright bayonet aimed at David's stomach. He was so close that David saw him with absolute clarity, noting that he had a large mole on his right cheek.

David lifted his pistol, pulling the trigger—and it clacked on an empty chamber. The keen blade on the end of the soldier's musket seemed to grow larger, but David threw himself forward, directly at the bayonet that the soldier thrust at him. As David twisted his body to one side, the blade sliced across his chest, tearing his uniform. David then swung the pistol, knocking the soldier to the ground. When he attempted to get up, David reversed it and struck him in the head with the butt of the heavy Colt. The man collapsed at once and David picked up the rifle he'd dropped. There was blood on the tip of it, and he saw he'd been grazed by the blade, which had a razor edge. Staring at it for one brief second he noted with relief that his nerves were steady. *You can't get closer to being stuck by a bayonet than that!*

"Are you hurt, Lieutenant?" Sam Watkins called as he ran to stand beside him.

"No, I'm all right. Let's get these Yankees out of here," David replied.

Since they were reinforced almost at once by the thirty-sixth and the fifty-sixth Georgia infantry, the fighting was shortly over.

Sherman at last halted the fighting. After suffering two thousand casualties, his troops still weren't any closer to taking Tunnel Hill than they'd been at the beginning of the day.

David helped gather the prisoners, who were soon herded off, and then assisted in carrying both Confederate and Union wounded to where the doctors could care for them.

Rupert Allen, who hadn't been scratched, said to David, "Let's see that wound."

"It's not much," David replied. Although his uniform was torn, when he unbuttoned his shirt there was only a thin red line on his chest. "Just a scratch."

Allen eyeballed the wound. "Better try to bandage it up, I guess." He studied it for a moment, then shivered. "I never could stand cold steel. I saw you go after that Yankee with nothing but an empty gun. I don't think I could have done that."

Amused, David answered wryly, "I don't think I could either."

Rupert stared at him, "But you did. You ran right at him. I thought you were a goner for sure."

As David Rocklin stood there among the frantic activity of the army getting ready for the battle they all knew would come the next day, he was suddenly sure of one thing: that he could stand as a man and face death without fleeing.

★ ★ ★

On the morning of November 25, Gen. Grant stood looking up at the heights of Missionary Ridge. At last his army was ready. He turned to Gen. Thomas and, with his teeth clamped on the everlasting cigar, said, "I think we'll see if we can take those rifle pits at the foot of the mountain, Gen. Thomas."

Thomas, an expert drillmaster, nodded and left. He formed his ranks precisely, the lines perfectly straight. As all twenty-five thousand men appeared on the plain, with bands playing and banners waving, the Confederates, watching from the mountaintops a mile away, were struck with fear.

At Thomas's signal this great mass of infantry began marching toward the Confederate line. They seemed remorseless and unstoppable. Later, Confederate Gen. Arthur Manigault wrote in a letter that the Union army struck with the order and regularity of a juggernaut.

Bragg had given orders that the Confederates should fire one volley, then move up the ridge. This order proved to be disastrous, for as the men fired their guns and then moved upward, it encouraged the Federals, who thought they were watching a retreat. It also disheartened the rest of the Confederate army high up on the hill who didn't know their comrades were retreating by Bragg's orders.

Grant watched as his army rolled over the rifle pits, capturing many of the Confederates who'd stayed. Then, through his binoculars, Grant saw an astonishing sight. Long lines of blue-clad Union soldiers were laboriously pushing their way up the hill.

Dismayed, Grant turned to Thomas, demanding, "Thomas, who ordered those men up the ridge?"

"I don't know," said Thomas. "I didn't."

Grant questioned the rest of his officers, including Gen. Granger, who responded, "They started without orders." Then Granger added with grim satisfaction, "When those fellows get started, nothing can stop them!"

Grant turned back, his jaw tense. This was a battle out of control—a general's nightmare. Never once had he considered taking Missionary Ridge, since it seemed impossible any troop could take it because of its location.

"If it turns out all right, fine," Grant said, muttering. "If not, someone will suffer!"

Someone *was* suffering, and it was the Confederates. David and the First Tennessee fired as the men in blue advanced up the side of the hill, then began rolling rocks down the hillside. But nothing could stop the force of the charge. As the Confederate men at the bottom of the slope raced for the safety of the summit, they made it hard for the defenders, who were afraid to fire for fear of hitting their own men.

There was something uncanny about the soldiers of the Army of the Cumberland. They came on, determined to reach the crest of the ridge, and as they did, the men of the Army of the Tennessee threw down their arms and fled.

As Gen. Bragg came upon the fleeing soldiers, he shouted, "Here's your commander!" But the soldiers only mocked him and ran past.

Gen. Breckinridge was cool enough. "Boys," he yelled, "get away the best as you can!"

David held his little company together along with the other officers, but soon saw it was a hopeless task. Flags from sixty Yankee regiments began to float along Missionary Ridge from one end to the other. As great cries of victory went up from the Federals, Col. Bleeker told David, "Get the men out! Make an orderly retreat, Lieutenant."

"Yes sir." David turned to his men and ordered, "Move back! We'll be all right! They'll win this time, but there'll be another day!"

The Army of the Tennessee moved backward and to their rear. No one has ever explained how panic can strike an entire army, but on that day, the First Tennessee was not itself.

As they retreated, David found himself, along with his company, trapped between two forces of Federal troops. Skillfully he maneuvered them back, but just as they were free of the trap something struck him in the side of the leg. There was no pain and he thought he'd run into the branch of a tree. But when he looked down, he saw that his uniform was crimson with blood and thought with shock, *Why, I've been shot!* Then the pain came, but he gritted his teeth and continued to direct the retreat.

It was Sam Watkins who saw it first. "Look, Lieutenant!" he said to Lt. Allen. "Lt. Candy—he's been shot!"

Allen rushed at once to David's side. "Are you hurt, Dave? Let's see."

"I'll be all right," David muttered. "Just don't leave me here."

"Here, you fellows! Help the lieutenant! Get him out of here!" Allen yelped.

Sam threw his musket down and, along with Sgt. Hickman, took David's arms and looped them over their shoulders. As they started moving, David protested, "It's all right—I can walk."

But he couldn't walk, and suddenly the rattling of guns and the booming of cannons was muted. He tried to say something to Sam, but his lips wouldn't work. His legs were also losing their power. After what seemed like a long time, he heard Corey say, "That's all right. I take care of you, sah."

As the darkness began to close over him, the last thing David saw was Corey's face in front of him. As Corey lifted him, holding David in his arms like a child, the blackness swept over him like a mighty wave and he knew nothing.

★   ★   ★

David's world had grown strange. For some time he had felt hands working on him, and sometimes there was pain. At other times he'd wake with a start. But through it all, he knew he was part of the wounded, of those who were moaning in a makeshift hospital about him. Only one factor remained constant: Whenever he awoke, Corey was by his side instantly.

"Am I going to die?" David whispered once.

"Die? Why, no sah! The doctor, he got that bullet out and you gonna be fine."

David smiled briefly but passed out almost at once.

He awoke again sometime later, but in a different place. Once again Corey was there, this time with food. "You got to eat, sah."

As Corey pulled him upright David noted they were in a room of some kind, but there were no wounded soldiers there.

"Where are we, Corey?" he said softly. Then, clearing his throat, he said in a stronger voice, "Where's the rest of the army? Is this the hospital?"

"No sah, the army done moved. Now here, you eat this, and if you eat it all, I tell you what you need to know."

David ate two servings of the soup, then looked down at the bandage that swathed his leg. "All right. Where are we, Corey?"

"The army done gone. The doctor got the bullet out and you didn't get no fever, which they said was unusual."

"Where's the army gone to?"

"Done retreated, sah. But you wasn't fit to go with 'em nor to ride in one of them wagons they took 'em in. So I kept you here. I used some of your money to pay for you a room with these folks. Them sympathizers to the South. Soon as you get able we gonna get out of here. I done 'ranged with the gentleman that owns this place to take us to the railroad."

"Where are we going, Corey?"

"Going back home to Virginia, sah."

"But I'm in the army!"

"Col. Bleeker, he done told me to take you home and get you all healed up. You ain't gonna be soldiering for a while, I don't reckon."

David looked down at the wound and said nothing. When he did look up, he smiled at Corey. "It'll be mighty good to get back to Virginia. You're gonna like it there, Corey."

The black face split in a wide grin. "Yes sah. And you and me, we gonna be the finest farmers in all the whole state of Virginia!"

CHAPTER TWENTY-THREE
"You Have to Trust Love!"

The grave had been dug in ground that was frozen at least a foot deep. Now the small company of neighbors and friends who had known Martha Rayborn most of her life stood silently as the tall, white-haired minister read passages from a worn black Bible.

Claire, Amelia, and Leah wore black, of course. Martha's death had come quietly. She'd spoken with them all on Thursday evening and seemed to be doing better. All three of the women had sat around her bed, and the sick woman had been more lively than she had been for some time. She'd asked Leah to read to her again the last chapters of Revelation, and when Leah finished Martha Rayborn had smiled, exclaiming, "What a time that will be when we all fall down and worship the Lord Jesus Christ and the Father!"

The next morning, as Leah was eating breakfast with Amelia, Claire had entered the room, her face pale. The other two women knew before she spoke. "Mother's gone. She died with a smile on her face. I don't think she knew a moment's pain."

Now as the cold breeze whipped Claire's skirt, she listened to the final prayer and then turned away from the graveside. She endured the duty of receiving the condolences from friends well, but she was glad when she was back inside the house. Taking off her bonnet she hung it up carefully, then removed the heavy coat and did the same.

The three women went about their duties at once, cleaning house in that unnatural atmosphere that follows hard upon the death of a loved one. They spoke little that day, but the next morning at breakfast Claire surprised them all. She waited until they were finished with the pancakes that Bessie had made, then said, "I've got to go back to New York. We can't stay here."

Leah nodded. The fond memories of this place had been replaced by new ones of war and hardship and now the death of her grandmother. "Are we going back to Father's house?"

Claire hesitated, then said, "Yes," and nothing more.

After Claire had left the table, Amelia said quietly to Leah, "I'm surprised we'll be going back so soon."

"Mother's been very quiet. I suppose Grandmother's death has hit her hard."

"It's more than that," Amelia remarked. "I think there's been some kind of change in her. I've never seen her like this before. She was always a little too—well—too *hard* in her ways."

Leah looked up quickly. "You mean toward Father?"

"Yes. I think she's been thinking a great deal about her life and the way things have gone."

After that, the two said no more about it. It took a little over two weeks to get ready to go. Martha had left the property to Claire and although it was devaluated by the war, still it had potential to be a good farm for someone. The farmer who lived on the adjoining place had expressed an interest in buying it, and Claire had asked the assistance of the local banker in concluding the sale. The buyer didn't have all the cash, but he had a good down payment and agreed to pay the rest in yearly payments.

The three women went through the house packing the things they wanted to keep—mostly pictures and letters and photographs. Finally they made their way to the station, relieved to discover it wouldn't be hard to get passage out. Supplies were pouring into the city now for Grant's army, and the trains were filled with troops, but they returned to the North mostly empty.

As they moved out of the Chattanooga station, the steam engine huffed coarsely, sending large clouds of smoke and steam against the iron-gray sky. But instead of looking around, Claire was thinking about what she would say to Matthew when they returned to his house.

★ ★ ★

New York was gripped in the fist of a hard winter. By mid-December, ice and snow were piled high on the sidewalks, having been cleared from the roads by plows and crews with shovels. The three women dismounted from the train, and Leah saw to the luggage while Claire found a carriage. When they were all inside, Claire gave Matthew's address, and the horses responded to the driver's cheerful, "Giddup, you lazy hosses!"

Leah noticed her mother was pale. Claire had spoken very little on the journey, which had been, as usual, difficult. Although a wood stove was kept blazing near one end of the car, the cars were drafty and cold and offered little comfort. Now as they moved along the streets of New York toward the residential area, Leah thought, *Father's going to be surprised to see us coming.* She herself had practiced her speech to him over and over, but now that the time approached, she felt uncomfortable and wished it were over. She had a rootless feeling that she hadn't been able to shake off. Glancing over at Amelia she noted that the older woman was more cheerful than she'd been in a long time. As they drove along the frozen streets, Amelia spoke of the future with some hope . . . but Claire did not respond.

★ ★ ★

Matthew was in his study going over his accounts when he heard a knock at the door.

"I'll get the door, Lucy," he called out. Stiff and tired of the book work, he stretched as he moved out of the room.

Down the hall, Lucy stuck her head out of the kitchen but withdrew it as she saw him headed for the door.

Opening the door, Matthew stood stock still, unable to speak for a moment. Disturbed by his silence, Claire was unable to speak. Finally, it was Amelia who said cheerfully, "Well, Matthew, you have a houseful of company, it seems."

Matthew at once exclaimed, "I'm so surprised to see you! Come in—come in, all of you."

When they were inside, Claire found her voice. "I apologize for barging in like this, Matthew—"

"Don't be foolish, Claire! Here, let me take your coats and hang them up." He took all of their coats but didn't inquire more than to say, "You must have had a hard trip from Tennessee. Come on into the parlor. I'll stir up the fire and we can talk."

Fifteen minutes later they were all seated in front of the fire, and Leah, standing beside it, held her hands out to the yellow flames. "That's good! I've been freezing to death on that drafty old railroad car!"

Matthew smiled at her. "Winter's not a good time to travel." He turned to Claire and said, "I was grieved to hear of Martha's death." He stroked his chin thoughtfully. "She was a fine woman. I loved her a great deal."

"She was very fond of you," Claire said quietly. "She spoke of you almost every day. I think it was one of the regrets of her life that she didn't get to see more of you during these last years." Embarrassed, Claire turned her face away, studying one of the pictures on the wall.

Matthew looked up quickly. From the time she'd stepped into the house, Matthew had sensed a new quality in Claire. But for the moment, he said only, "She's always meant a great deal to me. I'll miss her."

Lucy came in to ask, "I'm fixin' dinner. You all staying?"

"Of course they're staying," Matthew replied quickly, seeing a strange look cross Claire's face. "You are, aren't you?"

"If—if we won't be in the way," Claire stammered.

"Of course not," Matthew said with a smile. "I'll get Simon, and he can carry your bags upstairs. I think he's out in the back."

When he left the room and the three women were alone, Claire said miserably, "I don't know why I'm so awkward."

Amelia examined her niece, seeing a brokenness in Claire that hadn't been there before. *She's changed,* Amelia said to herself. *She's changed a great deal.*

The noon meal went well, though Claire hardly spoke. Matthew talked with animation. "It's good to have you here. I just rattle around in this big old house by myself." He looked over at Leah and said, "You and I may get to take in a play or two." Then he winked at Amelia. "A little bit racy for you, Aunt Amelia, but these young folks, you know how they are."

Leah, suddenly feeling warm, said, "I'll look forward to it." She was thinking ahead to the time she would have to speak to her father—and that time came the next morning. She'd gotten up early, dreading the thought of the meeting, and gone downstairs to find Matthew sitting in the kitchen. He'd built up the fire and made a pot of coffee. "I expected you to sleep late," he commented, teasing her. Then he studied her face. "You didn't sleep well?"

"No, not very." She took a quick breath and said, "Father, I have to talk to you."

"What is it, Daughter?"

"I've been very unhappy lately. I want to ask you to forgive me."

Matthew Cleburne was silent for a moment. "Forgive you for what?" he asked finally.

"I haven't been the kind of daughter I should have been. As I was growing up, I resented you a great deal. I blamed you for not being with us and I was lonesome. But it wasn't your fault; I know that now. I wish I could go back," she said quietly, hesitating. "But I can't do that. None of us can. Will you forgive me?"

Matthew stepped forward and put his arms out. Leah

moved into them at once. "Of course I will," he said. "We'll start from right now."

Leah stepped back, quickly wiping the tears from her eyes. "Well now, tell me all you've been doing." The moment was over. Later Leah would speak more about her childhood, but presently she wanted to get away from the tension.

As the two talked, he finally asked, "What about that young man, David Rocklin?"

"I don't know. He was with the army when they retreated. A great many men were killed and more of them wounded. I did let him know where I was, but I haven't heard anything."

Matthew examined her critically. "You were very fond of him, weren't you?"

"Yes. I treated him badly, too." Leah shook her head in despair. "Seems like I need a lesson in how to treat men. I haven't had much success."

"What about young Decatur?"

"He's still with the army in Chattanooga. I saw him before I left."

"He was pretty serious about you."

"Yes, but he could never be more than a friend. I told him that when I left." She smiled and continued, "He'll find somebody. I think he was really infatuated with the idea of having a Rebel sweetheart. He's a fine young man, but not for me."

The two talked for a long time and finally Matthew looked up at her from across the table, saying warmly, "It's good to have you here, Leah. We'll have to make up for lost time."

★ ★ ★

Claire Cleburne was more miserable than she'd been in years. She'd thought coming back to New York might solve her problems, but somehow she couldn't seem to fit in. She was happy to see Matthew and Leah growing close and had brought it up to Amelia, who said, "They always loved each other very much, but now it'll be different."

These words made Claire feel even more guilty. She'd struggled with her feelings for some time, and now that she was back in New York in Matthew's house, despair gripped her. Finally, she determined that she must leave for a while. At least knowing Leah and Amelia had a place made it easier. She waited, not wanting to tell them. But one Thursday evening, after Leah and Amelia had gone to hear a local minister, she stayed at home, knowing she had to speak to Matthew.

For over an hour she sat in her room, wondering how to speak of their past, then finally shrugged. "I've *got* to tell him! I can't stay here."

She walked down the stairs and went to his study. Once there, she stood in the open door and asked quietly, "Matthew, may I speak to you?"

Looking up from his book, Matthew got to his feet at once. "Of course, Claire. Come in and sit down over here by the fire."

"No, I can't stay long. There's something I have to say to you."

Matthew looked at his wife—for so he still thought of her—and saw that she was disturbed. Her smooth features were marked with signs of tension, and unhappiness shone in her gray eyes. "Is there anything I can do?" he queried.

Claire, her hair fixed in an old-fashioned way that framed her face, couldn't face him. She walked to the window, staring at the streetlight for a moment, trying to put her words together. Finally she turned and said with effort, "I talked with Mother a great deal before she died—and before that with Aunt Amelia." When she saw he didn't understand her, she continued with difficulty, "They talked to me about—my father."

When Matthew saw that the words almost had to be wrung from Claire, he waited. Finally, when she seemed to find no words, he asked, "What about your father, Claire?"

"He wasn't the man I thought he was. I always put him on a pedestal. I see that now." The words began to flow faster, and Claire put her hands together, holding them tightly to control the trembling. "Ever since I was a little girl, I thought he was the greatest man alive. I measured all other men by him."

Matthew Cleburne had long known this, but he'd never expected to hear Claire say it. As he stood there quietly, Claire shook her head and cried in despair, "I was wrong about him, and I treated you shamefully!" Her throat seemed to close up and her voice trembled. "I've got to say this to you. *I* was the one that ruined our marriage, not you. It wasn't your fault. It was me that drove us apart. I've ruined our lives, Matthew. Can you ever forgive me?"

For one moment Claire thought Matthew would leave her without a word. Then he came to stand before her. Putting his hands on her arms he said simply, "I've always loved you and I always will."

"Oh, Matthew!" Claire began to weep. She buried her face against his chest as his arms went around her. She hadn't been held like this by a man for years and it all but broke her heart. She wept until there were no tears left, and still he stood holding her as if protecting her from a storm. She felt his lips on her tear-stained cheek as he kissed her, bringing back memories. She clung to him fiercely then, and he lifted his head and said, "Of course I forgive you. We'll start all over again."

"Can love be put back together like that?" Claire whispered.

"You have to trust love," Matthew said gently. "Do you love me, Claire?"

Echoes of years gone by sounded deep within Claire Cleburne. She remembered the first time she'd given herself to this man. There had been a freshness in their love and a stirring in her that she'd never forgotten. And now she knew that she'd longed desperately for his love for years. As he held her tightly, she said, "Yes, I always have, but I was such a fool!"

He kissed her again, then smiled. "I think it's time for

another honeymoon. What would you say about a voyage to the South Seas? There would be warm breezes and blue skies, and we can get to know each other all over again. Would you come along with an old man?"

Claire looked up at him, returning his smile through her tears. "You're not old!" she protested, "and yes, I'll go with you. Oh, Matthew, I can't believe it. Can we really start over again?"

"If you trust love," Matthew responded, "you can always start over again."

CHAPTER TWENTY-FOUR
Freedom

Corey looked up from the forge where he was tapping a red-hot horseshoe with a ten-pound sledge. "Why, Mr. David," he said in surprise, "I didn't 'spect to see you down here the day before Chrissmas. Why ain't you with the family?"

David carried a cane. He still favored his left leg, but the weeks of recuperation at Gracefield had brought almost a complete recovery. He'd been released from the army, and for the past four weeks he and Corey had been together every day.

"Leg's getting better all the time, Corey. What are you doing?"

"I'm makin' a new shoe for that little strawberry mare you like so good."

"Nice to have another blacksmith on the place. Box is getting a little old for much hard work. He's been telling me that you're the second best blacksmith in the South."

"I lets him talk like that. He's a good man," Corey said. "You set down over there and let me finish this horseshoe. Then we'll see can we scare up some of them groceries they been makin' in the big kitchen." David sat down on a box turned on end with his leg stretched out in front of him. The minié ball had missed the big bone but had torn a deep furrow in his flesh. Now he watched as Corey tapped the horseshoe from time to time, reaching over to the bellows and sending sparks flying upward.

As he sat there, David thought of his return home. He'd been received with open arms by his grandmother especially, and with hands that had trembled—something that didn't happen often, for she was a steady person. His father, Clay Rocklin, had managed to come home once on leave and had listened carefully as David had told him the whole story of what had happened to him.

As Clay listened he was thinking, *He's so different from Dent, far more sensitive than he is—or me either for that matter.* He had a special love for this young man, so quiet in his ways, so unobtrusive. Now he saw something different in him, a firmness that hadn't been there before. Just then David said, "I couldn't stand being a coward. What I did may have been wrong, but I would rather have died than live with that."

"I'm glad you didn't," Clay said quietly, hesitating. "I could tell you some stories about myself—about the time I ran away once in the war in Mexico. But you're all right now. God brought you through it all." Then he'd embraced David.

As David watched Corey form the horseshoe, feelings of gladness and peace, which he hadn't known for many months, came over him.

When Corey finished the horseshoe and sat down beside David, he commented, "Lots of Chrissmas doin's up at the Big House."

"Not as many as we'd like. My brothers are still gone—couldn't come home. But still, it's good to be here."

"You got a fine family," Corey said simply.

"Yes, I do. . . . Liable to be pretty active tomorrow, Christmas and all, but I've got your present right here."

"A present for me?"

"Yes." David reached into his inner pocket and pulled out an envelope. He handed it over and watched as Corey opened it. Inside was a single sheet of paper. Corey had learned to read, despite obstacles, and now as he formed the words with his lips he seemed suddenly turned to stone.

Finally he looked up and whispered, "This says you done give me my freedom, Mr. David."

"I told you I'd wait a year, but I thought it would be a good Christmas present. Merry Christmas, Corey. You're a free man now," David said, smiling. "Go anywhere you want to; you're not tied to anything."

"That ain't right," Corey said, having trouble breathing. He stared down at the words on the paper and then repeated them as if they were an incantation. Finally he looked up. "I ain't belonging to nobody. That's right and I thank you forever for that, Mr. David. But I guess in one way when a man's got a friend, why, he ain't completely free. He owe that friend something, and nothing will ever change what I feel for you."

David's throat thickened with emotion, and he slapped the big man's knee. "Well, that's over," he said briskly. "Now all we have to do is make this into the best plantation in the South."

"I reckon we kin do that. Come spring you gonna see some plowin' like you never seen before!"

The two sat there for a long time until, finally, David rose to his feet. Corey stood also and put out his hand. When David took it, he gripped it hard. "Jubilee Day for Corey Jones! Free at last. Never thought I'd see the day. Thank you, Mr. David!" Corey said gratefully and reverently.

David left the blacksmith shop and hobbled back to the house. He could hear voices as he entered the kitchen, and for a while he joined his family. However, there was a sadness to the planning of the upcoming festivities, for the whole family wasn't there. David knew some might never be there again, but he kept these feelings to himself.

Christmas came the next day, and little gifts were passed around. There was good food, and they savored it to the fullest, perhaps even more so because they all knew it couldn't last long and they must go back to the grim specter of war. When Clay asked David, "Will you be going back to the Army of the Tennessee?" David shook his head. "I don't know, sir. Depends on how well this leg does. It doesn't look good for us, does it?"

"No," Clay Rocklin said firmly. He'd never been in favor of the war; he'd fought against the South's entering it with all he had. "There's only one end—they're just too strong for us." He hesitated, then said, "And we had the wrong cause."

"Slavery's got to go," David said. "I think it would have gone anyway if the war hadn't come." He'd thought a great deal about this and had talked with his father about it often. It was a bad system morally and even worse economically. "I'll be glad when it's all gone."

Clay examined this young son of his carefully. "It's men like you, David, who are going to have to rebuild the South. It'll be hard, but with God's help we can do it."

"Yes sir. We can."

★ ★ ★

Two days after Christmas David was sitting in the study going over the records and planning for the spring planting. He was surprised when his stepmother, Melora, came to say, "Corey wants to see you, David."

"All right." David put his papers aside, picked up his cane, and hobbled to the door.

"Put your coat on if you're going out," Melora scolded. "You're just like a little boy! That's all you'd need, to catch cold again."

He laughed and said, "You're too young to be my mother, and I'm never going to call you anything but Melora."

Melora sniffed teasingly. "You always were a disrespectful young man. Now, put on that coat."

David shrugged into the coat Melora held for him and saw she was smiling. "What are you laughing about?" he asked suspiciously.

"Oh, nothing. Go on along with you now, then come back and we'll have tea or coffee or something."

"It'll have to be 'or something' I guess. The tea and coffee are all gone."

"I'll make some sassafras tea. You always liked that."

"All right."

David left the house and saw Corey standing beside the area that held the scuppernong vines. Although they were stripped of leaves now, they were so thick they practically formed a wall. As he approached, he noticed that Corey was struggling to suppress a smile. "You're grinning like a mule eating briars, Corey. What are you laughing about? What's so funny?"

"Chrissmas gif', Mr. David!" Corey announced. "Two days late, but I got it for you!"

David frowned. "Christmas gift? Oh, you didn't have to do that."

"Well, no sah, but I thought you deserved it. You want it now?"

"Why, yes."

Corey waved his hand and said, "Go right in that grape arbor and you'll find it all waitin' for you."

Giving Corey a quizzical look, David moved past him, his cane tapping hollowly on the stone walkway. He turned the corner, not knowing what he would find, then stopped dead still.

"Hello, David."

"Leah!"

David heard Corey laughing behind him, and then he heard departing footsteps. The sun overhead was a pale disc and the air was cold as David stepped toward Leah, putting out his left hand. As she took it, he said, "I can't believe you're here!"

"You said in your letters you were lonesome for me," Leah said. "I hope you meant it, because here I am."

Leah had received three letters from David in New York. Each time he'd told her he loved her and promised to come to New York as soon as his wound healed completely. She'd finally talked with her mother and Amelia about it and it had been Claire who insisted, "If he can't come to you, you'll have to go to him. I don't know if you love this young man or not, but now's the time to go find out." Claire radiated joy these days. As she and Matthew prepared to leave on their trip in a week, she had told Leah, "I'll get the money from your father. You can go in style this time and dazzle that young man. If he's the one you want, then go after him and never let him go!"

Her mother's words—and the happiness on her face—had propelled Leah to come. But now that she was here, she was somewhat embarrassed at her own boldness and very conscious that he hadn't released her hand. "How—how is your wound?" she faltered, afraid that she'd presumed too much.

David stared at her. She was wearing a beautifully tailored hunter-green wool dress with a coat to match. A small black hat perched on her head, and her face flushed as she stood before him.

"Leah," he said huskily, then pulled her forward. His cane fell, but neither of them seemed to notice. He very naturally leaned on her, and she very naturally supported him. "You'll have to hold me up a little," he said, smiling at her. "My leg's not very strong."

Leah put her arms around him and looked up at him. "I was afraid to come," she said simply, "but I found out that I couldn't forget you."

"I hope you never do." He held her for a moment, searching her eyes, then drew her close. "You fit right here in my arms," he said. "Have you come to stay?"

Leah smiled impishly. "I've come to be courted. You needn't think you're going to get out of that! I'll be staying in town. You can bring your guitar and sing love songs to me in the middle of the streets of Richmond."

"I can't do that! I can't even sing!"

Suddenly he pulled her closer. As she felt the strength of his body, Leah Cleburne knew that she'd come home. She clung to David as he kissed her firmly. Then, when he pulled his head back, she said, "I love you, David. I don't know what's going to happen, but I wanted you to know that much."

He touched her cheek. "You're here," he murmured quietly, "that's all that counts."

For some time they stood there, then, suddenly aware of where she was, she struggled in his grasp. "We can't stand here kissing in this arbor! It would cause a scandal if anyone saw us."

David smiled. "All the Rocklin men bring their sweethearts to this arbor to be kissed. That's what it was built for."

She took his hand, bent down, and picked up his cane. "Come along," she said, "I'm anxious for your family to meet me. They'll say I'm some brazen woman come chasing after you! You'll have to protect me."

David laughed and hugged her tightly, then the two of them made their way out of the arbor.

Standing off to one side where he was concealed, Corey shook his head and grinned broadly as the two moved slowly toward the house. When they went inside, his grin grew even broader.

"Well, now! I guess I done brought Mr. David a Chrissmas gif' he ain't *never* gonna forget!"

GILBERT MORRIS is the author of many best-selling books, including the popular House of Winslow series, the Reno Western Saga, and the Wakefield Dynasty.

He spent ten years as a pastor before becoming professor of English at Ouachita Baptist University in Arkansas and earning a Ph.D. at the University of Arkansas. Morris has had more than twenty-five scholarly articles and two hundred poems published. Currently he is writing full-time.

His family includes three grown children, and he and his wife, Johnnie, live in Bailey, Colorado.

If you're looking for more captivating historical fiction, you'll find it in these additional titles by Gilbert Morris....

THE APPOMATTOX SAGA

#1 A Covenant of Love   0-8423-5497-2
#2 Gate of His Enemies   0-8423-1069-X
#3 Where Honor Dwells   0-8423-6799-3
#4 Land of the Shadow   0-8423-5742-4
#5 Out of the Whirlwind   0-8423-1658-2
#6 The Shadow of His Wings   0-8423-5987-7
#7 Wall of Fire   0-8423-8126-0
#8 Stars in Their Courses   0-8423-1674-4

RENO WESTERN SAGA

A Civil War drifter faces the challenges of the frontier, searching for a deeper sense of meaning in his life.

#1 Reno   0-8423-1058-4
#2 Rimrock   0-8423-1059-2
#3 Ride the Wild River   0-8423-5795-5
#4 Boomtown   0-8423-7789-1
#5 Valley Justice 0-8423-7756-5
#6 Lone Wolf   0-8423-1997-2

THE WAKEFIELD DYNASTY

This fascinating saga follows the lives of two English families from the time of Henry VIII through four centuries of English history.

#1 The Sword of Truth   0-8423-6228-2
#2 The Winds of God   0-8423-7953-3
#3 The Shield of Honor   0-8423-5930-3